HOUSE OF WAITING

House of Waiting

Marina Tamar Budhos

GLOBAL CITY PRESS

NEW YORK

THERE ARE CERTAIN PEOPLE WHOM I WISH TO EXPRESS MY HEARTFELT THANKS TO: JERRY BADANES, ELI GOTTLIEB, PETER KAUFMAN, DONNA MASINI, PHILIP RAIBLE, LYNDA SCHOR, SARAH WOLF, AND DEBORAH WOLFE. HELGA SCHWALM AND KIM VAETH OFFERED COMPUTER RESCUES AT CRUCIAL MOMENTS. THE VISION OF LINSEY ABRAMS AND LAURIE LISS AT GLOBAL CITY PRESS BROUGHT THIS BOOK INTO PRINT. MACDOWELL AND YADDO COLONIES, THE FULBRIGHT PROGRAM, AND THE WRITERS ROOM ALSO GAVE PRECIOUS SHELTER AND TIME.

SPECIAL THANKS TO MY MOTHER, SHIRLEY BUDHOS, FOR HER SUPPORT ALL THESE YEARS. AND PROFOUND GRATITUDE TO ROBIN BRADFORD, FOR READING AGAIN AND AGAIN.

In memory of my father

It isn't easy to turn your back on the past. It isn't something you can decide to do just like that. It is something you have to arm yourself for, or grief will ambush and destroy you.

—V. S. NAIPAUL

Should we have stayed at home, wherever that may be?

—ELIZABETH BISHOP
New York, 1953

HOUSE OF WAITING

I

The night before Roland left for the Caribbean, I dreamed of goldfish in his winter coat. It is a splendid coat: thick navy wool with wooden toggle buttons, Scotch plaid lining, each pocket deep as an old nest. In the dream fish flicked between the epaulets and the teeth of his zipper hung broken and open. I woke in a panic and shook Roland awake. "Tell me this," I asked. "Are there goldfish down there?"

Roland let out a groan. "Darlin' I have no idea."

"Parakeets then? I think I read that in a book."

"I believe so."

"And what about your coat?"

"What about it?"

"Isn't it too hot to take?"

Now he was wide awake and laughed, swinging an arm around my waist. "Come here," he said, rubbing his unshaven chin on my stomach. "That reading of yours gone scrambled your thoughts."

He hoisted my nightgown over my head and made love to me for what I knew would be our last time for a long while. All around us, in our one-room apartment, lay Roland's belongings, slumped in the dim morning light.

But I could not stay with him. My mind was a small white box: I was still thinking about the goldfish and what to send his mother and by the time we'd rolled off one another and were fully awake, I'd taken to thinking about food. Maybe a Loft's package tied with a green sash. "Chocolate?" I asked. "Is that something she eats? Or will it melt?"

"Sweetheart," he whispered. "All these things are good for my mother. " The puddle of his pajama drawers, crushed at the end of the bed, were drawn up over his loins, then he hoisted himself out of bed and started for the bathroom.

"Coffee!" I shouted through the bathroom door as I heard the spray of a shower on porcelain. "I've got some in the icebox!"

No answer. "Roland, please. There must be something. The way I was raised you can't go anywhere without at least two full shopping bags."

A rattle of a doorknob; he popped his head out, chin doused in shaving cream, one ribbon sliding off the razor. "Sarah, when you come down, you can bring all you want. But first my mother and I got some straightening out to do. " He shut the door.

Disappointed, I decided to pull on my clothes, even without a shower. I felt silly, sulky as a little girl, stomping around the cold floorboards, fishing up my good stockings and tweed skirt crumpled on a chair. But there wasn't much I could do to persuade him. Yesterday we'd gone shopping and bought what I thought to be a stingy showing of presents: a carton of Pall Mall cigarettes for his brothers, sweet-scented soap and a curling iron for his sisters.

Outside it had rained again, my old geranium pots glazed with water on the fire escape. I made some coffee,

4

which we drank in silence at the kitchen table. We were too nervous for the usual morning talk. Then we got ready: Roland stuffed the presents into his carry-on bag, I put the bedding away and an hour later, we stood on Seventh Avenue, hailing a cab. It was rare we took cabs, but the treat was worth it—we might sit back in the seat and hold hands for our last hour. The driver, though, was in a bad temper. "Goddamn traffic," he muttered as we turned the corner of Houston. "They got some kind of rally at City Hall. Gonna mess things up bad downtown."

"Take FDR Drive," I suggested. "It won't be so bad."

No reply; he adjusted the rear view mirror. Crew cut, spiny black bristles poking from a ruddy neck. He reached for the radio knob, pausing in the WQXR bulletin. The House UnAmerican Activities Committee were on—this made Roland nervous—a few days before, there were difficulties in getting a visa, then he showed them an old letter from home and everything was settled. Folded into his jacket pocket was temporary permission, signed at the British Embassy.

The driver began to fidget with the knob. Roland edged forward, opening his mouth to ask him to leave it, but then sank back with a soft grunt. The taxi driver settled on swing music, the sounds tinny. I kept quiet. I knew why Roland didn't press about the radio: a few minutes ago, as we were shunting the suitcase into the taxi trunk, the driver stared at my pale hand balanced on Roland's elbow, so I took it away. We were used to such moments.

"So where you folks off to?" The driver's tone was lighter, as if he'd decided to be a bit friendly.

Roland answered. "British Guiana."

"Never heard of it."

"Caribbean. There's a new leader there—"

"Roland." I nudged him in the ribs. This wasn't the place to talk about the new socialist government.

The driver didn't notice our little fumble. "I saw a movie the other day, 'Outpost in Malaya'—near there?"

"That's the Pacific."

He shook his head. "Pacific, yeah. Gotta cousin in Korea." Another shake. "The world's a damn dangerous place, hunh?"

"Not really," I said.

No answer. Roland and I stared out the window. Seventh Avenue, Houston, the Puck Building rearing up in a soft, clay-colored wedge. I nudged him again.

"Will you write me?"

He took my hand. "What you talking about, sweetheart? Every day I'll send you a letter. You'll be sick of hearing from me soon."

Then we sat back again in silence as the driver crossed town, and swung onto the East River Drive. Fifteen minutes later, we were crossing Manhattan Bridge, one tug moving slowly in the silvery, choppy waters; a trolley clanged and shuttled beside us. Gray clouds sat massed behind the strip that was Staten Island; a storm was predicted in the next few days.

Suddenly, I was furious again about the goldfish and chocolate. To make me feel worse, we were driving past my old neighborhood with its familiar stoops, the low-hanging Brooklyn sky. Last I heard of my mother she sat gossiping in a park about the dark grandchildren she would soon have.

My knuckles rapped the cold glass. "I know every inch of Eastern Parkway by heart."

"How's that?"

"On Shabbos I was so bored I would walk up and down with my girlfriends, wishing a movie director would suddenly appear and whisk me away."

He laughed. "I'm going to miss your stories, darlin'. Maybe this is crazy. Maybe everyone right. I should stay and be with you."

"No. You have to go." But I could barely get the words out.

Another silence. Roland fidgeted in the seat. Suddenly, he grabbed my hand. He was trembling.

"What is it?"

I could see the confusion working beneath his half-shut lids. "Tell me," I whispered. "I won't be angry. I promise."

For a moment Roland seemed to consider, then he leaned forward and put his cheek to my stomach. I wanted to giggle. "I'm so tired, Sarah," he whispered. "So awfully tired."

At the check-in counter, the man took one look at Roland's ticket and visa and gave a jerk of his head. "You'll need another approval on this." He pointed to the end of the hall. Immigration Inquiries, the sign read. Swearing under his breath, Roland heaved his suitcase off the scale and started to trudge towards the office. I hurried alongside him, but as we maneuvered inside the narrow room, the man said, "If you don't mind, ma'am, I'd like to talk to your husband alone."

"Why?"

Roland put a finger to his lips. "None of your fast talk, sweetheart. Hush now. I be with you soon."

I went to a candy stand, where I bought a Cadbury bar and crammed it into my mouth. Then another. I was starving. Ten minutes later my head ached. Roland was still inside the office. I could see his profile through the smoked glass window. I knew he had shown them everything—his passport; our marriage license; his letter from

7

home. It must have embarrassed him, the words of his
mother written by a neighbor, now sifting through the
pale fingers of an immigration officer. *Come home, Baba. I
know there are differences between us., but let us put it behind us.
The past is the past.* What differences? I wondered, pressing
my ankles together.

As he came out of the office, Roland stopped at a news-
stand to buy a paper, then flicked a comb out of his pocket
and quickly rearranged a loop into the swirl of his hair.
Before I knew it, he was standing over me, tugging on his
shirt cuffs. "Ready?" he asked. His voice trembled.

"Hardly."

The flight announcement came crackling over the
loudspeaker. Roland picked up his briefcase, folded his
coat over his arm; we approached the gate door. "Sarah,
forgive me. I be back soon. I promise." He squeezed my
arms so tight, they began to hurt.

"Oh my God!"

"What?"

"I forgot. I don't even have your family's address." I put
a fist to my mouth. Tears leaked out of my eyes. "I can't
believe I forgot something like that. This is simply
awful." I shook his arm. "Everything is so wrong, Roland.
I can't believe this is really happening to me."

"I gave you my address in Georgetown. I told you
before. That's where I'll be staying and working. I got no
business in my village."

"But your mother—"

"No, no Sarah, don't start fightin' now. Is important.
You stay with our friends, they your family now. They
going to take care of you."

"But what about your family?"

He hesitated. "Don't worry, my sweet." Then he let go
his grip, his mouth twisted into an ugly line.

A few minutes later, he was walking through the gate; soon he shifted across the tarmac, bent against wind, coat collar clutched to his neck. As he ducked into the plane's doorway, I felt the first real flickers of doubt about the man I had married seven months before. I pushed my fists into my coat pockets as the plane's propellers started to whirr. It inched forward, coasting down the runway. The plane lifted into the air.

2

Beautiful.

That's all I could think the first time I spotted Roland Singh in the library stacks. A smile split open his silky brown face; loose, rumpled hair swept into a pompadour. In his freshly glossed wingtips, he came sauntering down the aisle, hips swinging in his triple pleat pants, holding out a cone of greasy newspaper. I was sure he was a delivery boy. That, or a jazz musician. Definitely somebody I should not be talking to.

"Hey, book-lady," he whispered. "You try." He pointed to his package.

"It's against the rules to be eating here," I told him.

"And is against my rules to talk so rude to someone bearing a gift."

Giggling, I pushed my book to the edge of the carrel desk, then checked my watch. I had about five more minutes before my boss would look up from his desk and notice how long I'd been gone. Bored of typing reference cards, a half hour ago I'd slipped a novel under a stack of library books, faked an urgent search and went wandering to my hideaway, where I went almost every day. Usually there was no one else in the archaeology section, where now and then a sleepy-looking graduate student floating among the carrels, slid a volume from the shelves and vanished once again.

"Come on," the man now urged. Edging closer, he pointed to what looked like a turnover nestled in the paper and broke it open. Steam, pungent with spices, floated to my face. "See here. This is the pattie. It's just ground beef. And the outside here is coco bread. Nothing going to kill you." Seeing me hesitate, he added, "Go on. Give it a try."

My jaw tightened. "Why should I?"

"Because I brought it for you."

"Why me?"

"I saw you before. You need a little fattening up. Is going to make you read better."

"You noticed *me*?"

"You come up here, hide out like me." Again he held the package near.

"I don't get it."

"Look, darlin', where I come from we don't let a girl lie quiet when she so skinny like you. And I been tryin' for days. I push my cart, but you too stuck up, you keep your face in that book of yours. I even come by two times the other day and you still no look."

It astonished me that any man, even this man, droplets of grease sliding off his fingertips, would try to nab my attention. I didn't think of myself as much to notice. Sure, I managed a bit of slapdash, homemade style with my wide gypsy skirt. But my breasts were too little and I wasn't very good at small talk. I broke off a corner of the pastry and chewed. The taste was strange, but not unpleasant. I could feel him staring at me, as if he liked watching me eat.

"Still hot?"

I nodded. The taste of oil lay on my tongue.

"Just got this from Brooklyn on my way over," he explained.

"That's where I'm from."

"Yeah, but I bet you don't know my Brooklyn."

"What's that supposed to mean?"

"I see you chattin' it up with your girlfriends. Last thing you know about it is a fellow like me and the places I go."

"Now look who's stuck up."

"Not me. I'm not in this country maybe four, five years, I don't know much about the place. But I know a girl with a stubborn mouth like yours."

Embarrassed, I wiped my fingers and tried to give the pattie back to him, but he was ready for me, thrusting out a greasy hand. "Now you don't know me yet. My name is Roland Singh. But you call me Bump. And if you be nice to me next time, I bring you another pattie and tell you how I get such a name."

This made me hesitate—what an odd, crazy man he was, clavicle bone showing like a ledge through his shirt; his rush of words to fill the narrow space between us. "Nice to meet you, Bump," I said. "My name's Sarah Weissberg. Now can I get back to my reading?"

"That's the idea, sweetheart."

Before I could say anything more, he had sauntered to the elevator.

It didn't take very long to figure out that Roland Singh was following me. When I ate my lunch in the cafeteria with the other librarians, I spotted him stumbling into the cafeteria, the rounds of his spectacles flashing like bright white clock faces. He was so adorable, so child-like—the dimpled curve of his cheek, unruly curls flopping at the back of his collar. Each time he spotted me, his thin body seemed to stiffen with purpose, then he waved, giving me an impish grin, as if there was now a secret between us. I waved back shyly.

"Who's that?" my friend Nettie asked one afternoon. "I've never seen him here before." Nettie grew up in the same neighborhood as me. Right after high school she'd enrolled in librarian school and got engaged to Ernie Cohen, which now gave her permission to be a know-it-all about everything, especially my life. "Come on, Sarah, who's the stranger?"

"A man."

"No kidding."

"He works stacking books," Elaine put in. Elaine also came from our East New York neighborhood. In high school, Elaine was a cheery, popular type I would have steered clear of. Now we ate lunch together every day and I pretended to like her. Today the soft, loose bundles of her breasts were sheathed in yellow cashmere, showing off her good coloring.

"Is he Negro?" she went on. "His hair is kind of different."

A flush of anger rippled through me. "No, he's Indian." I wasn't sure how I knew this but it seemed important to impress on Elaine my newfound authority. "And you might try not being so obvious. He does have eyes."

"I think he's interesting looking. Sort of contained and off to himself."

"Stop it!"

"Somebody told me he's a graduate student," she went on.

Nettie shook her head. "You must be mistaken. His English couldn't be that good."

"I think she should talk to him," Elaine giggled.

"Sarah always has mysterious things happen to her."

Nettie flicked a bread crumb. "Mysterious! I think he's creepy. Did you notice his nails? They're dirty."

"If I didn't know any better, Nettie, I'd call you prejudiced."

"And you think you've found your Heathcliff, Sarah."

Though the three of us laughed, the two of them had managed to make me both ashamed and excited for my stranger. Across the room he sat with an enormous textbook flung open before him. I pitied the grin he could not wipe off his face. But by the time I folded up my lunch bag and rose from the table, my stranger had disappeared.

For days I waited for him to come up to me, or walk into the cafeteria with those loose, ambling strides, thrusting his hand from his jacket sleeve, offering his friendly wave. But he was nowhere to be seen. On a damp, dreary day a few weeks later, I slipped another book under a library pile and went wandering up to the archaeology section. As I was turning a corner, I spotted him. First his tumble of rough black curls buried in his arms. Then a column of textbooks perched on the desk corner, about to tip over.

I tugged on his shirt sleeve. "Bump," I whispered. When he didn't answer, I tugged again. "Bump, you can tell me now. About your name."

His shoulders stirred. He jumped up, shouting, "What's the hell!" His textbooks fell with a clatter to the floor; he grabbed for his glasses, peering at me. "Oh it's you." He tamped down the waves of his hair. "Why you have to scare me like that?"

I did not even recognize him. He had lost weight, his eyes rimmed with ashy circles. "Are you sick?"

"I was working hard. I had an exam."

"Then you are a student."

Roland's eyes narrowed with suspicion. "What you think? I'm planning on spending my whole life stacking books?"

"Why do you always put things in my mouth before I'm even finished with what I want to say?"

We paused, suddenly wary of one another. He seemed different, not the adorable stranger I'd fantasized about. An angry mask slid over his features, reminding me that he *was* a foreigner, coming from God knows where. Nervous, I took a step back. "Forget it, then. I guess I made a mistake."

His mouth opened, as if to say something, only it was as if his voice had suddenly evaporated. Our glances see-sawed, first to me with my books pressed against a neatly buttoned blouse, then he with his untied shoelaces, swiping at a lock of hair. I could tell he was trying to figure out what to do with me. I wished right then and there he would lean over and kiss me, so I might taste his soft, plum-colored lips. Instead he blurted out: "Food!"

"What about it?"

Roland was hopping back and forth, from foot to foot, like a child getting impatient on line. "I said it before. You too skinny, girl. Don't you get enough to eat?"

"I eat enough."

"You peck and fuss, I can tell."

I smiled. "So what's Bump?"

Now it was his turn to smile. "That's my nickname. My mother name me that 'cause I always knocking into furniture, running after my older brothers and sisters."

I liked the name and could easily see him as a clumsy, eager brother tripping over his feet, scrabbling after others with the same wavy black hair. It made me want to take him into my arms.

"Will you?" He crooked a finger around my wrist.

16

"Will I what?"

"Go to dinner with me."

I drew my shoulders up. It was one thing to nab his attention, but I didn't want him getting too arrogant on me. "If you promise—"

"Promise what?"

"Not to call me skinny." I grimaced. "I hate that word."

"Don't you worry, sweetheart. I'll call you a lot more than that."

I never had much luck with homes. They seem to sift through my fingers like a slippery fabric. For the first six years of my life I was shuttled between foster homes all over East New York. I slept in baskets and beds, next to radiators, once in a closet. I didn't learn what a real family was. I didn't know places intimately; not the turn of a doorknob or the shape of my father's coat on a rack. I learned to shrug off places; to love people dually since I knew that the hands that smoothed my hair each morning also got a check for keeping me. My real mother, an unmarried telephone operator, had left a note pinned to my blanket when she handed me over to the adoption agency: Just remember: my daughter is Jewish.

I can still remember the day I first went to the Weissbergs, an old couple from Russia who'd told my social worker, Ruby Markowitz, that they wanted to adopt me. I was living with the Steins—Mrs. Stein wore dresses made of tablecloth fabric and Jacob Stein used to pinch my knobby knees and tell me I would one day die of scarlet fever in a Ward's Island hospital. That morning I combed my hair into two pigtails tied with pale ribbon, put on my only good dress, velvet with lace and stepped into the full luxury of a beaver-tipped coat given to me by the

Stein's oldest girl, Rachel. With Rachel's head of yellow-silk hair, the coat seemed glamorous, Shirley Templeish. On me the sleeves hung too long and the color brought out my sallow face. Sitting on the streetcar, fists bunched in my pockets, I wondered if my new parents would change their minds when they saw how scrawny I was. As we got off the streetcar and trudged up the block, there was the old guy Samuel, crouched on his stoop, thin hair blowing up on end. He'd put on a suit and bow tie—which touched me—to wait on the dirty concrete, the air raw with wind. My heart quickened. I even broke into a skip.

But as I hurtled toward him, cold air streaming at my cheeks, I noticed Samuel's face turn pale with fright. He yanked his shoulders back, as if bracing for the full impact of me. It was all wrong. I was too boisterous, too noisy. My knees stopped pumping. My head lowered as if someone had pressed a hand against my neck.

Inside the apartment, the old man's wife Frieda stood by the dining room table, hair done in pink-yellow curls that lay flat against her cheeks. I noticed her hands were smooth, fingers long, with two glamorous rings.

Shyly I followed her into the living room and climbed onto an overstuffed chair. On each end was a table. The right table held a shallow glass dish filled with nuts. While the adults were busy talking, I began sliding the dish back and forth. Then I switched it to the other table and started to take the nuts out and arrange them in a row. Frieda pushed the dish away from my fingers. "Darling, are you hungry?"

I shook my head.

"Something to drink, then."

I shrugged.

A few minutes later, the old woman had hurried back

from the kitchen with a glass of warmed milk on a saucer. I gave the milk a tentative sip. I hated warm milk. It always made me queasy, frothing sourly in my stomach. And this room seemed too dark. I was sure the walnut doors of the armoire in the corner were going to fling open and swallow me.

Ruby Markowitz, though, had settled on the sofa across the room, and was gushing about my grades in school. "She's a little genius!" she exclaimed. "Ninety-seven in history! Ninety-five in spelling!"

The old man and lady glanced at me, like embarrassed winners of a lottery. I could hardly open my mouth to speak. I tried to remember what Mrs. Stein had told me before I left. "Watch that big mouth of yours, Sarah," she had advised. "Don't pick your cuticles and remember to agree with everything they say." But the milk had made a sticky web across my throat, making it hard to murmur even a few syllables of gratitude. Ruby Markowitz was getting on my nerves.

Then the old lady noticed my glass. "Why didn't you tell me you don't like it?"

"Because you didn't ask," I said, before I could help myself.

A furrow appeared between her eyebrows. "Such a waste!"

At that moment, I felt all my apologies, my good manners, drop like pebbles into my stomach. Milk went sloshing out of the glass, scalding my wrists. "It's not my fault!" I cried and jumped up from the sofa.

"Ah!" the old lady cried, her hands flying to her mouth. She jumped up from her seat to open the doors to the armoire. I began to shriek some more. "Don't!" I wailed, watching her arms disappear into the frightening dark mouth while a white stain seeped into the carpet.

Embarrassed, Samuel looked away while Mrs. Markowitz kept her eyes on her hat.

The rest of the afternoon didn't go much better. During lunch, I didn't want to eat the borscht and creamed herring, either. None of those foods ever went down right with me. But I noticed the old lady's lower lip pull over her teeth when she saw my untouched plate. Terrified, I picked up my fork and forced myself to eat.

At night I would lie in my bed, fists tight against my thighs, listening very hard, as if my whole life depended on believing in those sounds. If I could shape them in my mind—a radiator shriek, the shuffle of the old lady's slippers as she passed my door—then I could be normal. The Weissbergs would be my home. I would not be alone.

But there was always something to keep me apart. Frieda and Samuel seemed nice enough, but they left a chill that stiffened into a cold knot at the bottom of my spine. The first day, I unpacked my suitcase and hung my few dresses in the cupboard in the tiny bedroom which was now mine. Frieda let me tack an Ann of Green Gables movie poster over my bed. But otherwise she was a tyrant about the apartment: don't move the dining chairs, the lamps, and even my tea cup had a special hook.

Samuel wasn't much help either. Kneeling on the floor, he clasped me by the shoulders and said, "You will stay with us. We are not easy people, but you seem a good girl."

"What does that mean?" I asked.

"You wait," he smiled. "You are with us now."

Frieda and Samuel were odd people, coiled snail-like into their ways. Samuel owned a grocery on Pennsylvania Avenue, a narrow strip of a room, a terrifying double-handled cheese knife hanging slant-wise behind his head at the counter. Back in Russia, he'd been a shy, prized son sent to a yeshiva, not meant to coarsen his hands in shop. Then one summer night five Cossacks came crashing through his village; the next morning he woke to find his own father lying face down dead in a neighbor's hay loft. He fled with his mother through a maze of relatives and friends, pocketing his dark, angry star of difference, arriving in East New York where he married the first woman his mother found for him.

And it took a while, but that ice cube of my heart did start to thaw, guilt leaking through my body like any other kid. Samuel became papa; Frieda ma. In the schoolyard, when the kids asked me who made my sweater with the pearl stitch yoke, I let those strange syllables slide off my tongue: my parents. *My parents.* I grew to love small things about my new parents. I loved Frieda's nails. They were slender and immaculate-pink. And there were the lullaby words I'd never before heard—*mama shaynala, sleep my sweetest*—drops dissolving in my tired mind when I lay under the quilt each night, freshly bathed, Frieda smoothing my damp hair flat. She taught me how to sew and knit; evenings, we sat by the window, chewing knots of thread, French-stitching, hem-stitching, needles clicking, gathered into a strange blue peace that lifted us far up from the stormy tantrums of the day. I loved her then for her soft white arms, her yellow hair, her competence.

But then came Fridays. Our apartment pulled tight with new rules: no friends, no singing, no sitting in the front room, no radio; God forbid, we might die of pleasure. Frieda flew about the kitchen like a startled canary, beautiful hands trembling over the countertops. Nothing was ever right—the challa, her stewed cabbage, the roasted chicken.

I only made matters worse by doing everything wrong.

I mixed up dishes, used the wrong candlesticks, dropped a chicken bone near a smear of Farmer's cheese. I chafed under my mother's constant, worrying gaze. Friday afternoon Samuel would arrive home, shrug off his shopkeeper's jacket, put on his prayer shawl, and disappear into the living room. I couldn't understand why he did this, since it didn't seem to make him very happy, his prayers rising through the glass-pane door in soft, depressing waves. I wasn't allowed even to put a toe in the living room.

To revenge them, the next morning in the temple balcony, I let the Hebrew sounds slide right through me. There was the spine of the book on my palm, the still, airless heat, but none of it ever seemed real to me. My mind wandered and dallied on other, better things. My movie magazines. I was in love with Clark Gable. I loved his great black brush of a moustache, his long earlobes. Squeezed on the bench between my mother and the wide-hipped Rose Saltzman, I used to practice my Vivien Leigh swoon, imagining Rhett Butler would part the curtain to the women's balcony and sweep me into his arms, take me far away from this sweaty room.

Sometimes, when no one was looking, I scraped up my dimes and nickels and ran to the corner candy store run by Joe Mahoney. Then I would order a vanilla egg cream and a BLT and suck them down in ten minutes flat. Afterwards I'd push through the glass doors and stand on the pavement, sweat pouring down my legs, as I waited for a delicious crack of sky, the lightening bolt to strike me down dead.

I couldn't help myself; I was always trying to run away. Thirteen years in a rear tenement where the furniture didn't change once. Even the pile of hairpins in my mother's crystal bowl I could count on. If I closed my eyes I could say exactly what she was cooking for Thursday supper and how many times she would complain about my father leaving his slippers in the living room. Under my bed, I kept a small suitcase with my dog-eared copy of Wuthering Heights and a black lace shawl. Gypsy, my mother called me. If only she knew. I used to fantasize that I wasn't the daughter of these apple-cheeked, melancholy people, but a gypsy child left in a basket at their door. I should be so lucky. Even though I was adopted, I was cut from the same genetic cloth: I had my mother's widow's peak and my father's grim Russian mouth.

And I took myself very seriously. During dinner, when guests collected around our huge mahogany table, the legs curved and dimpled like lions' paws, Samuel would lean under the wavy bonnets of the over head lamp, stabbing his butter knife in the air. Samuel loved to argue, especially with Jennie and Mosel Friedman, my parents' unlikely best friends—real radicals, whose oil painting of Lenin over their sideboard used to terrify me. My father hated unions, crowds, rallies, anything that smacked of optimism. "Like children you are with your demands," he liked to grumble.

"And you're like an old man hiding in his books!" Jennie chided. "All that reading and you can't see a thing. This is *life,* you silly fool."

Though my father had left his own home long before the war, before the worst had happened, his flight had left a wound that seemed to flow darker and angrier each year. He bandaged himself up, suspicious that anything unknown must be dangerous. Even the jazz programs I used to listen to he found repugnant. But it was Samuel I most liked to listen to. Mosel, with his rump of silvery hair, his slogans, bored me. To his statement, "Religion is the opiate of the masses," I smiled, "But I'm hardly one of the masses, Mosel." Samuel smiled too. In his voice, I heard the grown-up elegance of a solitary mind that rendered for me a world, though bleak with ailments, complex, unsolvable. At the dinner table, he poked two bony fingers into my back—"Loud like a trumpet, kindela, speak up." Giddy from wine, I heard my own words forming like perfect bubbles on my lips. First in Yiddish then in the more enticing syllables of English, which I began to impose on them, like a general with new routines. "Stop talking like you're in the old country!" I would shout. "Speak in English! You've been here twenty years!"

"So the American girl thinks she knows better!" Frieda laughed as she bustled around us, clearing the dishes. That was how my nickname—American girl—got started.

At school, I worked hard to please Samuel. In my essays, I believed myself just like him, stubborn with challenge. Trundling through the Jefferson High corridors with this onerous intellectual destiny, I thought of myself as a cross between Jane Austen and a sultry Joan Crawford. Graduation day, sweating in my pancake makeup and Peter Pan collar dress, I felt like a forty-year-old wobbling on fourteen-year-old ankles to the graduation stage to take my honors prizes.

When we came home later, Samuel slid off the ribbons and spread my honor certificates flat on the table, peering at my name hand-lettered underneath. Smiling, he said, "I have a surprise for you, American Girl."

"What?"

"You have to wait until Sunday."

"Tell me now."

My father put a hand against my cheek. "What, the world will change in a week that you can't wait?"

*

On Sunday we took the streetcar without Frieda. I sat beside my father, my hair still chemical-smelling from my new permanent. I'd worn my graduation dress, and sat with my coat across my knees. I was ecstatic, for everything seemed so right: my father by my side, the two of us going out for a meal like two grown-ups in Manhattan. Everything lay in bold colors before me.

At the restaurant we chose a table in the window where we could make out the downtown clock tower and people walking by in their spring coats and hats. Samuel wore a herringbone jacket, his hair combed sideways to cover his bald spot. To me he looked like the thoughtful professors I'd seen walking across the Brooklyn College campus the other day.

After we ordered my father pushed a box across the table. It was slender, no wider than my wrist, wrapped in gold paper. Inside, resting on a strip of blue cotton, lay drop-shaped earrings, stamped with dark eyes of onyx. I held them up, light snatching and grabbing at the filigreed silver. Amazed, I put them on, admiring my upside down reflection in a spoon. "They're beautiful!"

"It's nothing." His fingers brushed me away.

"I can wear them on my first day of college." My words spilled out of me in rush. "I told you about the classes I signed up for, right? French philosophy and the Enlightenment and George Eliot. I did tell you about her, didn't I? She's this wonderful writer, papa. She wrote this book called *Daniel Deronda*. It's all about a man who doesn't know he's a Jew. And then he finds out later and he's all mixed up."

"What does an Englishwoman know about being a Jew?"

"But she does! She understands his outsideness."

"There have always been those who pretend knowledge, Sarah, with their fancy words."

"It's not fancy words! It's a book. It's intelligent. It has *feeling*."

He didn't answer. His spoon scraped the soup bowl. How much older he seemed to me: his facial flesh shrunken against bone, the blue-puckered veins crinkling under his eyes. After a while he wiped his mouth and said, "I have a surprise."

"Another one?" Soup warmed through my ribs.

"This one is even better." Placing both palms on the table edge, he said, "Guess what I've done for you, Sarah."

"What?" It seemed like a game; the lunch, the earrings, this grown-up feeling.

"Guess."

I shrugged. All I could think was maybe he knew I wanted my own two-volume Oxford English dictionary. Or tickets somewhere. I was always complaining that I wanted to go out, to the theater. How was it I grew up my whole life within minutes of Manhattan and I'd only been with my parents twice to Radio City Music Hall? Finally my parents were understanding it was time to enjoy life.

"A job."

"What do you mean?"

"I got you a job."

My spoon lowered to its bowl. "I don't get it."

"I lined up a bookkeeping position in Stewart's company. Everything's arranged."

Globs of fat were turning solid in the broth as I took in his words. My thoughts bunched together, dark as violets, then sprang apart. "But when will I have the time?"

"That's what's so wonderful, Sarah. Stewart says you can work out whatever hours you like."

"Bookkeeping?" The word spun like a coin in my mouth. "I don't get it. Do we need money?"

"Of course not." He leaned in a little further, eyes

sharp. "But even with your fancy classes, you got to have a vocation, Sarah. A vocation fitting a girl."

"That's not a vocation," I heard myself saying, my voice lifting into its smug, Debate-Club tone. "That's more an *avocation*."

A noise of disapproval whistled through his teeth. "Don't play around here."

"I'm not even that good with numbers."

"You'll learn."

"But what about my education?"

"Didn't I pay the registration fee last Thursday?"

"But papa—"

He looked up from his soup, glaring at me. "Sarah, this is not an argument! You understand?"

The restaurant flew into a roar around me. I could not even lift the spoon to my lips.

"Always, everything has to be a discussion with you. It's a bad sign, thinking yourself so big."

I tried to dip my spoon in the soup, but the broth was thick with fat. "Excuse me," I muttered and ran out of the room.

In the bathroom I crouched on the floor, staring at the rusty eye of a toilet. I wanted to flee, anything to stop the hateful burn in my chest. Didn't he know? I was great, an editor, an A+ English major with a head for metaphors! I tried a few dry noises. Nothing.

In front of the mirror I undid the top pearl buttons, took off my belt and scrubbed off all my make-up until my face turned blotchy and pale. I put on eyeliner extra thick, so my eyes became owlish and Joan Crawford sad. With a comb, I began to attack my hair. The more I straightened my curls, the more they sprang back in ferocious, wiry puffs. When I checked myself in the mirror I was glad to see I looked hideous and strange.

Samuel frowned at my appearance. "Why must you make such a spectacle of yourself?" he asked.

"I'm in the mood."

He shook his head. "Always such dramatics."

The sun shone on our faces, thick as butter. We didn't talk much after that. More dishes arrived, food stacked in oily heaps. I ate up everything, trying to swallow down my little scene in the bathroom. I could not get enough. I was ravenous.

I lasted two years as a bookkeeper. I hated it—five hours wedged on a secretary's stool, listening to the old ladies in the front room complain about their arthritis and their kids in Long Island who never visited. I started to keep secrets. I slept with my boss, a refugee who had a wife and kid back in Rumania. Joseph was a rake, but he did set me up with a doctor for a diaphragm. I had to lie and say I was Joseph's wife, but it was exciting. A few weeks later, I decided to quit my job for good. Frieda was horrified— she sent me to see a local doctor who told me I suffered from a "nervous condition."

Through Nettie I got the job at N.Y.U. library. The job was dull too, but I loved the chilled, empty stacks; the feel of print under my hands when I snuck upstairs to read. Evenings I walked the Village streets, calmed by the narrow lanes and elegant stoops, fingering book spines in second-hand stores. There was something reassuring in this neighborhood. It reminded me of James' *Washington Square*, of a genteel life I pretended to be having. Back at home my mother began inviting boys over for supper. They were nice, acceptable guys at Brooklyn College who majored in accounting and weren't the least bit attractive to me. My mother fired questions at them such as what kind of salary they could expect after they graduated.

After each of these ordeals was over, I marched into the kitchen and threatened to board a Grayhound to California if they did that again. My father, sitting in the living room, rattled his newspaper. "Too much restless," he complained.

As Roland and I walked through the doors of Bombay Palace, a musky smell of spices filled my mouth. Before us lay a long room, blazing in red and crimson, booths hung with cork beads that made a soft, clicking noise as we pushed them aside. Once I settled into my seat I stole a glance at Roland. He looked different, dressed in a clean white shirt, hair slicked back into a blue-black shine, showing the charcoal bruises of his eyes. He seemed more foreign and remote than ever.

"So you're a student in economics?" I tried.

"That's what they say. I'm in a program through the Indian Consulate. They say they going to promote me when I finish my courses. That is, if those jokers wake up from drinking their tea and notice me." It was meant to be funny, but Roland wasn't smiling. He kept tugging on his shirt cuffs, glancing around the restaurant. I tried again.

"What part of India are you from?"

"Don't know. "

"You don't know?"

"I never been to India. My grandfather come over to Guiana a long time ago."

"Where's Guiana?" I asked, feeling foolish.

He laughed. "Don't worry, sweetheart. Not many people know about my country. It's a little patch of mud with some palm trees on the top of South America. "

"I don't understand. Why did your grandfather go there?"

"In the last century, a lot of us Indians sent over to

work the plantations as coolies. British Empire. You know, the sun never sets and all that."

"But I thought you said you work for the Indian Consulate." I tilted my water glass to my lips and smiled. "You'll have to forgive me. But it is confusing."

"No kidding!" Roland laughed. "Is confusing for me too. I'm what you call a colonial Indian. We kind of in-between folk in an in-between place. But beautiful nights they got there."

"You must miss it."

"All the time."

"You planning on going back?"

"Back? Darlin', the only thing they let me be down there is some clerk in a suit pushing papers." He rubbed a finger along his cuff. "That's why I hook up with these Consulate folk. Where I come from, a man not a real man. You inferior from the day you born, so you got to prove yourself ten times more. You can't reach for what's easy."

"And you?" I smiled.

"I reach for what's hardest," he admitted. "That's why I bloody my nose so much."

I guess this might have been my cue to try some more questions, even petulant ones, but I didn't. We sat in silence, me staring at my newly polished nails, while all around us fell the sounds of other people talking, knowing something about one another. Dreamily I wondered about his world; if there were coconut trees and sweet-talking men like him. Nor did any waiter come and rescue us, until Roland began to mutter under his breath. "Typical," he complained. "Take them a whole day to write down your order."

"What do you mean typical?"

"Always do things they own time."

"It's all right. They're busy."

30

"Not with me it's not all right," Roland said as he thrust himself out of his seat. Through the crazy clicking of beads, I watched him angle through the dark restaurant. My mood sank. I got the feeling he was leaving to get away from me.

A few minutes later, loud voices came keening over the other diners' heads. Roland strode down the restaurant aisle, face grim, a short man hurrying behind.

"See here! This lady been waiting for how long for you to come!"

"Please lower your voice sir," the man replied as he nodded and bowed. "We are very busy tonight and we try the best we can."

"But we been waiting half an hour!"

The man continued in the same patient, pleading voice. Barely reaching Roland's shoulders, his wide, smooth-skinned face crumpled and smoothed itself like a paper bag as he spoke in flustered spurts. "Please accept my apologies, madame. I am owner of Bombay Palace. We are open three months." He spread his fingers. "At first no one came. Now every night more and more." He let out a big sigh. "I'm not used to the fast way here."

"Fast way!" Roland exploded. "You got to learn a different system here!"

"May I be taking your orders now?" I could see his face working into an expression of graciousness as he added, "And if it may please you, all appetizers are on the house."

I thanked him, irritated by Roland's bad manners and ordered a chicken dish. Roland named a few dishes I couldn't make out. After the owner had left, I remarked to him, "That was quite a scene."

"I tell you Sarah, is a backward way of doing things."

"Your rudeness or the man's slowness?"

A wry smile came to his lips. "You think I just a raging

bull? Maybe. But I know what this man comes from. They don't like to change. They close themselves off with their ways and they want everything to come to them. None of us ever going to get ahead if we can't change."

I watched sweat ease down his temples. "You don't have to do that," I said quietly.

"Do what?"

"Show off for me. I'm not going to judge you because of one slow restaurant."

Roland began to laugh. "You sharper than I thought, book-lady," he murmured.

His gaze went to my chest. I had worn a white silk shirt—the sort of shirt my mother would cluck her tongue over. Now I regretted it, feeling him stare right through the thin fabric to my sweaty breasts. "I like that," he added.

"What?" I pressed the rim of the water glass against my neck.

"You talking back to me. No woman back home would do that."

I also laughed. "That's what I'm always getting in trouble for. Stop hitting your head against a wall, my father always says."

"That right? What else he tell you, sweetheart?"

It was as if our table, with Roland and me, was now dangling high above the dark rooms with my parents waiting inside. "That troublemakers are unhappy people."

"I see it different. Take my sisters. They raised to bring their brothers food and stay quiet. Now they good on the first count, but the second they have trouble with. So they cut me in the back all the time. You cut me right up front. That's good."

Slowly he lifted his knife and pointed it at me, the

blade flashing red with candlelight. "Does that mean you'll stop showing off?" I asked.

His eyes shone. "I'll do anything you tell me, darlin'."

After that our words flowed more easily. Roland's bad manners had riled me but during the next half hour, as we waited for our food, I began to detect that underneath his tantrum lay a darker, more serious cause.

"Tell me about your books," he said. "I see you reading all the time."

"My father thinks they're ruining me. Not only do they make me forget who I am but it means I'll forget to be depressed about how rotten life is here in America."

This made Roland smile. "Where I come from, that's the best thing about books. You learn what they won't tell you. I remember the first time I read Balzac I understand I was poor. Can you believe it, we don't have enough fish on the table and I didn't know that before? And then I read everything I get my hands on. I read Tolstoy and Marx and the Cambridge History of the West Indies. I read until my eyes go bad under the kerosene lamp."

Our gazes met for a moment. This is extraordinary, I thought. I feel as if I have known him my whole life.

"That father of yours," he went on, "he got the wrong idea. A girl like you, she got to read. She got to get mad."

"But I'm not mad," I faltered.

"Maybe not now."

"Honestly, I'm not. I don't even like politics. I just want to be left alone. I want my parents to—" But I broke off. I didn't know what else to say, how to explain myself. If Bump had leaned over and whispered to me, Your family does not exist, only you and I do, I would have believed him. Or if he had pushed me away from the table, chiding, Go back and marry one of the boys they find for you, I would have done

33

that too. I could hear what my mother would say of him: Big talk and no bank account, Sarah. What's he got to be so mad about? But I listened. I wanted to listen to him.

Our dishes arrived and his face lost its hard expression, softening into eagerness. "Man, am I starved," he sighed. "Haven't eaten for a whole day."

"Why not?"

He looked away, a crease forking between his eyebrows. "No time, I guess."

"Why?"

"The truth of the matter is, I too busy studying my head off." He patted his stomach. "But I tell you what my mother used to say. Is no cure for an empty head but a good meal."

Amazed, I stared at the array of plates put before me: in aluminum cups no bigger than a tablespoon, orange chutneys, gluey sauces and cabbage doused in red oil. Roland took a fried dumpling and dipped it in one of the cups. I did the same. Next the entrees came, piles of steaming rice, and I realized with dismay we were supposed to eat with our fingers. I studied Roland as he tore off a corner of soft bread, pinching rice and meat inside, and shoved it between his lips. His mouth worked fiercely. An occasional grunt came from his throat, but otherwise, conversation had come to an abrupt, agonizing halt.

Napkin spread on my lap, I tried to do the same. Only each time I pushed food into my bread, clumps of rice and meat went tumbling to the tablecloth. When I raised my eyes, I found Roland laughing at me.

"What are you laughing at?"

"Take a look at yourself," he gasped.

"Take a look at me! You don't even stop eating to breathe! Much less say a few civilized words."

This set Roland going even more and he let out

another loud, rollicking laugh. A smudge of grease shone over his left eyebrow.

"You're a mess!" I insisted.

"That I am," he agreed.

"Your manners are abominable."

"And you like a schoolteacher who can't stop teaching."

Smiling, he got up and sidled next to me in the booth, stuffing bread into my hand. My knuckles rested in his greasy palm as he guided my hand to my mouth. "How's that?"

My head spun, not just from the spices. Our thighs were touching. I noticed his hair smelled of pepper. Once again Roland was guiding my wrist to the food, only this time I bit the tips of his fingers. They were soft and rubbery. "Like this," he said, and suddenly, my own fingers were swimming inside the moist cave of his mouth.

In his Chelsea boardinghouse room, we stood pressed against one another, feverish, scented with dinner. My mood swung a curve from nervousness to irritation. The urgency of his body frightened me. I could hear voices floating through the thin wall. Roland pulled me on top of him, onto the mattress. I struggled at first, worried, for some reason, that someone was going to walk in on us. Roland was kissing my neck. One hand ran under my skirt, up the back of my thigh, untugging the skein of stocking from a garter. "Bump!" I whispered, trying to squirm away. A garter came unsnapped, his fingers loosened the other and I felt my stocking peeled off like a layer of skin. Then the other, and we lay back down on the bed as he unbuttoned and rolled down my silk blouse to my waist. My breasts, stuffed into their wire bound cups, seemed to lunge out, ridiculous and absurd. I covered

35

them, but Roland pulled my hand away. As he undressed I found myself shivering in sweat, as much with arousal, as fear that the strange voices next door would stop and hear us. Waves of excitement passed over me as I fumbled with his zipper. But Roland was slow and methodical, folding his trousers on the floor.

Then he returned and pushed his knee between my legs, his mouth making rough circles on my skin. I wasn't ready to have him enter me, but as he stripped off my panties, a strange thought cut through my mind: *He is a hole and so am I.* Roland thrust deep inside. A flash of heat stung my legs. We were moving, as if hugging something hot and painful between us. A moment later he let out a shout, and collapsed with a long shudder. We lay catching our breaths, my fingers clutching the oily strands of his hair. Neither of us could speak. He was crushing my leg; one fist clutched a clump of my hair. My eyes were growing thick with sleep. I could not even muster the energy to push him off.

What seemed like hours later I jerked awake, imagining a thundering chorus of footsteps, my mother's fists raining on the door. Where was I? I pulled myself up. The air hummed with silence. A burbling noise, followed by a sharp pain, cut across my stomach.

Hurrying into the bathroom, I crouched over the toilet. A second later, an oily stream of curry and peppers came gushing out of my mouth. I wretched again, fingers massaging my belly. Over and over. After I spat out the last yellow flecks and flushed, I foraged around for a glass to wash down the sour taste in my mouth. The bathroom was greasy with neglect: a shower stall edged with yellow mold, sinuous black hairs scattered in the sink basin. On a shelf, ringed with a suspicious film, sat one glass.

I found Roland sprawled on our tangle of clothes.

Squatting, I tried tugging my blouse out from under Roland's hip, but he wouldn't budge. I hissed softly, "Move."

He did not. I said it again until the thick brushes of his lashes swept open; he moaned out my name, his fist opening and shutting like a baby's.

"Roland, I have to leave. My parents are going kill me."

But he grabbed me by the arm, so I went tumbling down next to his warm, naked body. His hands idly stroked my breast.

"It's late." I added, in a low, urgent voice, "Besides, I got sick."

"How's that?"

"The curry was too hot."

Roland's fingers gave my breast a quick squeeze. "You just nervous, sweetheart. Come, Bump make you feel better."

I was about to protest, but another pain tore up my spine and my stomach began to churn again. "Oh no," I moaned, and with a gasp, I fell to my knees. This time all I could do was squat and wretch while Roland kept his arms around me. When I was done, he shoved something into my hands to wipe my mouth. I looked down at the crushed silk in my hands and let out a shriek.

"This is my blouse!"

He smiled, sheepishly.

"What about a towel?"

"They dirty."

"So you gave me my blouse?" I tossed it down in disgust. "What kind of place is this?" I gazed at him. "Who are you?"

"I'm a country boy," he smiled. "I'm not too good keeping up."

"Keeping up!" Thrusting myself up from the floor, I

stamped into the bathroom. "And what about this bathroom of yours? Is it against your country's religion to
wash a glass?" I filled the basin with water, but when I
looked at the blouse, it was hopeless. A ragged yellow
halo stained the front. Roland had come up from behind
in the bathroom, the florescent light making his skin a
drab olive color. He put his hands on my backside and
began rubbing up and down. I struggled to keep the heat
from lighting my skin again.

"Go away."

He did not stop. "Roland, this isn't funny."

But his touch was insistent. Not angry as before, his
fingers warm and softened with sleep. He rubbed every
tired, baffled inch of me and I could feel the stale rhythm
of my heart start to quicken with hunger. My thighs softened. Gently, he raised me to the cold sink ledge, my toes
curling in surprise.

"You leaving now?" he grinned.

"Oh my God, no, yes, I am leaving."

"You are?"

But it was too late, I saw. Warm basin water frothed
and sloshed against my back, and my blouse went sliding
with an outraged thump to the floor.

3

My friends thought I was crazy. I was crazy.
But before I could help myself, I adored everything about
Roland Singh. I loved his loping, clumsy walk; his
Caribbean accent, each sentence cantering into a sunny,
open-voweled lilt; his muddled fumblings for a phrase,
for he wasn't as quick with words as I was. I loved the
very feel of him: his hair, greased into a luscious pompadour; his suits swimming in heavy folds from his shoulders; his nut-brown thighs and peppery smell and the
splayed, broken rhythm of his anger. And his laughter—
God, how that man could laugh. At theater one evening,
while watching The Importance of Being Earnest,
Roland's guffaws blasted across the theater like a hearty
shiphorn. The other people turned in their seats, gaping
in astonishment. "What's the matter?" he called out.
"You never hear a man take his pleasure?" After, he fit
my elbow into his and whispered, "Listen to this, book-
lady. I never have such a good laugh but with you." He
rubbed my cheek. "What's the matter, I say something
wrong?"

"No. I've just never laughed so much, either. In my
house, they used to act as if God was upstairs counting

39

how many times I laughed." Then I added, "I've also never kissed a poor boy who owned so many suits."

He pulled away, feigning insult. "What you know about that?"

"I saw, in your room. I swear, Roland. How can you afford them?"

"They make me feel good. Anything wrong with that?"

"I suppose not."

"I see your face. You're offended."

"No."

"You are, silly girl!"

"It's so extravagant."

We walked in a silence a few minutes. "Sarah, the way I was raised you supposed to feel grateful for ever little crumb they give you. They always telling us to do this or that to be good. My father, he convert to Presbyterian Church so we can go on to school. I get the best grades, get my overseas exam. But when I come back, what is there for me? Same old sleepy village and nobody movin' on. It's a trap, this idea if you good enough you find your reward. You understand?"

I nodded. I understood only too well.

We were walking quickly now, Roland gesturing in the air. "People like us, we need more. Change got to be bigger. My life down there never going to be better if I do as I told."

But I didn't know if I could believe in something bigger than me. I only knew I wanted to have Roland take my arm as we strolled down Fifth Avenue. I felt proud of the two of us, unmoored ships, at home nowhere. Only with Roland could I feel this delicious pull in my veins. My skirt blew like a sail. For the first time in my life I thought myself truly beautiful.

I had my idea of political people: they led austere, painfully unattractive lives. There was Mosel, with his extra copies of *The Freiheit* he carried in a shopping bag. His friends wore drab suits from Kleins. Their niece Maxine returned from Camp Kinderland each summer with overdeveloped calves and a righteous assortment of Paul Robeson songs. Now I saw it was my own parents who lived with real deprivation. They worried. Every article of clothing was dissected and revivified into some Frankensteinian creation: doilies lumpy with used wool, old shoulder pads floating like lab specimens in herring jars over her sewing table. Even our new Singer sewing machine—that monstrous, expensive machine with its clacking wheel—provoked a torrent of fear that we had sinned in American laziness. Roland never worried. Besides his twelve suits, each of them meticulously tailored, he owned a beaver-fur-trimmed wool coat. His drawers teemed with a jumble of silk ties and gold and topaz cuff links.

Roland steered me to a boutique off Madison Avenue which was open late. It was exactly the kind of store I would never dare enter: a few dresses hung from a nearly empty rack, the latest poodle-cloth coats hung on walls the color of a pale rose. Roland strode to a rack and picked out a red silk dress. "That's my favorite color," he said.

"I can't."

"No arguing, girl. Give it a try."

The saleswoman held back the curtain and I stepped inside. Quickly I shrugged off my dress and stepped into the new outfit. The fabric shimmered; the tailoring made clefts of my waist. Outside the dressing room, Roland held out a belt with an enormous brass buckle. Flicking the supple band between his fingers, he clasped it shut around my stomach. "It's all yours," he said, stepping back.

"How can you?"

"Take a look at yourself." I stood before the mirror. I hardly knew who I was. My breasts brimmed into the scoop neck, my arms hung thin and elegant at my sides. But my skin began to burn. I began undoing the belt. "This is crazy. I can't wear this."

Roland came up from behind. "What you doing?"

"I can't Roland. I feel so cheap—"

"What you mean, cheap?"

"My father—"

His hand stilled on my buckle. "Don't you worry," he whispered. "Next time you come visit me you wear that dress."

A few days later I found myself hurrying up Sixth Avenue to Roland's rooming house. In the library bathroom earlier, I'd slipped on the new dress, now concealed under my black wool coat. I hoped I wouldn't run into Pandu, a very fat man who'd found Roland the place when he first arrived in New York. Every time I tried to pass Pandu in the hall, I could barely squeeze past his enormous belly, wood panelling digging into my back, but I couldn't avoid his oniony breath or the eyebrows he wriggled at me in a sneer.

Back in Guiana, Pandu had been a house servant for Roland's uncle Lionel Lal, a wealthy Georgetown barrister. When Roland was nineteen, he went to work for his uncle, though it wasn't long before the two of them clashed. "I have no time for his sweet-talking British airs," Roland told me. "He and the fat-headed sugar men runnin' that country to the ground." For two years, Roland continued to work as a law clerk, all the time remembering the world of his village, reading his revolutionary books, and plotting to get away. And he found some comfort in the simple company of Pandu, who lived on the top floor of his uncle's house with his gramophone and stack of 78 jazz records.

Pandu was extraordinarily ugly, with fly away black hair that made a straggle of a rooster's tail down his nape. And his head—almost like a sculptor's oversight—the brow too massive, hanging heavy over smudged eyes; his mouth lost in the folds of chin. When he spoke, he poked out his neck, spitting words. If I ever came a few minutes early, the door across the hall would fly open and Pandu would shout, "Singh not here! Come back later!"

Now, the door to Roland's room swung open by itself. I found Pandu standing in the middle of the room, heaps of Roland's belongings on the floor. The mess did not alarm me—Pandu often scrubbed Roland's room for him—but the panicked look on Pandu's face surprised me. He held in his hands a half-wrapped cardboard box, odd bits of stuff spilling over: what looked like a checker print dress and a blond-haired doll, one loose arm reaching down Pandu's thigh. His neck jabbed forward and he started to rumble. "Wife!" he shouted at me. "You are not wife!"

"So what?" I tried to keep my voice cool. "Roland will come soon."

He stared wildly around him, not sure what to do with the box. Suddenly, he loped across the room, dumped it on the bed. Returning to me, he wagged a threatening finger. "You must wait. You must not go anywhere."

"Roland told me to come."

"Yes, yes. But you stay. You do not go."

I stood there while he wrapped up the package, taped it shut and wrote an address out with a thick marker. "Your daughter?" I ventured to ask.

Pandu gave me a quizzical look. The corners of his mouth drooped. "No."

"I can help, if you like."

Pandu didn't answer. By now, he shambled about the room, fishing Roland's old trousers and shirts from the floor, folding them in a careful stack on a chair. I saw now that his movements were sudden because he almost did not trust his own massive body, his long arms which reached and yanked, his stomach bumping against bedposts and walls. With a sneer of disgust, he picked up our two smudged glasses from a few evenings before. Watching Pandu's elbows jab the air as he scrubbed them with a bristle brush in the bathroom sink, it was as if he meant to wash us away, an unmarried man and woman not only making love, but talking face to face, drinking! The room seemed suddenly too small to hold us both.

Pandu dried his hands on a towel, slapped his palms together and shrugged on a colorless sack of a jacket. Before he left, he held up a finger and said, "You wait."

Picking up the package, he left. I stood listening to his footsteps echo down the hall, the front door shutting, then a channel of silence. I waited perhaps one minute before rushing out of the room, and out onto the stoop. By now Pandu had reached the corner, package tucked under his arm.

I began to hurry. I wasn't sure why, but I wanted to follow him, to see what he did with the package. By now he'd turned left down Eighth Avenue and was headed downtown. I kept several paces behind him, following the urgent swing of his legs. He kept his head tipped back, as if his brow was too heavy to carry, and I was sure that at any moment he would tilt around, thundering more orders at me. We made it to 18th Street without his noticing me, and then he was slipping inside the post office.

Crouching, I watched as he shuffled up to a table, and

began to write out an insurance slip. At the window, he yelled at the clerk that the last time the package took too long. Then he turned back in my direction, face calm. As he was shoving the insurance slip into his pocket, it fluttered from his hand, making a playful loop in the air. I lunged forward.

But Pandu was ahead of me. He snatched the slip up from the floor. "Ah no," he laughed. "Mistress cannot have."

"Why not?"

"Mistress must wait."

With an odd, bleary look, he pushed past me and through the door. I remained, not sure what to do. I felt miserable, foolish for letting this bully of a servant trick me. Slowly I got up from the floor and went outside. Pandu was nowhere to be seen. I crossed the avenue, then crossed back again. I had no idea where to go next. I followed my feet until they brought me back to the rooming-house stoop. But I would not go inside. Why all these strange secrets?

Suddenly, the front door opened and out stepped Roland, sweeping a comb through his hair. He looked dazzling today, pink collar bright as a shell against his skin.

"Roland!"

"Where you off to, darlin'? I been waiting here twenty minutes. "

Then I was folded into his arms. "Roland, it was terrible. I saw Pandu and he—"

"He givin' you a hard time?"

I couldn't tell him. "He's so fierce."

Roland's fingers stroked the back of my neck and I softened with relief. "Oh sweetheart. Don't pay that fool any mind. He come from the old country. He just a little jealous, that's all. He can't get used to the idea that I moving on with my new woman."

"Sarah," Nettie groaned. "Not again. "

"Just cover for me one more time. I promise."

"But Elaine will be disappointed."

"You know I can't stand events like that. They're so bourgeois."

Nettie laughed. "Listen to you!"

"It's true. Do I really want to stand around and pretend for the zillionth time that Elaine's diamond ring doesn't look like an ice cube?"

"She's your friend, Sarah."

I shifted the receiver to my other ear, listening for my mother on the other side of the wall. "It's just that Roland and I never have a whole day to ourselves. On Shabbos I'm with my parents. And usually he has to study on Sundays."

"Can't you bring him to the restaurant after?"

I let out a laugh. "Oh, right. I can just imagine. Elaine's mother will think he's the waiter and talk to him like he's a schvartze with a pretty accent."

"That's not true. You don't give anyone a chance."

"Look, I'm not ready for that. Roland isn't ready. Maybe another time. "

"Where are you two going?"

"He says he wants to surprise me."

She sighed. "He is sweet. Okay, I'll tell them you joined us for the shower, if your mother asks. But you really have to tell them one day."

"I know, I know."

Excited, I hung up the phone. Roland and I had a rendezvous outside Judson Church at ten o'clock. This was the first time I would spend an entire day with him.

"So where is Miss Gal About Town going in this shmata?" Frieda asked as she set down a plate of eggs and toast. I had worn a full blue skirt, cinched with the belt Roland had impulsively bought me a few weeks before.

"With Nettie to Elaine's shower."

Frieda didn't answer, but began pulling dishes out of the china cabinet.

"What are you doing?"

"The other day you put the regular dishes with the Passover china." She shook her head. The strings of her apron made dents in her waist.

"Sorry."

"You've been so busy, I didn't get a chance to tell you. We're all set with the bungalow for the second two weeks in August." Her fingers worried a handkerchief. "Not that we can really afford it. It's ten dollars more a week this year." When she saw my glum expression, she added, "You are going, aren't you?"

I stared at my eggs floating in runny pools on the plate. Every August we went to the Catskills with Jennie and Mosel. We never even visited the big hotels; that would be too indulgent. I didn't want to go. I had a crazy idea of two weeks, all to myself in the city, left to Roland. I could even bring him here, away from that awful Pandu—I imagined the extravagance of our forbidden time, like Dante's Francesca and Paolo, entwined on my floral-print bedspread.

"Sarah!"

I looked up. My mother was standing in the kitchen doorway, her mouth in a grim line. "Just like your father says. So careless these days. Do you know, the other day you forgot about visiting the Rosens? They're sitting shiva, Sarah."

She went inside the kitchen. Hearing the clatter of

dishes in the sink, a slow miserableness swept through me. I got up from the table and stood behind her. The yellow cotton of my mother's dress had been washed to almost white. Her emerald ring perched on the soap dish. It wasn't her fault that I couldn't stand to spend time with them anymore; that their lives seemed so shrunken and ordinary.

"Ma," I said. I brushed my mouth against the top of her hair.

With a cry, Frieda swerved around. "My God, Sarah, you scared me. What is it now?"

There were wrinkled white circles under her eyes. "I'll go to the Catskills."

"So you're going, so what? You make an announcement like Benny Goodman is coming. Fine. I just hope you can be civil to us for more than an hour." Turning back to the sink, she thrust her hands into the sudsy water.

On the subway over, I could not help thinking about what Roland would think of the angry scene at home. They trying to control you, Sarah, he would say, and make me feel small and weak for having agreed to go. I squeezed my knees together, the subway windows flashing black. But it wasn't the same. I couldn't give everything up as he did, just like that.

It was extraordinary: I had been with Roland now over two months. Nothing was the same anymore. Judson Church's spire shot above like an Italianate tower, the sky overhead an azure blue, like the dome of tropic blue I imagined arching over Guiana. Everything seemed possible, my life now connected to this man with peppery-smelling skin and the sound and smells of a place I could hardly fathom. Then I heard the shy, high beep of a horn and swivelled around to see Roland sitting inside a red roadster, grinning at me. We both giggled. He wore a

cheap crimson ascot around his neck. Shading my eyes, I
looked at him with suspicion. "Where'd you get the car
from?" I asked.

"A friend."

"Roland, for once tell the truth."

He tapped the horn once more. "Come on, girl. We got
a lot of things to talk about."

I climbed into the bucket seat and we screeched out of
town. We drove and drove, out of the city, past Westch-
ester, the car gobbling roads like a hungry insect. Up and
down small mountains, tires spitting gravel as we arrived
at some vague destination: a broken-down dairy; a boy
leaning under a bucket. We hardly spoke, letting the
weight of the afternoon, the sun-drenched fields, fill our
heads with a dreamy carelessness. By one o'clock we had
ventured to Mohonk Lodge and sat on the splintery, ram-
bling porch. Well-dressed couples strolled by like nine-
teenth century figures. We were given odd looks, but left
alone. I didn't care. There was something in Roland's
manner that kept people away. I only wanted to sit there
and hold his hand.

"What was it you wanted to talk about?" I asked.

He hesitated, drank from his glass. "This country turning bad, Sarah."

"Such big statements," I laughed. "Don't you ever
think small, Roland?"

"Wait a minute, woman. Listen to this. I ever tell you
about a man named Cheddi Jagan?"

"Is he the guy we met on West Eighth Street one day?"

Roland laughed. "No, no. Cheddi famous down where
I come from. He's a man—same as me—come from the
same poor start, live in a house with kerosene lamp and
wood floor, and he come to America. He see all of this,
Sarah. Places where one meal cost your food for a month.

He go to all the fancy parties. He get around in New York, Chicago. He even marry an American lady." Roland hesitated, as if letting the weight of temptation sink in.

"But the thing of it is, Cheddi don't suck up to the dollar. He get an idea in his head, he and his Janet lady going to turn things around back home. Back when I working for Lionel, Cheddi just getting started in politics. He get himself on the legislature and he fight like hell to get those sugar wages up. You should hear my uncle Lionel curse him! And next year his party going to run for the big time. That's what Pandu tell me."

"I haven't seen Pandu in a long time."

"He's goin' back to Guiana soon. Now he gone to live with some people in Brooklyn."

I giggled. "Is it because of me? I don't think he's very fond of our being together."

"None of his business if he like you or not."

"I'm sure he thinks it is. The way he yells at me all the time, saying I'm not your wife. It's really quite dreadful, Roland."

Roland was silent a moment; his fist opened and shut on his knee. "I going to talk to him," he mumbled.

"Honestly, it doesn't matter. I don't care. As long as we're together."

"Sarah, you don't know what you talking about. You not married by the time you twenty to some shy little village girl, they put the knife in you. That's what you and me got in common. We don't take things the old way. We choose our own path. Like Cheddi and Janet."

I wanted to say, I can't be so sure, but Roland had already stood, slapping me on the knee. "Come on. I promise I give that Pandu a good shake and tell him I'm a free man now."

Though I returned his laughter I could see, as we

walked off the porch, Roland's face was troubled. He fiddled with his keys, then started the car, easing us out of
the lot. We turned down a long drive winding up the
mountain and when we reached bottom, Roland hesitated, as if not sure whether he should head back to the
city or go further, into the country, away from our compli-
cations. He fingered the turn signal. I said nothing.
Roland steered the car to the left, away from the main
road.

"So what you think about coming down?" he asked a
moment later. His voice was low, hoarse.

"Why?"

"Because I got to go back."

"Is it that Cheddi guy?"

"Is more than that."

I stared at the telephone poles spearing by, the hills,
hunched and wooly against a late spring sky. My fingers
spread in the folds of my skirt. "You're not telling me
something."

"And you not answering my question. You with me
here? If we got married, you come down with me?"

I was flattered, made giddy by his insistence. But it
seemed too hard to explain it all to him. The business
with Pandu, now these new heroes, Cheddi and Janet.
Who were they? What did they have to do with my life?
As the car spun on, it was as if pieces of me were shred-
ding under the tires. My thoughts, dark with worry,
pushed at my teeth. "This is so fast, Roland. My parents
don't even know about us."

"You ashamed of me," he declared.

"Of course not!"

"Then why you not tell them?"

"It isn't that easy."

"It's easy to know the chains that hold you down."

"Roland. This isn't a political speech. They're my family."

Roland pressed down harder on the accelerator pedal. A pocket of chilled air sucked into my mouth. After that, we stayed silent. It had come out then—what we couldn't work our way around: his stubborn rebellion, my attachments. Several times as I reached in the back for the thermos, my hand brushed his. He flinched. I could see the confusion working under his cheekbones. With the trees feathering past, something different lay between us. I was afraid and he was too. Leaning my head back on the seat, I watched the dizzying rise and fall of hills. Overhead the sky spread into a slate blue.

We parked at a valley dabbed with black-eyed susans, grabbed a blanket and moved across the field. There was no one around, no signs posted. We fell down exhausted, listening to the tick and rustle of insects.

"It's crazy," he observed, grabbing me by the waist. "I don't mean to talk so harsh. But I can't live without you, Sarah. You a girl never even seen a mango tree and I feel as if I've known you my whole life."

"And you're everything I'm supposed to watch out for. Arrogant. A dreamer who can't balance a checkbook. And sometimes a liar, Roland."

"You like that too," he grinned.

I hesitated. "Maybe we wouldn't even like each other, if it weren't—" I realized what I was saying and had to look away.

"That's all right. No use fooling, ourselves, huh, sweetheart?" Sitting up, he half turned away, showing me the dark muscles of his back. "Maybe all this works because it can't be."

"Don't be clever."

"You sounding bitter."

52

I was silent. I didn't mean for this to happen, did not want, at the very moment when I lay stretched near to him, hungry for his touch, to be thinking of what lay ahead.

"I know all that," I insisted. "But I feel differently than what I think. Or have we decided to do away with feeling once again?"

He smirked. "Your second bitter thought."

"It's not funny, Roland."

"No use fooling ourselves, hunh?"

"Why keep saying that?" The last few months telescoped into a lump of hardness. "And why bug me about coming down? Why not get yourself a nice village girl and she'll keep the home fires burning? She won't fight with you or give you a hard time."

Roland's face darkened. "I did."

I rubbed a stalk between my thumb and forefinger. So this was it, then, what I feared. But now he was turning towards me and his face was smooth, mouth opening in laughter. Roland had risen on his knees. Putting his head on my lap, he took my wrists into his hands and squeezed them, hard. "Don't pull away," he told me.

"And the village girl?" I asked.

"What about her?"

"Who is she?"

He put his mouth on mine. "You," I heard him say but the sound was muffled, for he was rolling—and I was rolling too—down the slope, his hand sliding up my leg. I was shocked at how easy it was to forget what we could not know about one another, all we might hide. I only knew that after pulling at our clothes, how little time it took to find him naked beside me, his breaths in my ear, a faint disturbance spreading outwards into pain and pleasure, I wasn't sure which.

*

The bus swung around the curving country roads. Frieda had brought two shopping bags of fried fish filets and latkes wrapped in wax paper, and the smells lingered like a misplaced odor. Jennie sat next to me, Mosel in the seat across the aisle with a Yankee cap jammed over his bald spot, and my parents in front of us. "What are you reading?" Jennie asked.

I held up my book: Wage Labour and Capital. Roland had found a copy for me in a used bookstore off West Fourth Street.

"I thought you only read English authors who write about what Jews live like," Samuel remarked over his shoulder.

"Hush, Samuel. Sarah always reads good books."

"The revolution happened, folks. They're just the same old thieving Cossacks dressed in red."

"God forbid you should have a hopeful thought."

"And you an original one, Mosel."

I leaned forward, my forehead grazing the back of his seat. "There are other places, papa. Places where these books matter because they're not even treated like human beings."

"What do you know of such things?" he asked.

"Thatta girl," Mosel winked. "One of these days your father will be whistling the Internationale."

"Nonsense. And for someone who's never gone farther than the New Jersey border, I don't know how my daughter has become such an expert on international politics."

Insulted, I slumped down in my seat. Lennie nudged me in the arm. "Don't listen to them." She lowered her voice. " So, darling, what's new with you? We haven't seen you in a long time."

"I've been busy."

"Working?"

I shrugged.

"You have a boy?"

"No. No. Not really."

"No one?"

I was sure Jennie knew I was lying. But this wasn't the time, not yet. Leaning my head against the chilled glass, already I felt antsy. I wasn't particularly thinking about the heavy volume opened on my knees. In truth, I could hardly remember what I was reading. The pages blurred with categories I could not absorb: use-value, production. I was thinking about Roland, how much I wanted to please him. I imagined myself trundling down the roads in his country, dressed in a safari dress, hair tied in a dramatic white scarf, all the village people smiling with gratitude at Roland and me. I wanted to be as good, as pure with purpose as Janet Jagan.

Inside the book he'd stuffed news clippings about the Jagans, so I could learn more of who they were. Self-styled socialists, they'd started their own party in Georgetown in '47—the People's Progressive Party—and after Cheddi's success in the legislature, were now plotting next year's campaign, much to the chagrin of the British authorities—and the U.S. press. I lingered over the delicious words of censure. Misty-eyed subversives, one article called them. Janet Jagan organized propaganda cells and dared to leave her four-year-old son to attend a socialist conference in Denmark. In a newspaper photo the Jagans were leaning out a window. Cheddi showed a loose, easy grin similar to Roland's, and he wore a wide-lapel suit like I'd seen black men wear.

It seemed plain how Roland might be like Cheddi. But no matter how hard I fantasized, I was not really like Janet Jagan. Our faces were similar—we could be cousins, the two of us lying thigh to thigh on park grass, sharing dark mouths of gossip. She, too, wore her hair tucked behind her ears. There was something different, though—I could see it in the set of her jaw, the way she offered her face to the camera—Janet Jagan had faith. That scared me. I had no faith, not her kind. I wanted something else, a hard bone of sureness knit from within.

At the bungalows I did my best to act as if everything was normal. I helped my mother set up the beds and washed the linoleum. I sponged down the windowsills since the dust made Samuel cough. I was good at doing these things, showing my devotion through activity. I even rearranged the living room, spreading a gold-fringed scarf Roland had given me over a beat-up table and placing it in the center of a cozy circle of chairs. When Frieda saw what I had done, though, she lost her temper. "What are you thinking?" she cried. "Your father will bump his knees on the table!" Her hand flicked at the dangling scarf. "And what is this? We have to live like gypsies now?"

"It looks better this way."

Even Samuel was surprised at my mother's vehemence. "It's just a little fix-up, Frieda."

Frieda waved a hand. "Go! The two of you talk your important thoughts. Leave the housekeeping to me."

Banished outside, Samuel and I sat on the front steps. The air was porous with the scent of evergreens.

"So now you're decorator," Samuel smiled.

"It's just so boring. Always the same thing. Just like the holidays. I could cook the entire Rosh Hashana dinner in my sleep. And it still wouldn't mean anything to me."

Samuel laughed. "So change is always better?"

"Definitely."

"You're so sure?"

"Of course I'm sure," I snapped.

Samuel tipped his head back, watching the lake deepen to a silvery black. We could hear Frieda inside, pushing a chair across the floor. "What about loyalty?" he asked in a quiet voice.

"That's different ..." I faltered.

"Such as the other day. I thought you would come with me to visit the Rosens. I thought you like the Rosens. Hiram reads the that rag, *The Forvets*—he even meets your high intellectual standards."

"I just forgot."

He shook his head, back and forth. "There's a lot more you are forgetting."

"Papa, please. We're having a good time. Don't start."

But Samuel had begun to steer his course of reprimand. "I know we can be difficult people, Sarah. I *know* that. We're old, we're set in our ways. But remember, you came to us a little bird with no direction, no idea of what it means to belong to the people around you. We raised you to be responsible. That's not foolishness."

"I never said it was."

"Youth is a terrible thing. It blinds you to the future, to the consequences of your actions."

"Or maybe it shows you that the future is yours."

He was silent a moment.

"Papa, you remember the time Mosel came by with a new Ford? You were so nervous you jumped out of the moving car? So who's afraid of the future?"

Samuel laughed. "I did that?"

I giggled. He put a hand on my cheek. "This will be a good holiday. No more fights, nu?"

I wanted to touch him; to throw my arms around his neck and beg his forgiveness. But that wasn't the language between us. Instead we rose from the steps and turned into the bungalow. For a moment, we stood with the screen door half open, watching Frieda drag a rocking chair back across the room.

The second week, after the five of us spread out our blankets and arranged the folding chairs, my mother turned to me. "Come, stranger," she said in her efficient voice that meant I had no choice. "Make your mother feel like she knows you. We'll go swimming together."

I drew off my sunglasses. "Can't you see I'm reading?"

"And I'm waiting."

She stood from the blanket, brushed the sand off her suit and held a hand out to me. I blinked, almost as if seeing my mother for the first time. My mother had a healthy, round-waisted body, her hair a pile of silver-gold waves. Wading into the water, her suit darkened like a flower over the lush curve of her belly. Only her arms seemed strangely withered. Patting the water, the skin on her upper arms shook, loose and white.

The water was warm and shallow here, the lake bottom soft with loosened pebbles and algae. Frieda's palm was soft too, like a baby's. It was as if I never really bothered to notice what her hand felt like. Now we stood in waist high water, hands clasped, as if we always did this. We looked back at Samuel, who sat in a folding chair with the newspaper across his knees. "Don't go so far!" he shouted.

"Sha!" Frieda shouted back. "You think we can't swim?"

She turned to me, green eyes flashing. "To the float, no?"

I nodded. That was what I had done every day, swimming the quarter mile to lie on its silvery, sun-warmed planks. It was something I liked to do by myself while

Frieda and Jennie splashed around in the shallow area. As we headed out, I also realized I had never gone to the float with anyone; it was where, once I hauled myself up onto its splintery boards, I could safely be alone.

I'd also never seen my mother swim with such determination. Each time she lifted her head, I caught sight of the stark "O" of her mouth, its smear of red lipstick. We plowed on, the water cold. She must be getting tired, I thought. But Frieda fought her way across. Even at the halfway point marked by two evergreens—when I usually slowed myself down—Frieda kept on. Finally we reached the float and climbed onto its boards, exhausted. Neither of us could speak. We lay gasping for breath, water pooling around our suits. After a while, Frieda opened her eyes and remarked, "I can't keep up with the American girl, hmm?"

Often they called me that nickname. It was meant to be sweet, showing me off, but I hated it, as it was also laced with guilt, all the trouble I'd caused them. "It's a long swim."

"And there's Samuel and the others. I wonder if they can see us."

"It's too far."

"Your father looks good, no?"

"He sure does," I agreed. Then I added, "Maybe this year he'll try swimming."

"Your father doesn't like the water. You know that."

"I *know*. But maybe this time—"

"He will not." The words came out abrupt. I shivered in the sun.

"Always, with the remarks. Wanting to change us."

"For Godssakes, ma. I was just talking about swimming."

"I see you. Not enough fancy talk, we bore you. Even

59

Mosel you're snide with, rolling your eyes when he talked about his liver problems before."

I refused to reply, not wanting to grant my mother her small triumph of observation. She began to rub her thighs, roughened and red from the swim. "So Miss Girl About Town, what's it like?"

"What's what like?"

Her eyes didn't waver. "To have so many lovers."

I bit my lip and glanced away.

"Don't give me that cold shoulder of yours. I'm not your father, who closes his ears and wants to know as little as possible." She added, "At least I show an interest."

"Interest," I grumbled.

The color had returned to my mother's cheeks and she sat with her feet dangling in the water, float tipping in her direction. I remembered all the stories about my mother in Russia, the Frieda I never knew, a champion runner, a real athlete, pretty unusual for a girl of her upbringing. There was even talk of sending her to school overseas until, when she was twenty-four, a few years older than I was now, Frieda's world as she knew it ended. Possibilities ended. She had survived, but no longer wished to distinguish herself. All she wanted was to get married and live the most orderly life possible, even without the Godly mission of having children. She and Samuel did not like change. They liked children. I was never meant to change what they had.

"I'm sorry."

"Don't talk foolish."

"Well, what the hell do you want me to say?"

"Don't swear at me, young lady." She turned so she was facing in the opposite direction, sun striking her face, showing crinkled, loose sacks under her eyes. "Why must you talk to me as if I'm your enemy?"

I couldn't answer.

"I don't always think the same as what your father says. But you know nothing of what we come from, Sarah. You only want to do things your way. It's disrespectful."

A sigh of impatience—how many times had I heard this self-pitying answer. "I can't do everything the old way."

"You think I'm forbidding you pleasure just because I'm old-fashioned?"

"What else?"

My mother gazed at the sky as it spread its dark and cool light. "If you could see the look on your face, Sarah. Such hatred. It scares me." Her voice was very quiet when she spoke again. "There are just some things you must resist."

"Such as?"

She reflected a moment. "Such as this American belief that you should have whatever you want."

"That's wrong?"

"It is untrue." She stretched her arms around her shins and hugged them to her. "Look, it's no accident we call some things shmutzik. Before you came to us, the other families observed, no?"

I nodded.

She put her face close to mine. "I am telling you, Sarah. There is something that means more than this crazy movie love you are always so ga-ga over." Leaning closer, our breaths, warm and moist, mingled. I could see the sweat dripping from her upper lip, sliding off the flushed edge of her chin. The air between us went close, without light. "My own mother used to say it to me. I know you."

When I didn't respond, she repeated the phrase, rapping her knuckles on the boards. "I *know* you. Do you understand the difference, kindela? I know everything that went into you. Everything we taught you."

"You don't know me." I tried to pull away, but Frieda had grabbed me by the arm, and began shaking me, hard. "Do you understand that a man could lead a thousand lives but was chosen for only one? That any other choice will bring him only the worst kind of pain?"

"You know I've never believed any of that stuff. And it doesn't matter who I marry. If he doesn't live around the corner and sit with his mother every Friday night, you'd still be moaning and groaning."

Frieda sat back with a sigh. We watched a feather-shaped shadow dance across the lake. "All this impatience," she said. "It makes me afraid."

I pressed the heels of my hands into the wooden boards. We both waited a few minutes.

"What about your new job? Do you like it?"

"You know I'd rather go to college full time."

"You could work for Stewart again. I'm sure they'll offer you better money."

"I prefer the library."

"Is there a reason?"

For an instant I thought of getting it over with and telling her about Roland. Instead I let the silence between us lengthen. The sun began to roll behind an evergreen ridge, leaving Samuel and the others sunk in shadow. The water, now roughened with waves, was like a sheet of hammered steel. I knew it would be cold. I hugged my arms, rubbing some warmth into them as I moved to the edge of the float. Frieda was doing the same. We dove in and swam back.

A few weeks later, after we'd come back to the city tanned and relaxed, my mother with a peeling burn across her nose, I was sitting in the living room after a shower, reading the newspaper when she came up to me, holding something on an outstretched palm. Then I saw what it was: the discolored yellow bubble of my diaphragm. Carelessly—or perhaps not so carelessly—I had left it on the rim of the tub.

Slowly I rose from my chair. "Don't say a word," I told her.

Then I stomped into my bedroom and flung everything I could into my suitcase: all my handmade skirts and blouses, my honor certificates and movie magazines, the red silk dress. Later, my father came into the bedroom. He had not even changed out of his street clothes. He said only one sentence to me: "You have shamed us." I could hear the sounds of my mother weeping in the next room.

When I went to Roland that night at his roominghouse, he took me into his arms. "I have no one," I sobbed.

"I'm your family now, sweetheart," he whispered.

And he was right. Within a week, we decided to get married. When I called my parents to tell them, my mother paused a few seconds, then declared, "This is no news I want to hear." Then came the abrupt whine of a line gone dead. I tried calling once, twice, three times, but it was always the same. A few weeks later, a brown paper package with the black lace shawl and dog-eared copy of *Wuthering Heights* arrived in the mail. Each time I tried my parents again, when they heard my voice, they hung up.

There was only one wedding photograph. In my white linen suit with big shoulder pads, I look like a top-heavy sail straining against the wind. My eyebrows are plucked and arched. I'm not carrying flowers, but a single rose is pinned in my lapel. A matching rose gleams in the buttonhole of Roland's suit. He looks like an immigrant. Ashy-eyed. Underfed. Pandu took the photo: he caught us just as we were running down the City Hall steps, me clutching Roland's arm, the two of us pitching forward, stumbling into a bright and unknown light.

4

Roland and I couldn't even find a decent apartment. No matter how hard Roland worked at his looks—slicking his hair down with Brill cream, putting on a clean shirt—there was always the wince of surprise each time a door swung open and the landlord took us in. How clearly I saw the two of us: my pale face, Roland looming darkly behind. As I hustled through the empty rooms, checking water taps and gas burners, Roland stood helplessly by, too scared to make small talk. When I came back to negotiate, I could see the problem was not so much that Roland was dark and me white, but that we were together and somehow uncategorizable.

Finally I found us a fifth-floor walk-up on 10th Street, off Seventh Avenue. Our wedding furniture consisted of two ladderback chairs, a kitchen table and a sofa that doubled as a bed. I tacked up some cheap Gaugin prints on the walls and lined the paint-crusted sill with a scrappy box of geraniums. Sequined pillows were tossed on the floor and six carved brass goblets—wedding gifts from friends at the Consulate—crowned the fireplace mantle. At the Salvation Army I bought Roland an old mahogany desk and a Remington typewriter.

But I was thrilled. My Bohemian life had begun. I had finally run away and this would be our home.

Anxious to please Roland, to live up to this new, daring life, we began to give parties all the time. Those who came were rootless like ourselves—usually men around Roland's age, either foreign students at Columbia or N.Y.U., or moving up the diplomatic rungs at the Indian Consulate. Many of them were well-educated bachelors, vain and a little spoiled but in a pleasant, harmless way. A party would start when Bump idly suggested to a friend that he drop by our apartment that night. Then he'd call me up at the library, saying, "Look it, Sarah. This Ghose fellow hasn't had a decent meal since he left his mother's house in Calcutta. What you say he join us tonight?" I would always say yes, and usually left the library early to wait half an hour in an uptown store for a sullen-faced Gujarati woman to sell me jars of mango chutneys and bitter-tasting achar. I began experimenting with fried pakoras, learning how to dip slices of eggplant in the chicpea batter and dropping them swiftly in bubbling hot oil. Somehow, in the short time between Roland's call and my return home, six of these men would shoulder their way through our door, praising me lavishly. "Thank you for your gracious welcome," they greeted me, tipping their long, serious faces. As a joke they began calling me the green-eyed Punjab.

But it wasn't all good. In the beginning Roland and I would make love at all hours: after the men left, with a gentle sheepishness, we pulled out the sofa bed; in the early morning after the alarm rattled and sun gilded the fire escape outside we again found each other. But as the months passed, Roland became distracted, unhappy with each day he had to rise and face. Though he loved our nights, sitting on the floor with our dirty dishes around us, arguing politics with his friends, underneath he hated his work at the Consulate. For one hundred dollars a month, he spent most of his time organizing their hopeless filing system. His boss Srini kept promising Roland a better spot so he could quit his extra job at the library, but usually Roland found himself cutting out ads for washers and radios Srini wanted to send back to his relatives in Madras. Roland shared an office with another graduate student, Ranjit Thapar, and Roland complained that the Cambridge-educated Ranjit was shamelessly favored by Srini—paid three hundred dollars a month to go to parties in the new U.N. headquarters and flirt with diplomats' wives.

In March, with the House UnAmerican Activities Committee hearings in full swing, the U.N. was put under interrogation. Since India's five year plans were modeled on the Soviet Union's economic plans, Roland was handed his first bonafide assignment: writing a short report that defended India's domestic program as democratic and "pro-Western." For five nights, he came home early and sat hunched at the desk, scribbling furiously. All day Saturday, before Ranjit Thapar was scheduled to drop by and read the report, Roland recited out loud while I typed on the old Remington typewriter. It was terrifically exciting—Roland pacing the room, arms flying over his head; my steady, careful corrections of his grammar. Afterwards, we made love on the couch, the upholstery buttons grinding into our backs.

"What extraordinary luck," Ranjit remarked as he strode into our apartment a few hours later. "You do the work and I get to come and enjoy your wife's marvelous cooking." He dropped down on our couch. I tried not to get too excited, having Ranjit here. He was a handsome man: solid, North Indian looks, a sharp profile, his cheekbones forming a smooth, oily plane. It was hard not to feel that he was going to make a much better foreign service type than Roland. "What about a spot of something to drink?"

"Tea or coffee?"

"My goodness, Sarah, you can do better than that. You've got some whiskey?"

I fixed Ranjit his drink while Roland hunched down in a chair, annoyed. Ranjit had by now loosened his tie and sat relaxed on the sofa, legs outstretched. There was an awkwardness between us. Ranjit's long lashes fluttered as he took in our one-room apartment, as if he floated in a serene, abstracted space. I knew Roland was too embarrassed to say something.

"Aren't you going to take a look at the report?" I asked.

He set his glass down. "My goodness, Roland, your wife is quite a taskmaster." After a few minutes, he glanced up from his reading. "This is fine. A bit high on the bombast, but it will do."

"What do you mean, bombast?" I asked.

Ranjit's head tilted, as if surprised to hear my voice. "This business about the colonial legacy, it's rather old hat for our purposes. Fine for the salt marches and the Mahatma."

"It's a beautiful paper," I said. "It isn't dry. It has passion."

"Yes, it does have that." He leaned toward Roland. "You've taken up agricultural economics?"

"Not yet."

"Our biggest problem right now are those fat landlords who won't irrigate their land properly. What do you think they're all squabbling about? Water."

"I know all about that. Guiana got its share of sugar landlords."

Ranjit waved a hand, a silver and amber ring flashing

like a yellow eye on his finger. "It's not the same. Guiana is still a colony. You can blame everything on a political system that's milking you dry."

"That's right! And this time the folks down there going to change all that."

"Honestly, Roland. Your earnestness is almost touching."

"No, listen, Ranjit. I hear on the BBC the other night the Jagans leading by twelve percent. He got both the blacks and Indians going for him. Is not so different from Gandhi's movement. I was thinking maybe I can ask Srini for some time off and go down—"

"Don't be ridiculous," Ranjit interrupted.

Roland's head jerked back, as if struck across the chin. I pushed down the urge to lean over and kiss his neck. It looked so thick and vulnerable.

"Roland, what can you be thinking? Srini isn't going to pat you on the head for your volunteer work."

"But Cheddi's damn popular."

"In the meantime, you'll be out a damned good job." Ranjit turned to me. "So Sarah, what do you think about these windmills your husband is tilting against?"

I tried a nervous smile. I perched on the sofa, one arm barely grazing the back of Roland's head. Their talk excited me. Like concentric circles, widening out from this small, overheated room, all these words floating toward all these places I had yet to know. But I could see the difference between the two of them: politics was a dry and practical business to Ranjit—Roland was interested only if there was a risk, a chance to make himself over again. "All I care about is that Roland is happy. Maybe his paper wasn't in the right bureaucratic language. But Roland has a lot to say. If working for Cheddi makes more sense," I hesitated, "I'm behind him."

69

"Hardly a proper answer from a wife," Ranjit laughed.

"Then you shouldn't ask me. Neither Roland or I are very good at doing what we're supposed to do." My fingers teased Roland's curls. "Isn't that right, sweetheart? It's probably the only thing we can agree on."

"Now that's worth another drink." Ranjit raised his empty glass. "A marriage without a speck of conventional good sense."

But was that what I really meant? I wondered the next morning, when cleaning up the apartment. In the drawers, crumpled into old trouser pockets, like some tide he could not sweep from our new life, I found all the the newspaper clippings about Guiana and the election coming up. A few weeks before, Roland's uncle helped draft an onerous piece of legislation: The Undesirable Publications Law, which forbid the import of any "Red" publications. I'd said the words—*I'm behind him*. Was that true? Did I really think that our future lay in such big ideas— Guiana unshackled, Roland hurrying back to a house he'd never been allowed to own?

Stooping, I fished another wadded paper from under the sofa. Now I wasn't sure I wanted to be like Janet Jagan, molding myself to Roland's troubled past, this vengeance he felt toward village life, where even his choice to move to the big city of Georgetown took massive effort. I cared more for more ordinary triumphs: our braided rug, the gold-rimmed glasses I found in a thrift store, now lined up next to the brass goblets. Each of these things were a buttress against the world, all the rude looks that fed Roland's wellspring of rage. And in ordinary things the rage would again gush forth. Last week he'd flung a coffee pot across the kitchen. It was only later he confessed to me a counterman wouldn't serve him and he'd come home to realize he didn't even know how to work our pot.

In these clippings Roland found hope that his pain might be gathered into one whole. And for me, too, they seemed to coax me out of my loss. Now six months since I'd married, my parents and I hadn't exchanged a word; the package they'd sent still sat under his galoshes in the closet. For a few weeks Nettie tried to play go-between but my parents wouldn't talk to her. Roland felt bad about the whole business. The break with his family had been easier. His mother wrote every few months—blue airmail letters that nested in our mailbox like robin's eggs—a few words scribbled—*The steps are broken and the taxes went up this year. Son, we are looking forward to your return and we can all be family again.* Roland always tore them up. That's why he brought people over so much—to drown out the silences of our marriage. There were other friends, too, from Guiana and Trinidad. When dashing out of the apartment that morning, Roland had scribbled down the telephone number of a man I had yet to meet— Charles Magalee—a friend from Georgetown who had moved into the neighborhood a few weeks before. "But they don't even know me," I objected.

"Listen here, we going to take care of you. In the Caribbean everyone related. Everyone minding each other's business. Now you give Charles a call and stop moping around here so much. He talk your ear off like real family."

The telephone sat on my lap. Several times I tried to make my fingers dial my parents' number—just as many times I let my hand drop. I finished my tea on the table and tried again. All of a sudden my mother's voice crackled on the line. "Hello?" I heard her ask.

I couldn't speak.

"Hello? Hello? Who is this? A bad connection? This is 237-5497. You want to speak to someone?"

Heart pounding, I slammed the receiver down. It took several minutes before I dared to dial again—this time I called Nettie.

"So stranger, too busy to have any time for your old friends?" she greeted me.

"I'm sorry, Nettie. It's been crazy these days."

"Obviously." There was a moment of uncomfortable silence. "Did you hear the news?" she asked.

"What?"

"Elaine is pregnant!"

I couldn't help myself: I was shot through with envy. "She is?"

"It's really great. Joe got a raise so they're moving to a new place in Queens next month. She's been running around picking out baby clothes. You know Elaine."

"That's wonderful," I said, my voice tight.

"And how's Roland?"

"He's good. Working too hard. Hopefully he'll get a promotion soon."

"And when are all going to go out?"

"Soon," I said. "But I better go. I'll see you on Monday."

I don't know what I had expected, I thought to myself as I set the receiver down on the cradle. Something to reassure me, to make a link between my old Brooklyn world and this muddled one-room life? I got up, swept the papers into the garbage and rearranged Roland's books. Then once again I dialed—this the number on the slip of paper Roland had left. One, two, three rings— when the line picked up, a man with the same honeyed accent as Roland answered.

"This is Sarah," I rushed in. "You may not know me—"

An explosion of laughter burst on the other end. "Hey, hey! Finally we hear from the mysterious lady! Why you got to keep yourself so scarce?"

"I hate to barge in."

"What you talking about? Here it is, Roland go and get himself married, and I haven't even met his damn blessed wife! Where he keeping you?"

"You know Roland," I laughed, sinking back against the chair. "Always off doing what he isn't supposed to be doing."

"That sound like the Roland I know. But now he busy with his books, stupid boy, and you a free bird. Why you not visit us now? We just round the corner."

"You sure?"

"Come, darlin'. My wife Sarita is dying to meet you."

I took down Charles' address, which was just two blocks away on Jane Street, and left a note for Roland. As I was turning the corner, the same voice came blasting out of the cool dark night. "Wait a minute, wait a minute!" he yelled in a burst of musical outrage.

"I'm waitin' until me arms drop off!" a woman yelled back.

"What you think, I'm Moses climbin' a mountain?"

"No, you the mountain about to fall down on me! Come on, move it, old man!"

The mutterings came from a bald man, who was trying to hoist a huge bureau up the stairs to an apartment building, drawers sliding open, brass handles jiggling. A woman gripped it from the top, but neither seemed able to budge it any further. "Damn blasted thing," she complained. "Why you can't pay a mover for this thing?"

"Wait a minute," Charles repeated.

He shifted his end of the bureau, so it rested between his

73

thigh and the rail, pulled out a handkerchief and mopped his face. Then he spotted me. "Hey, hey!" he shouted. "I bet I know who you are!" Grimacing under the weight of the bureau, he added, "Wait a minute now I put this thing down. My wife thinks she married a weight lifter."

He grunted and swore, but could not seem to get in the right position to let the bureau down.

"Is it that heavy?" I asked.

"Everything heavy when you married!"

There was a loud crash as the woman let her end go. "*What* did you say?" she screamed.

"Nothing, darlin'." He pointed to me. "Don't you see? We got ourselves a guest. Be good now. This is Bump's wife." Wriggling free of the bureau, he hopped down the stairs and hurried over, grabbing me by the hand to give me a peck on the cheek. "Now I see why that old man of yours hasn't introduced us. The devil wants you all to himself."

I stepped back, smiling. Charles looked about forty years old, with creases etched around his mouth and eyes, his belly making a soft, drooping U over his beltline. "And now I know you're one of Roland's friends," I sallied back. "Always with the compliments. And you don't mean a thing you say."

The woman, having extricated herself from the bureau, squeezed her way down the steps. She pushed a thick shock of hair out of her face as she leaned over and also kissed me on the cheek. "I'm Sarita," she laughed. "And you right. Don't you dare listen to a word this man says."

"Now I got two of you!" Charles groaned.

We all laughed, as if we had known each other a long time. Sarita seemed much younger than Charles, with a wide, saucy face, a mouth resembling Sophia Loren's and a frivolous polka dot scarf cinched around her neck. "I say to him, if you going to pay for furniture, pay for the delivery as well," she went on.

"The man wanted five dollars. Where you think I got five dollars?"

"Hmph."

Charles mopped his face again. "Time for a little break, girls, now that Sarah's here. I be right back." He went inside and brought us cool drinks which we sipped while leaning against the fender of the truck Charles had borrowed for the move. The bureau remained stranded halfway up the stairs.

"So I'm from Trinidad—" Sarita explained.

"And you probably heard I'm from Guiana. That's why we sound like fools with our bloody heads chopped off."

"Somehow I never got to meet Roland," Sarita said. "Which part he from?"

"Berbice," Charles put in.

"Oh, he from the bush! What's his family name?"

"Singh."

"You know the Singhs! Roland got some that uncle— Lionel Lal—up in Georgetown running the whole show. You wait, Roland going to be a big man like his uncle one day, with his fancy degree and high talk." Grinning, he patted me on the shoulder. "But what I want to know is how a country boy from the Berbice end up with a sophisticated lady like you."

"Sometimes I ask myself," I laughed.

"Yeah, I can see it. You a smart lady. I bet you talk a pretty circle around that husband of yours, huh?"

I shifted in my shoes. The ribbing didn't bother me— Charles sounded a lot like the rest of Roland's friends, with their cajoling and joking—but still, he made me wince. Behind the slack, smiling face, I could see a man smarter than he wanted to let on.

"I only teasin' you. You must know by now us rum-headed boys can't talk serious even if we want to. Look it your husband there. He big on talking politics, but I know he just a lot of hot air." Straightening up, he put his glass down. "Not like me! I'm a man of action!" He clapped his hands together. "Come on, woman!"

"This man." Sarita shook her head. "He drives me *crazy*."

The bureau was finally moved into Sarita and Charles' apartment on the first floor, then they invited me in for a drink. Their place was not that much bigger than ours—a railroad flat, three dark rooms leading one into another, the walls in need of a paint job, a bedroom hidden by a rough blue cloth hanging from a rod. The Magalees decorated as if for a real house: wedged into the narrow living room was a large sofa, its back carved into a braided twist of wood, green velvet seat cushions sealed in new plastic covers. A vinyl-upholstered bar loomed in one corner and an atrocious oil painting of a barnyard hung over the bar. "What's it going to be?" Charles asked, holding a liquor bottle by its neck in each hand.

"A little whiskey and soda." The sofa crackled as I sat. I wasn't sure I wanted to drink—it might make me moody, thinking about the muddle of the last few weeks.

"What's Roland up to these days?"

I faltered. "He works a lot. And he's interested in Cheddi Jagan's campaign—"

"Jagan!" Charles set down his bottle. "What kind of foolishness is this? His uncle know?"

"I doubt it. He and Lionel don't even talk anymore."

Charles shook his head. "Roland got a future working his big-time Consulate job, getting a good degree. Why he want to go back to that little dirt place for that crazy communist?"

76

Before I could answer, there was a soft knock on the doorjamb and Roland came striding into the living room. His briefcase bumped against his legs. He looked tired; ashy circles rimmed his eyes. He dropped down with a sigh next to me, and took the drink Charles offered him. "So how you doing there, big man?" he said to Charles. "They treatin' you well on that salesman job of yours?"

"That's right. I'll be running that place soon enough." He nodded to Roland. "Why you not come work for us? Is a good company, there's a real future in pharmaceuticals. We start you out at a dollar an hour plus commission."

"A dollar," I murmured. "Can Roland do this part-time?"

"Why not?" Charles nodded toward the room. "You'll be able to buy this wife of yours nice things."

"I've told you a hundred times, Charles. I come to this here country to study."

"And how that going?"

Roland shrugged, staring at his briefcase. "Fine." Flicking back his head, he gulped down his drink. "That reminds me." Out of his briefcase, Roland pulled a small white envelope. "That there is an invitation to Srini's house in two weeks. He's having a party, for the Indo-American Club."

"Well what do you know! Those professor types mix with a fellow like me." As he read the invitation, a slow grin spread across Charles' face. "What you say, Sarita? How's that for us country boys?"

"You do all right for yourselves." Sarita stared sourly at the drink he handed her.

"Come on! Aren't you happy for us?"

"I'm happy," Sarita replied. But she did not meet her husband's eyes.

Roland and I stayed for well over an hour. It was hard

for me to concentrate, though. I felt as if I were floating underwater, unable to surface, with an unknown weight tugging me down. And somehow, the conversation never steered back to the Jagans.

As we were climbing into bed, I said to Roland, "I liked the Magalees. They're very lively."

Roland grunted as he peeled off his socks and slid under the covers. "They all right."

"And it'll be nice for you to have a friend so nearby—"

"Sarah," Roland interrupted. "Let's not talk about Charles right now."

He had switched out the lights and we lay silent in the dark. For weeks we had lain this way and my limbs longed for his old touch, for something to root us back into the here and now, what we knew of one another.

"You can just tell me if you're mad," I blurted out. Rolling over, I punched my pillow. "I just thought it was really nice to see them. It's been so strange. I never see any of my own friends. And I was looking forward to the party—"

"Sarah, you don't know Charles like I do."

"What's to know?"

Roland sat up. I could see one strand of hair slowly fall into place. He brushed it aside. "Charles is a nice man, you right about that. But I'm not a salesman."

"Is that what you're upset about? The job he offered?"

Roland turned to me. I could hardly make out the features of his face, so I listened to his voice fall in disembodied waves around me. He let out a laugh. "My friends back in Georgetown would laugh at a man like Charles. Back there, Sarah, he what you call a simpleton. He got his eyes on one thing only. The high and mighty dollar. He like a dog with his snout to the ground all the time, eager for what the white man give him." Leaning a little closer and with his knuckles, gently brushed my cheek. "You see why a man like Cheddi Jagan so important to me? He don't ask to us to be dogs."

"Oh, Roland. You know I believe in all that stuff. But it's so crazy, all your talk—"

"You doubting me now?"

I didn't answer, thinking about Charles and Sarita and the phone call I had tried to make to my parents. Nothing made any sense anymore—I was still left with the uneasy sense that I was no more at home, no more secure than before—not with Roland's ambitions, keeping him restless and unfocused. "Roland," I whispered. "What, sweetheart?"

"I tried to call my parents today."

He sat up. "You did?"

"I don't know what got into me." But I couldn't finish what I was saying.

"Oh, darlin'. I'm sorry."

"I'm just so mixed up. I don't know where I belong anymore. Like, why can't I write your mother? Maybe we can make up—"

"Hush. One thing at a time. You got a lot on your mind and here I am with my big mouth."

He took me into his arms and I leaned into him, into his smell, his rough cheek against mine. "I'm so tired. All this talk about the elections and then Charles. I can't keep track. Could we concentrate on a few simple things? Like, we need milk and chicken tomorrow and I'm out of cash. And maybe—maybe you could ask for a raise at the Consulate."

Roland kissed me on the forehead. His breath smelled of rum. "My sweet, practical wife," he whispered. Then he began kissing me in earnest. Roland had not been this

ardent in weeks and it took a while for me to untense, as if
the long chaste nights that had stiffened my spine were
slowly melting into a stream of remembered embraces.
We moved slowly, pausing for the other to catch up. As
Roland's hands stroked the hollow at the bottom of my
spine, there swirled before my eyes an image of Ranjit
slumped on our couch, Charles holding up his liquor
bottles.

"You with me here?" Roland asked.

"I'm trying."

Then we began with more concentration, like athletes
who have faltered, a knowledge of disappointment in our
bones. Roland seemed to be keeping his energy at bay,
focusing, then letting us drift into a shallow bath of
caresses. Then we went deeper, farther out, gasping, as if a
line had been let loose as I foundered in waves I had
pushed aside. Roland crushed himself against me. I began
to weep for everything that had been lost and gained in
the last few months: for my father sitting before the lake
in the Catskills and the newspaper clippings piling up on
Roland's desk.

"What is it?" Roland wiped strands of damp hair from
my face.

I cried some more. My thighs shook.

"What you want, sweetheart?"

I touched his shoulder, his cheek. "I don't know. I'm so
mixed up. Nothing is the way I thought it would be."

"I know."

"And I want—"

"What?" he asked. "Tell Bump. What you want?"

Finally I could speak. "I want a child," I replied. I did
not even know until I had said it.

*

A shrill clatter of a telephone woke me. "Good morning!" Sarita's voice rang out. I put the receiver to my ear and rubbed my eyes in confusion. Roland was gone from the bed, leaving a space in the sheets. "I hope I didn't wake you, sweetheart, but I got to do some shopping today for the party at Srini's. Thought you might be wanting a new outfit too."

"I don't have much money, Sarita."

"What's the fun if we girls can't be a little frivolous?"

Rolling over, I looked at the apartment, drenched in winter sunshine and filled with the fresh, raw scent of new rain on pavement. Noticing Roland's raincoat and brief-case gone, disappointment stirred through me. Did we really talk about a child last night?

A half hour later Sarita stood pivoting in the middle of my apartment, candy-striped skirt swirling around her calves, as she peered with curiosity at my books, which lay in a heap on the desk. With her flashing black eyes, a huge straw pocketbook tilting from her elbow, she was all style and mischievous angles, a fox-like intelligence darting beneath the surface. At Saks Fifth Avenue Sarita pushed through racks of dresses, while I became bored. I had never much liked to shop in department stores and today there was a stiffness around my eyes, as if I hadn't completely woken up. Besides, everything was too expensive here.

"You are funny," Sarita remarked as we left empty-handed. "By now I'd be racking up a bill and Charles would be tearing his hair out, the little he's got." We stepped onto the escalator going up, since Sarita wanted to try Better Dresses. "Charles says I got to look the most ravishing in the whole place," she explained. "The party is through the Indo-American Club. You know about them?"

"Some. But Roland is always busy with his two jobs and school we never get a chance to meet everyone."

"That's because there aren't many to be knowing. More in Canada, I think. That's where my father and brother are. We got out, though. I say to my brother, 'John, what you want to stay in such a cold place for? How your thin blood going to survive?'" As she talked, we were passing the coat department and Sarita's eyes fixed on the displays of dyed white fox and beaver coats. "Now, if I lived in Canada," she murmured, "that's what I would get. A fur coat. Not one of those cheap ones, though. A long, mink coat."

"Is your brother still there?"

"He got himself hitched to a nice Canadian girl. He got a good thing going now. He don't have to go back."

"Is that what you think I am?" I asked suddenly.

Sarita turned to me in surprise. "What you mean?"

"A nice girl Roland hitched himself to?"

She looked embarrassed. "What you saying, dear? Charles tell me Roland is crazy about you!"

I trudged after her into Better Dresses where she began rifling through the dresses, as if she only had five minutes to steal what she could. Flicking the price tags into my palm, I was astonished by their prices. Seventy-five dollars for a dress! Sarita was already lugging a pile toward the dressing room.

The dressing room was also unlike any that I had been in before: a long row of doors striped in gay colors, beach-cabana style. Before the arched entrance, a woman with teased yellow hair and a pink smock held out a silver tray with keys. As we approached, she stared right through Sarita.

Sarita cleared her throat. "I'd like to try these on, please."

The woman shook her tall, coiffed head. "Now what's the point of bringing all those here? You don't need so many."

"Of course I do," Sarita replied. "How am I going to choose which one I want?"

Another abrupt shake of her head. "Go on, put the rest back."

"I will not." Sarita voice had gone high and stiff, like a bird trapped in a narrow chamber. "And you will unlock one of the doors for us."

"If you don't like it, you can go somewhere else." She added, with some belligerence: "*Miss.*"

Shifting the dresses to her other arm, Sarita pulled her face close to the other woman's. "I don't want to argue about this. I got a party I got to go to and I want to pick out me dress. I ask again. Please open the door. Now."

"Three a piece." It was as if the details of the scene had gone watery and magnified, a coin of sweat shining on Sarita's cheek, the woman's blond lashes. I lifted some dresses from Sarita's arm. "I'll take these. She'll take three. And can you please hold onto the other two? We won't be very long."

The woman shouldered past us to unlock one of the doors. Without a word she grabbed two dresses from Sarita and marched back to her place. Left in the dressing room, we stood in silence a moment inside the bright cubicle. As she began to undress, Sarita turned her face away.

"I think she was mad because of the way you talked to her," I whispered. "You could have been more polite."

The ends of Sarita's hair swung on her bare shoulders as her head jerked up. "Oh, you stupid, stupid girl," she murmured. When she turned around, tears leaked out of her eyes. "You don't get it, don't you?"

"Get what?"

"What's going on out there. How many women with my brown skin come in here acting huffy and bossing her around?" She turned away and snuffled into a tissue.

Embarrassed, I sank down on a stool—how could I have missed that? I knew, from being with Roland, how swiftly the world changed into a hostile, racial place. It was as if I didn't want to know, as if I was pretending everything might be like before. We did not talk for several minutes. And Sarita seemed to have shrugged off the incident. She stood perched on the balls of her feet before the mirror, cupping her breasts in her palms. Her tears were gone, her face screwed tight in concentration. "They're too small," she complained. "Nothing like that lady in the swim suits. We used to see her down at the cinema in Port of Spain."

"Jane Russell?"

"That's her."

"Oh God, Sarita, she's such a floozy."

Giggling, she swivelled around. "Well, who you want to be?"

"You know my type. Katherine Hepburn. I've seen The Philadelphia Story six times."

"You must be kidding! Why you want to look like her? She flat like board and act like she got a stick up her you know what!"

We burst into laughter, and the bad moment between us evaporated. To think of Sarita watching the same movies, hundreds of miles away in a place I could hardly fathom! We could be any two friends, crammed into a tiny dressing room, giggling over the dresses Sarita tossed on her long, willowy body.

For the next hour Sarita flung on dresses. She chose a stiff, lame dress that made a V-line in the back, a wide rayon chiffon skirt billowing to her calves. The top kept sliding off her shoulders, but Sarita told me she could stuff the cups with tissues.

After she paid for the dress, we trundled back downstairs with our big package to the shoe department where she picked out yellow high heels sporting green bows on the tips. By this time, my legs hurt from all the walking, but Sarita put a hand on my arm and begged me to make one more stop, back upstairs to housewares where she purchased two bath towels. When we dropped down on our seats on the bus a half hour later, she pulled her packages onto her lap, brought out a pair of sewing scissors and began snipping off the price tags. Crumpling the dress into a ball, she stuffed it inside her new towels, shoving the whole thing into her big handbag.

"What'd you do that for?"

Sarita was now rolling her shoes in the other towel. "Look darlin', my husband may want me to look ravishing, but he certainly don't want to pay for it."

"But why spend all that money if you're only going to lie about it?"

"You talk just like an American girl," she said, chin lifting.

"What's that mean?"

"Maybe you haven't noticed, but things is different with our men. You can't say everything out front."

I thought for a moment. "Do you think Roland is like that too?"

"I don't know, darlin'. I only know they want everything this place have but they don't like their wives getting the wrong idea."

We both turned our gazes to the women strolling down Fifth Avenue, out for a Saturday stroll in their white gloves and new spring hats. When we got off the bus a few minutes later, I had the sudden urge to grab Sarita by the arm, ask her to take back what she'd said, but she was pressing a perfumy cheek against mine. "Now don't you be moping about what I told you," she whispered. "Roland is a good fellow. He's not like the others." A moment later, she was gone.

Sarita, Charles, Roland, and I sat on their apartment stoop, the night air damp and close. Occasionally a truck rumbled by, our hems lifting from our ankles. In the past couple of weeks, we'd been out with the Magalees a few times. Sarita was a pain, every gesture of hers meant to call attention to her looks, and Charles played the oafish, clumsy husband, sometimes too insistently. But they were good people with wide, generous hearts and the moment they adopted us, they held on for good. Tonight we were waiting for another couple—Vijay and Claire—to take us to the party at Srini's.

A raggedy tin noise scraped the air as a red convertible, sleek with long fins and enormous fish-eyed headlights, came screeching around the corner. Behind the wheel sat a man with a thin, excitable face, his hair a wild tousle of black. He gunned the engine once until it sputtered off with a rusty groan. "Well, I'll be," Charles muttered under his breath as he rose from their steps. "This Vijay fool gone and got himself a new car."

"Come here, you old man!" Vijay was waving us near. "See what your nobody boy gone and got himself!"

"How you pay for like this?" Charles passed an admiring palm along the shiny fender.

I instantly liked Claire. I liked the way she ambled out of the car, light brown hair swinging across her chin, moving her body with frankness as she gave my elbow a familiar tap. "Don't pay any attention to Vijay. We just got the car on Tuesday and he's gone a little crazy."

Vijay had flung himself across the white vinyl seat, rubbed his fingers along the car's fake wood panelling, and popped open a silver triangle of an ashtray while we waited with amusement. Then there was the roof itself: the rest of us watched from the curb while he pressed a button and the canvas tarp hummed and swept backwards, collapsing like a fine-ribbed parasol on the back hood. "How's that for a boy gone barefoot in Port of Spain, huh?"

Charles laughed, his face breaking into tiny waves of delight. He relished the great fat loudness of American things—huge fin cars and Westinghouse ranges and radios. "I tell you, Vijay. You make me feel good. You make me feel like we bastards really in this country now."

The six of us clambered inside and screeched on to Seventh Avenue—top cranked down, even though wet air stung our faces. But it was as if I were piled into a high school joy ride—better, since these were people who, down in the Caribbean, could not imagine such lavishness. Squeezed in the middle, Sarita's kerchief snapping in my face, a giddiness rose in me too. I liked them all, terribly. They were all like Roland, who for the moment sat between Charles and Vijay, laughing—so much easier than my parents.

As we were bumping off the 59th Bridge, raindrops fluttered into our eyes. "Uh-oh," Sarita murmured, slumping down in her seat. The drops became thicker, drenching our cheeks, then our shoulders and arms. A ribbon of water skimmed the windshield, fanning backwards in a fine white spray. "Quick, do something!" Sarita yelled as Vijay slowed the car to the curb.

Charles, Roland, and Vijay held a conference, heads tipped forward as rain soaked the backs of their shirts, but no one seemed to know what was wrong. Each time Vijay pressed the button, the folded canvas top trembled, but did not budge. Roland tried the dashboard, but to no avail. The upholstery was turning gray from the falling rain. Murmuring under her breath, Claire twisted around in her seat and began fiddling with two latches on either side. As if by magic, the roof sprang over our heads and clicked into place. Vijay gazed sheepishly at Claire while Sarita gave Charles an angry shove in the shoulder.

"Don't bother me, woman," he grumbled as he mopped his head dry with a handkerchief.

The rain had stopped by the time we pulled up before a two-family house—plain brick with white trim, a gate bordering a narrow plot of grass. Mist drifted off the asphalt, the only other movement in the streets a huddle of three boys, one of them flashing a pocket comb out of his jeans as he threw us an impudent stare. As the rest of us began climbing out of the car, Sarita perched on the edge of the car seat, legs thrust out. "I can't walk on that," she declared. "My shoes will get ruined."

"Come on. It's only a few steps."

"They made of silk."

Shrugging, Charles bent down and scooped his wife into his arms. Sarita giggled, doing a tiny flutter kick as they knocked through the gate and lumbered up the path, the rest of us watching in amusement. "Let me in! Let me in, my wife is drowning out here!"

"They quite a couple, huh?" Roland whispered to me.

"Do they always act like this?"

"You haven't seen nothing yet, sweetheart."

The front door creaked open to reveal Srini standing in a blurry halo of light, dressed in pyjama pants and silk tunic. "Hush up!" He waved us all to come inside. "You want to get me the bloody hell kicked out?"

"I want the whole world to know who has come to visit you!" Charles laughed as he deposited Sarita on the door step and swabbed his face with a handkerchief.

"Please, Charles. I have enough trouble with the landlord." Then he led us inside a narrow hall smelling of tomato, up some thinly carpeted stairs and through a plywood door.

The Srinivans' apartment was a type I'd seen before among Consulate families: furniture that strained to be ethnic but somehow fell short for trying too hard: an ostentatious carved-wood and brass table, Kashmiri carpet and a few garish silk hangings on the walls. It was the kind of room that left me cold, because it was so obviously temporary, scenery meant for show, as if the real lives took place in some hidden, chaotic corner. And as we came into the living room, everyone rose, almost on cue. This I also recalled from other parties. It always took a little getting used to—a formality of introductions, this sudden animation of the scenery. After the first greetings, everything flattened again; the men withdrew into small urgent groups and the women rearranged themselves onto the chairs and couches.

Roland sidled up from behind. "It'll warm up soon enough, darlin'. It always does." He tapped my elbow. "Go join the others. I'm going to say a word to someone." He sauntered away and was soon absorbed in a conversation with a man I didn't know.

In a corner, by a table set up with plates and glasses, I found Charles and Vijay complaining loudly about finding only a few warm beers. "This Srini fellow don't know how to have a good time," Charles grumbled as he uncapped a bottle.

"Charles, quiet. They just got a different attitude, is all."

"Different. All these fellows, I seen them nipping on the whiskeys all the time."

"Then it's Srini. You wait, everyone going to slip away and take their fill in the other room. I never seen one of these parties where everyone don't fall on their face dead drunk."

From the other side of the room, Tara, Srini's wife, came hurrying toward us with a plate with pakoras and dipping sauce, neat bun straggling out its pins. I had never liked Tara. Even when she was trying to say something nice, her mouth turned downward. She didn't like Americans too much. And she was bossy, without an ounce of restraint.

"Sarah!" she cried. "I've been meaning to give you a call. Maybe you can talk some sense into that husband of yours."

"What do you mean?"

"I overheard from Srini that he's thinking of returning to Guiana."

I must have looked startled, because she added quickly, "Oh, I *am* sorry."

The blunder was intentional. "We haven't really talked about it."

"It would really break Srini's heart if he did leave. After all he's put into Roland."

Neither of us knew what to say. I stared at her plump fingers bent around her tray, and I hated her at that moment. With Tara, I was only allowed to be one kind of wife—like a model machine being tested for its adaptability in a new climate. Did I know how to make parathas? Was I planning on learning Hindi? The flesh and blood balance of living in two worlds—watching my husband shove rice and meat into his fingers, that strange and wondrous repulsion, knowing how utterly relative our souls really are—was kept tucked away. Now Tara grimaced as Charles drained his beer glass. "And Charles, tonight I won't even argue. No heavy drinking tonight. I already told Srini. We've had enough of that. It's awful. These boys come over here and they lose all sense of proportion. They don't know how to handle themselves."

"And mother Tara going to show us how!" Charles was already reaching for the next bottle.

"Come, put some food in your stomach." With a perfunctory toss of her sari, she drifted back to the others, leaving us by the table.

I searched the room for Roland. Only he could bridge the divide that forked across the Srinivans' expensive carpet: the Consulate men—delicate, careful intellectuals standing with their knees together, absorbed in their urgent talk—on one side; Charles and the others—men who had scraped together plane fare, made do with restaurant work or if they were lucky like Roland, a college scholarship—planted near the drink table. Charles was now bullying Srini about the new television console, which sat against the center of one wall. "Come on, man!" he shouted. "Show us some of your modern technology!"

"The way he goes on about it, you'd think Srini has discovered the bloody picture tube himself," someone else laughed from a chair.

Several people had turned around to watch the two men. A few of the women on the sofa craned their necks to see. Aware he was being challenged, Srini tugged off a cloth with a flourish, then explained: "The best part about this set is it's a Zenith, with thermostatic tuning." Obviously he had no idea what he was talking about.

Conversation ground to a halt. Everyone waited for something, anything, to happen. Tara had paused in the doorway with another tray of pakoras. I almost felt sorry for her—Tara meant to keep things smooth, and here came Charles, blundering into her living room in a heat of anarchic, immigrant passion. Now Srini was fiddling with the console knobs. A silvery dot popped onto the screen, then puffed itself out into a whitish cloud. Intrigued, several of the guests began inching up from behind.

Tara set her tray down. "Srini, use the horizontal," she commanded.

"If you recall, dear, the set needs to warm up. Then we'll get a beautiful picture. I don't know why I have to explain this to you every time."

"First it was the shortwave in our bedroom. Srini is up all nights, listening to the BBC. Though I prefer the television." She giggled. "My favorite is the George and Gracie show."

"Who's Gracie?" someone asked.

"Gracie Allen. George's wife. She's the one who always—"

Just then there was a shout—"I see something!" and the crowd stumbled forward, leaving Tara stranded in the doorway. With a jerk of her chin, she picked up the tray from a table. Everyone had by now gathered in a tight circle around Srini and the console.

A face was emerging from the cloud, soon shoulders and a torso. We could just make out a man—he wore a suit and was talking into a microphone. A moment later I realized it was Milton Berle, doing his comedy show. Another pulse of interest; chattering, they inched nearer, making it impossible to hear him. Small questions began to pop up. How many sets had made it to India? And what about sending one home?

I found myself pulling back from the group. Berle was cracking a joke about buying a pink Cadillac for his wife, even though she'd asked for a mink coat. "Well, the wife

says, Good thing you got a convertible so I can wear my
fur coat in the car!" Not very funny, but the others tilted
back their heads and let out peals of child-like laughter.

He started to launch into jokes no one quite understood. The ones about a mother-in-law brought out a few
familiar grunts. But the other were harder to follow. They
were schticks, American, vulgar. No matter—still the
group pulled tighter about the console, its blue light
flickering on their faces—still they laughed, though in all
the wrong places. I stared in amazement at the women,
the tips of their braids cutting across midriffs, the men's
open mouths as if drinking in the blue, blue light.

Now I was backing away in earnest, jostling against
hips, the coarse warmth of hair. I couldn't tell who was
laughing at what. Where was Roland? I took myself into
the hall and then another turn and through a door into a
largish bedroom. Here the air smelled of perfume and
perhaps the deeper odor of Tara. The bed, covered in a
garish red bedspread overflowing with a stiff barricade of
sequined pillows, looked like a respite from the party,
which had made my head ache. Over the headboard hung
a painted miniature of turbaned men and women in veils,
looking as if caught in a strange, elliptical dance. One
knee sank into the mattress, then the other until I collapsed across the bed. Through the walls I could hear the
garbled buzz of television. I was tired and confused. It was
as if I didn't know who I was anymore.

A few minutes later something thudded, not far away. I
sat up with a start, the air speckled white. A moment later
a closet door opened and a woman, dressed in a loose
white sari, pulled herself up from the floor. Her arms were
thin, the skin about her elbows slack and ashy. Her mouth
opened once, then shut again. One finger rubbed inele-
gantly at her nose.

"Sorry, is this your room?"

No answer. Stifling a yawn, she bent over what I now saw was a bedroll spread on the floor, folded it in a half and shambled nearer. The odor I'd first smelled—perspiration and a deep, woody scent—came from her. She made her way up to the middle of the bed, putting her face near mine. Her lips were thin and bloodless, flecked with black.

The woman kept pointing at my stomach, so I nodded. With a broken smile, she pulled her face close. I could feel the bone of her cheek pressing down; hear the alert draw of breath, one hand fisted into my skirt. We fumbled into a kind of embrace, arms loose about one another. She kept her ear pressed on my stomach, as if listening to a message shouted down a steep well. It was strange, but I shut my eyes an instant, listening to her breaths.

She muttered some words.

"What is it?"

Again she spoke but I couldn't understand.

Just then the door banged open and with it came a garbled rush of noise—the television, which was blaring too loud—and voices, mounting energetically in the hall. Tara stood in the doorway, hands flashing about her face. "What is this?" she shrieked. "What is going on?"

But we could not seem to uncouple from our embrace until Tara broke into a stream of Hindi, scolding the old woman, who had barely managed to pry herself loose. By now Tara had completely dropped her social graces, telling me coldly, "She's an ignorant servant. You shouldn't be bothering with her." With a flick of her wrist, Tara sent the poor woman scuffling off to the kitchen, where Tara informed me, "she wouldn't dare trouble our guests."

In the hall I came upon Sarita, looking strangely beautiful and aloof in her new dress, the top slid off her shoulders. Putting a hand on my arm, she whispered, "What was that about?"

"I don't know. The woman put her face to my stomach."

"You say something to her?"

"No."

Sarita giggled. "Oh, Lord. Mother Tara got all upset, she think her servant going to cast a spell on the Yankee lady."

As we were turning to go back to the living room, from down the hall, there was a shout. "You hear that!" Roland yelled. The television sound faded. I could hear the crackly noise of a shortwave radio. Roland came rushing out of another room, Ranjit following behind. "You hear that Sarah? Landslide! The Jagans got a landslide victory!"

"Well, well," Ranjit said with a rueful smile. "Looks like someone got their wish."

By the time we returned to Manhattan a few hours later, everyone was in a more light-hearted mood. Roland could not contain himself with excitement; stepping out of the car, he told me he was just running up to Sheridan Square to see if he could find a copy of *The New York Times* to see if there was any more news. As we watched him bound up Seventh Avenue, Claire gave my wrist an affectionate squeeze, brushed a kiss on my cheek and whispered, "I hope you two will come to our apartment some time." As the car roared off and we turned to walk down the avenue, I remarked to Charles and Sarita, "They're awfully nice."

"Claire's a good woman. It's Vijay that's got the devil in him."

"Sarita, you be quiet now."

"What you shutting me up for? Sarah can know if she wants to."

"Know what?"

Charles' pace began to hasten a few steps ahead, hands shoved in his pockets. Sarita did not hurry to catch up. Tossing her hair back from her shoulders, she told me, "Vijay's got a wife in Trinidad." She seemed to sing the words. I wondered why. I tried not to feel hurt.

"He married very young," Roland said.

"Yeah, young enough to leave behind. Not young enough to take with him."

"Sarita, why you always have to go on?" Charles had stopped walking.

"I know this sounds naive, but how can he have two wives?" I asked.

Sarita shrugged. "The other girl don't kick up a fuss so long as he keeps the dollars coming."

"And Claire?"

At this everyone both fell silent, a slight wind lifting off the rain-blackened pavement. Embarrassed, Sarita wound her scarf around her hair. "When he and Claire got married, he kept promising to tell her. He promise and promise. I tell him I don't know how many times, you can't be going around with a lie like that. It catches up to you."

"It's his business," Charles grumbled. "And he sends money for the kid."

"He's got a kid?"

Sarita nodded, biting her lip.

"I think it's mean. He has to tell Claire. It isn't right."

"It's true, it's wrong," Charles interrupted. "But what you think is worse. Knowing or not knowing?"

"I'm no fan of lying, Charles. Not knowing, of course."

We had taken up walking again. Charles watched me with a gentleness that embarrassed me. When he spoke his voice was low. "You wait. Age gives you plenty to be ashamed about."

And I would have offered an angry retort, but we had arrived in front of our apartment house, the three of us staring at a row of garbage cans, bent metal tops upended, like hats blown off school girls' heads. Discomfited, Charles drew Sarita towards him, almost like a father to a daughter. We said our good-byes with this odd, painful confidence jostling between us.

Left standing in the hallway, I had the urge to see my new friends one more time. But when I turned around to peer through the narrow window, I was surprised to see the Magalees walking as if indifferent to one another, at least a foot of space between them. Nothing like the gallantry or bickering I'd seen before. I walked upstairs in silence. Pushing open the door, I saw our apartment, exactly as we'd left it a few hours before: blinds drawn, newspaper clippings stacked on his desk, Roland's wingtips with their turned-up toes, as if caught in midstep. Exhausted, I dropped down on the chair by the window, raised the blinds and sat gazing at the empty street where Sarita and Charles had just walked.

Then I began to cry. First with embarrassment, wiping my face with my wrists, letting out delicate, self-conscious sniffs. I was crying as much for myself, as for the whole mess of the last few weeks—for me and Roland and my parents and the baby I wanted; for Sarita and Charles, Vijay and Claire too, and even the old woman sleeping in a closet—for all the lies and things kept hidden, for everything that can't be said between people.

And just as abruptly as I started, my crying stopped. A cab had come gliding down the street, its roof silvery pale under the street lamp. As it discharged a passenger, I felt all the air and hope of a reasonable life together go out of me. Rising from the chair, I went into the bathroom and ran the taps full blast, watching the water bubble and froth about the drain. After undressing, I stepped in, hot water circling my waist.

The tub was my favorite feature in our apartment. It was narrow at the bottom, opening white and wide like a dahlia. I loved the way the sides rose high above my shoulders and the blue-ringed bottom hugged my hips. Still I didn't feel any better. I sank down further, gazing around the bathroom. *My* room, I told myself. The chipped mirror, his shaver propped on a shelf. A few minutes later I could hear the key turning in the lock. Then there was a bashful tap on the door and Roland drifted in, a thicket of worry-lines spread across his forehead.

"I guess you know what I come to say," he whispered.

Fear shot through me. "Go ahead."

"I got to go and see what's happenin' down there, Sarah. Things are changing fast. Do you know more people voted in this election than in Jamaica, Barbados, and Trinidad. What I would give to have seen that!"

"But what about us, Roland?"

He was silent.

I stroked the water, palms down. "Is there something you're not telling me?"

His fingers twisted at his sides.

"Why do you always tear up the letters your mother sends? And why won't you talk to your uncle?"

Roland's face smoothed itself out. "Sarah, I tell you before. My family don't understand me, they tryin' to hold me back. And see here, Sarah. Now's the time to go down there and maybe make a little money helping out."

"Of course." I flipped the soap out of its dish, watching it make a slow, cloudy spiral before bobbing up again. "You've got to be where the action is. Damn you, Roland."

Roland collapsed on the toilet. "Please, Sarah. They need me down there."

I let my hands part and peered at myself in the water's reflection, aware of the ridiculous figure I cut: naked and apple-pink. I patted my skin. "Darling, I believe you are good, but not stupid. Don't you see you're doing a lot more good if you just stay and finish your degree?"

Roland began pacing the room in short, abrupt strides, turning sharply as he reached the towel rack. "It's easy to laugh at us, no? Village boys scrappin' over something bigger?"

"I'm not laughing at you, Bump."

"I tell you frankly. I'm afraid." The long curl of his pompadour had come unravelled. "How many men like Charles I see come here and a few years later, they forget the earth that gone weaned them. They come down flaunting their American dollar, shaming their relatives, shamed by the dirt roads and house they born to." He stood on the ragged oval of a bath rug, cocking an eyebrow at me.

"You done with your little speech?" I asked.

"I'm not going to be like that," he warned.

"First my family, now you," I murmured.

"That's not true!" He came closer to the tub. "It's a hell of a lot different. I take care of you, child. I no turn you away." A grin slipped over his teeth. "Besides, you going to stand in the way of big things?"

Nudging down further in the water, I was silent for a while. "Why can't I come with you?"

"Now look who's talking crazy! We can't both close up shop, just like that. I promise you, Sarah, if it lookin' good down there, then we figure out how to bring you down too." Reaching into the water, he stroked my stomach. "You can be the next Janet Jagan, hunh?"

"So when will you come back?"

"As soon as I can."

99

"Do you swear?"

He gazed at me, incredulous, his worry lines splintered into surprise. "What you saying, angel? Don't you know none of this means anything without you? You going to throw away everything we have?"

Then I couldn't help myself. I cried once more in the cooling bath water, considering this absurd, little existence, my parents and their brown paper package sitting under Roland's galoshes in the closet. Damn them all. But when I wiped my eyes and saw my husband, sitting on the turned-down toilet lid like a small boy exhausted after a tantrum, I simply couldn't muster up the same rage I harbored toward my parents. His shirt was buttoned wrong. His chin shone with chicken grease. I reached a hand out and patted him on the thigh. "Do I hate you sometimes."

To myself, I thought: What an idiot I can be.

Roland was already standing, shaking out his trouser knees. "I promise, Sarah. Cheddi going to win. I'll go see what's happenin' down there. Then we figure everything out. Everything going to be good and sweet." His breaths made moist rings on my neck. "You believe this Guianese fool?"

Wincing at the familiar, sunny bait, I thrust myself up from the tub, ribbons of water streaming off my legs. "You are a fool," I whispered.

5

A sulky, early summer fell on the city that year. Women walked down the streets, looking stiff and irritated in their crinoline skirts. I kept my windows open and could hear radios warbling on other sills. The first POWs were exchanged—it seemed the war was about to be over as fast as it had started. The news we heard from Guiana was mixed. During Crisis Week, trouble between black and Indian interests threatened to crack the party apart. But they negotiated, and in the end a set of ministers were chosen with the legislature set to open at the end of May. Even Janet Jagan held a position. The impact of the Jagans' win was not lost on anyone: as the first government in the Western Hemisphere with "socialist leanings," it was being watched closely by both the American and British press. In Manhattan, we watched swollen rain clouds jam against the skyscrapers, refusing to burst, while inside our apartments the air scratched with exhaust-smelling breezes.

Most nights I joined the Magalees and the three of us would head uptown to Vijay and Claire's, a dingy apartment they shared with another West Indian couple. Their bedroom was really an old dining room with a faded curtain tacked across a bevelled glass door; the ceiling fixture old gas lamps with bulbs stuck inside. Our evenings had the feel of improvisation, of a rehearsal before the real performance, which was always taking place somewhere else under bright lights, in other apartments, richer, more American than ours.

None of us had much money, but we tried our best to make ourselves feel luxurious. We knew the tricks: Claire bought half-price daisies from the florist five minutes before he closed up, Sarita found a butcher in Chinatown who sold hacked goat for our curries and Charles bought bottles of rum from a wholesaler in New Jersey. Then we would gather in the living room, on pillows and chairs, stuffing ourselves with curry and roti bread until our ribs ached. We forgot how outside of things we really felt; how Charles sold on a circuit two hundred miles wider than other salesmen to make up for slammed doors; Sarita's best job yet was as a receptionist at a candy company.

I would sit on the floor, legs tucked under my skirt, Broadway's traffic insistent as a wakeful child below, thinking to myself: Don't go anywhere. You belong right here. It never mattered that Charles always wound up arguing with Vijay or that the calypso records we listened to scratched and skipped. Images would float from their mouths. Sometimes about Trinidad or Guiana or about being dirt poor. Or gossip about others on the grapevine who'd gone off to London or Toronto, working as hotel maids or some lucky enough to get office jobs.

They were different from the immigrants I'd grown up with, their talk bright and lusty with plans. Every other week Vijay came up with another outrageous business idea. Though his luck was rotten and he'd lived only in shared rooms and bought his convertible on a high interest loan, he believed in the wild, extravagant dream of this country, the magic proportions he could imagine himself into. "We can start wholesale," he declared once, having dragged a battered suitcase into the living room. For the occasion, he'd put on a fedora cocked low over his eyes and his only suit—brown with dark brown piping and pegged legs. Only the contents of his suitcase were dismally disappointing: inside lay dozens of cheap printed scarves, edges unravelling. "We can open a store when we get enough capital—I have a friend, he owns a place in the East 60's, very posh. Lots of rich ladies come in buying," he continued.

"Vijay," Sarita laughed. "What makes you think a fancy lady going to buy a head scarf her maid wear?"

"You hush," Vijay made an insulted face, holding the cloth up to Charles. "What you think, man?"

"You show me the business plan." Charles said, rubbing a tumbler on his knee. "Then we can talk."

Of course this never happened, for the next week Vijay trotted out yet another scheme. One week it was smuggled gold necklaces from Guiana; the next time he brought us a man named Edgar from Guadeloupe who carried in two expensive bottles of champagne, which we drank while he explained his spectacular plan—something to do with leasing private airplanes. Far too exotic for our taste, but our heads were giddy from the champagne and we each scrounged up fifty dollars. Not that we ever heard from him again.

Each time, as we sat on pillows, a bit drunk, and Vijay came up with another dream idea, we would go through the same pantomime of excitement and ridicule, as if to reassure ourselves that we too were making good on the promise of America. Vijay would pace the living room, arms flying over his head, his talk pitching higher and higher. The more Vijay gushed and flailed about, the more Charles picked at the flaws in his logic until the fighting got terrible between them.

"Ass-licking brown-white man!" Vijay shouted at him one night, when Charles laughed outright at his suggestion of opening a shoe store. "All you want to do is work for the white man!"

"No good silly ass dreamer!" Charles shot back. "Whoever going to take a fool like you seriously?"

These fights frightened me, but in the kitchen later, our arms elbow-deep in suds, Claire leaned close and whispered, "Don't worry about them. Vijay wakes up the next morning and he's forgotten all about it."

I liked Claire. During all the conversations and dinners, she was the one who stayed quiet. She and I could admire each other without saying so; both of us were women for whom sacrifice was the easiest thing, selfhood troublesome. In public, we skated reasonably around our whiteness.

Claire had an open-prairie face, lake-blue eyes and a curious way of shrugging off her husband's crazy, nervous energy. She dressed in clothes from thrift stores: cardigans the color of faded typewriter ribbon, pocketbooks with another woman's lipstick crumbled in the seams. She kept on through our long meals, cutting her meat into tiny pieces, always smiling. I'd heard the story of their marriage from Sarita; how Vijay was married off at eighteen to a neighbor girl. But after five years of living in her mother's house, he'd skulked off to America where Charles hooked him up with a job as a janitor in a doctor's office.

It was there he met Claire and soon enough, they were a steady thing, though Vijay didn't mean it to last. But Claire made it too easy; she was reasonable to the point of blindness. Before he knew it, she'd moved her one suit-

case into his furnished room, lining a shelf with memen-
tos of their hurried marriage: a champagne cork and two
photos from the Circle Line boat tour they took after the
City Hall ceremony. They got comfortable, spending
Sundays watching his friends play cricket in Van Cort-
land Park. No one ever breathed a word about Vijay's
other wife.

Sarita, too, once told me her side of her ill-matched
marriage: she was seventeen, working in a dress shop in
Port of Spain, dreaming of becoming a designer, when a
cablegram came from her father in Toronto which said,
COME ASAP. GOOD CONNECTIONS FOR YOU. When
she arrived, her father dumped her with friends and disappeared for a few days, none of whom seemed to know why
she was there. A few days later he returned with a strange
man named Charles, the cousin of the man they were staying with. Sarita disliked him immediately, for he wore a
cheap, daffodil-yellow shirt and stank of cologne. Only
that night while they were playing poker and Charles was
winning everyone blind, Sarita's father put his arms
around him and laughed, "What a son this man going to
make!" Sarita bolted upright from the table and fled to
the bedroom and locked herself in a closet. "What's the
matter with you?" her father had yelled at her. "Charles
here is going to buy you anything you want! He's going to
get you citizenship!" And though she cried for hours, it
wasn't much longer before she gave in and found herself
in car next to Charles.

And then there was me, the odd, extra wheel. For better
or worse, I'd settled in with my new friends. From all the
eating and drinking, I'd gained a few pounds—everyone
said I looked better, less morose. I discovered something
in that West Side apartment, the streets a dark river running below, flecked with bits of foam, white faces that

arrogantly told us we did not belong, reminding us we were always outside the real pulse and tide. Listening to their rum-tinged talk gave me an honest feel for the life that had bred Roland, the simple pleasures of a moon rising over a rice field. It was almost as if I had joined him on those mud-clay roads.

Vijay was pacing. He stomped back and forth on the restaurant's red carpet, patting his trouser legs. The five of us—Charles, Sarita, Vijay, Claire and I—had been browsing in Times Square, arguing about which movie to see—either a Doris Day movie or Niagara with Joseph Cotten—when a sudden downpour broke upon us, needles of rain clattering against car hoods. We'd fled across Broadway, hopping over puddles streaky with neon color and took shelter in a Chinese restaurant. Now sitting slumped into a booth, we listened to the wind bellow against the gratings outside.

Wet hair poking into stiff black spikes, Vijay collapsed into a seat and whispered, "I got it. I got *the* idea."

"Uh oh." Sarita shook her fingers through her hair, which had frizzed into glossy ringlets. "Vijay, when you going to learn is no good idea but someone else's?"

"Listen you, fancy lady, don't be writing me off just yet."

"So what's the plan now? Racehorses or cards?"

"Not funny."

"Then speak up."

Sarita groaned. "I am so tired, Vijay. Can't we have one quiet night?"

Vijay swabbed at his hair, which kept spiking up in the back. His hands were fine and slender, always touching things, like a jazz piano player fingering his scales. "No man, I'm talking about a house. We can get ourselves a summer place. Fix it up and rent the rooms and the like."

"What you know about fixing houses?"

"Plenty. He knows how to tell the workmen what to do and where he's going to take his nap." Charles clapped open his menu, as if to indicate that Vijay's suggestion wasn't worth wasting much more time on.

"I'm serious! I can fix a roof!"

"Claire, is that true?"

"It's not a question if he *can* do it. It's if he *will* do it."

"Now you also against me!"

"Come on already," Charles grumbled. "Let's eat."

He flagged the waiter and ordered heaps of food: a round of egg drop soup, egg rolls and dumplings, then chow mein, sweet and sour pork, fried rice and barbecued ribs.

"If you're really serious, Vijay," I said after the waiter left, "there's a lot of bungalows and empty houses in the Catskills. It's not so far-fetched."

His face brightened. "See there!"

"All right, all right," Charles laughed. Unclipping a pen from his pocket, he started to scribble figures on a red paper napkin. "Okay, Mr. Idea-Man, what we get ourselves, half a dozen families from the Indo-American Club?"

"A dozen."

"Always the optimist," Sarita laughed. "Vijay, how many Indian families you think living in New York?"

"Hush, Sarita. Okay, we say one dozen. Total maybe thirty people and we charge thirty-five a couple for a week. Twenty-five dollars start-up fee. We got to cover costs."

"I don't see how you can talk costs when we don't even know how much a house rents for," I pointed out.

"The smart lady speaks." Charles winked at me.

"Two hundred!" In a burst of excitement, he had

jumped up from the table and began to pace once again, arms jerking at his sides. The family at the next booth looked up, throwing us curious looks. "I know, I talked to a man the other day!"

"Sit down, you old dog!"

Luckily our soup and dumplings arrived. This was when we did our best talking anyway—around food, abundance. Vijay jabbed his knife in the air as he pleaded and argued, while Charles shoved forkfuls of noodles into his mouth, taking in Vijay's confused suggestions. By the time our dishes were empty, Vijay's dream house had escalated to extravagant proportions: he saw us luxuriating in a plantation-style house with its own private cricket lawn and a swimming pool.

"Wait a minute!" Charles gasped, holding up a palm. "You on a cloud, man. Where you think we going to get enough money for such a place?"

"Inconsequential," Vijay shrugged.

"Inconsequential to you. Not the bill collector."

Claire seemed to wake at this. A furrow appeared between her eyes and putting her arm around her husband, she asserted, "What are you saying, Charles? Vijay pays his bills."

"Yeah, what you mouthing off, man? You doubting my credit rating?"

"And why not?" Sarita asked. "How you pay for that car of yours anyway?"

"You be quiet. Isn't only Charles who can make the money decisions around here."

This dropped us into a well of silence. There were bad feelings between Charles and Vijay about money; twice already Charles had bailed Vijay out, and it was he who secretly mailed the check down to Trinidad every month. When the check arrived with five fortune cookies, Charles cracked his open, and smiled. "Well, that settles our problems," he said, passing the slip of paper around. The fortune read: WHEN IT COMES TO MONEY, A FRIEND CONSULTED IS A FRIEND LOST."

Relieved, all of us laughed. Except for Vijay, whose fist went crashing to the table, forks rattling off the empty china. Before we could stop him, he had shot up from the table, snatched the bill from its plastic tray and paid for everybody's meal.

The next Saturday we filled up a cooler with Coca Colas, a bag of oranges and fresh somosas wrapped in newspaper and took Vijay's car. Thick, bulging clouds blew across the sky and shadows danced on the ground. We drove with the windows cranked down, cool air skimming our elbows. After the crowded streets of the Bronx I began to recognize some sights from my family trips—rich, suburban towns like Larchmont and Scarsdale, glimpses of Tudor houses rising grandly through a slender curtain of birch trees. No one we knew lived there.

We crossed over the narrow Bear Mountain Bridge, wound through the park and were soon in different territory. First the new houses, their unpainted sides raw as skin, sunk in green trim lawns. Next came older towns and soon we were rising in elevation, with sparse clusters of houses, the Catskills settling in a fuzzy blue mound on the horizon.

By one o'clock we'd made it to a diner named Monty's for lunch. It was a clean, upstate place, a small jukebox fastened to each booth table with three songs for a nickel, posters for the Monticello Races hanging over the grill and peeling from the bottom up. Even though we'd already gobbled down the somosas, we were all ravenous, so we ordered the day's special: open-faced roast beef sandwiches, the bread soft with gravy. Vijay purchased a newspaper and spread the classifieds on the table.

"The newspaper won't help much," I told him. "We've got to get ourselves a real estate agent."

He made a sucking noise with this teeth.

"Don't get mad, Vijay. What we need is someone who knows the scene. To give us the inside scoop."

"I'll take care of that." Vijay shot up from his seat and went sauntering down the aisle. "Hey!" he shouted to the waitress. "Hey! I got a question for you!"

A few heads rose. A man in a plaid flannel shirt twisted around to glare at him. By now Vijay had positioned himself by the counter and was trying to look casual, but there was something studied and awkward about his posture. I let my gaze fall to his feet, the ashy rim where ankle met paler, brown skin, and felt a wrinkle of unease. Vijay had rushed his question, his intonations falling in all the wrong places. The waitress did scribble something on a scrap of paper. It was the name of a realtor, Ed Rowe, whose office was in Phoenicia, a town a few miles up the road. We finished up and paid and got back into the car.

Phoenicia sat in a sharp wedge of a valley, a river running on one side, and a mountain rising in a steep thrust on the other. Phoenicia itself looked as if a bakery box assortment of building styles had been dumped on the ground: Swiss houses clung to the hillsides, while along the main street were several log-camp rough buildings housing a Five and Dime, a gun and tackle store, a library and an Italian restaurant named Roberto's. Ed Rowe's office was in the same building as the Phoenicia Inn, a sagging white clapboard which more resembled a pioneer movie set. The clock sign hanging on his doorknob read

BE BACK SOON and pointed to 1:00. It was 2:15. We decided to wait anyway.

Minutes crawled by, sun hot on our heads. Now and then people slowed their cars, leaned their elbows over the door and stared. Sweat trickled down the back of my neck; Sarita began to check her lipstick. Then a woman ambling down the street stopped to talk to us. At first she seemed friendly enough, tilting forward at the waist, one palm raised, like a tour guide greeting her group. She had one of those outdoor, sunburned faces which show the roughened creases, her skin soft-boiled white around the eyes. Only when she spoke, her voice was sharp, not friendly at all. "You live here?"

It was Charles who answered, a tentative finger on his belt loop. "No. We here to see Ed Rowe."

"What about?"

"Renting a house."

The gray of her eyes seemed to darken. One palm folded and pressed against her hip. "It's a busy season," she explained. "Nothing much left. Every year I rent a little cottage to a nice family." I noticed her gaze kept flipping up to me and Claire, going right through the others.

"We'll take our chances."

"Same people rent year in, year out, to the same families. That's the way it's got to be. Can't be no other way." She shrugged. "We're a small town, you see."

No one replied to this. The woman had made herself plain. I wished Charles at least would come out of the glaring sun. But he stayed rooted to the steps, as if he meant to be a challenge to the woman. Thankfully, Rowe did come striding across the street a few minutes later, newspaper tucked under his arm. Charles shot up from the steps and thrust his hand out, and Rowe had no choice but to shake it. "What can I do for you folks?" he asked.

"I'm Charles Magalee. Deputy salesman for Watson Pharmaceuticals. Got myself two hundred accounts, more than any rookie out there."

Rowe was not impressed. "And?"

"A house. We aim to see your listings for the season."

One corner of his mouth lifted. "That right?" As he trudged up the stairs, he let out a low laugh, shaking his head. "Not a good time. Not at all. But we'll see what we can do."

Keys clanking, he unlocked the door and led us into an office with two metal desks and a map of the Catskills region hanging on the back wall. The drawn blinds left wet strips of shadow on the floor, the only bit of brightness a small fish tank in a corner, swatches of tropic yellow and orange circling in cold blue. We waited while Rowe took off his hat, went over to sink and washed his hands, drying them on a nearby hanging towel. He kept moving very slowly, as if aware of being watched, trying to stall us as long as he could. When he sat down at his desk, he made a big show of rifling through the files, only none of them ever seemed right. He coughed several times. He never asked us how large a house we wanted or for how much.

"There's a couple of bungalow places that have openings." He smoothed out one folder, squinting at a sheet of paper inside. "The advantage is someone else does the maintenance. You got linens, everything taken care of."

"How long?" Charles asked.

"Two, maybe three weekends. I got to talk to the folks over there, of course. It isn't easy getting in."

We all fell silent. Vijay shot Charles a surly, schoolboy challenging look, as if to say, Go ahead, disagree with the man.

"Maybe I didn't make myself clear, Mr. Rowe. We need

our own place. We want everything just for us. Rooms, lawn, the works." He slapped his knees. "All those hours I work is time we enjoy ourselves."

Rowe slapped his folders shut and grabbed up his keys. "Don't say I didn't try.".

Then he brought us to plenty of houses, all of them wrong. We could tell right away, even before we slid across the warm upholstery and trudged into the hot sun outside. Either they were on some far off, rotting patch of land or they wallowed in bulrushes, weeds grown thick over the shutters. He took us only to the abandoned and neglected, not even the slightly run-down, inside which a small promise hunched. We knew we didn't have much money. There might be some trouble with the town. But *this*. The last place was an old bungalow camp with a few acres of land and a pond in the back. As I stood turning in the muddy driveway, I tried to imagine the life of summer here—badminton racquets tossed on a lawn, a line of bathing suits dangling on a line. The place must have been built in the twenties and was long since let go, thorn bushes sprung up between buildings, a rash of poison oak creeping up their steps. There were six military buildings in all—one crude eating hall, and five bungalows looking like stunned birds flopped to their nests. The mud was so bad we had to stand on wooden pallets to peer through the broken window screens.

"The toilet is an outhouse," Rowe admitted. "But you got to understand. You people come up here in May, and there's not much left."

The phrase, "you people" was like a window, shutting firmly, trapping us in a bare aquarium of evening light.

"That's all?" I whispered.

"That's all, Miss. Don't have much more." He'd spread his fingers wide, as if to indicate a kind of factual helplessness. A brisk, hard note of impatience in his voice.

I turned away, the man's stare nudging me between the shoulderblades. Only Vijay seemed able to rouse himself—he bounced forward on his feet, making tiny, challenging steps. I noticed Claire's wrist go to her mouth. She squeezed her eyes shut.

"You know," Vijay shouted. "We not stupid!"

I stiffened, waiting for the dense thud of bodies. There was a scuffle of feet in dirt. Only it wasn't Vijay who had gone close to Rowe—it was Charles. The two men's chests nearly touched. Charles crushed something into the other man's hand, and when Rowe swerved around, I saw it was Charles' business card, floating like a small white medal in his palm.

A glum dinner—chicken and boiled spring potatoes. For dessert there was canned pears floating in sugar gravy. Charles looked old, his pink polo shirt a bit ridiculous now, and Sarita's hat slumped on the table like an ugly centerpiece. None of us talked much, the night air an unfriendly space that came pouring through the huge plate glass windows.

"Now I remember why I ran so fast and hard from home," I said to Claire.

"What's that supposed to mean?"

I shrugged. "All that summer colony stuff. I know these people, Claire. They're so narrow-minded. Do you really think they want us as neighbors?"

" I think we did all right," she asserted. "Who finds a house the first time around?"

Then she brought her coffee cup to her lips, as if to show that she wouldn't dare bring up this afternoon's ugliness. Her face had settled into its usual calm, blue eyes dropping like stones to the distant bottom of her mind. Out of all of us, Claire could ride this either way—to success or failure. With her farmer blue skirts, hair hanging straight to her chin, she kept things in an unemotive balance. Each time she tugged her sweater over her heavy hips, she seemed to dutifully remind us that none of this mattered, not even the humiliation we were still trying to swallow down with our bland meal.

Turning from her, I listened to Charles and Vijay, who were beginning a low argument, though their hearts weren't really in it. "Why you have to act so friendly like?" Vijay demanded. "That man there wasn't going to help us!"

Charles put his hands on the table and asked, "And what kind of help you is wanting, man?"

"You know what I mean."

"No, I don't. Speak your mind."

"I don't take no yes say from a man who don't treat me no better than dirt."

Charles scooped up the last of his potatoes. "Fine. You do that. You save your precious thin skin. But when it comes to getting a house, you better buck up and let me do the talking."

"What you mean, huh? What makes you the big man?"

"All right! I tell you what I think! One thing you got to get into that proud head of yours, Vijay. Is no one going to *give* you something, just because you got a pretty face." He swallowed. "You got to bite that prideful tongue of yours. And you talk a beautiful silver streak and don't let those damn fools come under your skin. That's what they be wanting."

As their talk went on, I could sense them working at it, rehearsing what they would say to the next realtor, trying to smooth and polish themselves into a mosaic of acceptable speech. To me it all seemed so terribly pointless. The trees outside had turned to spears of black. The overhead lamps burned a ghostly white.

When it was time to leave, none of us wanted to clamber back into the car. "Maybe we should take a little walk," I suggested. "It's such a long drive ahead."

I began strolling, the others following behind in a loose, raggedy line. We made our way down a road and crossed a bridge, a cushion of air lifting off the stone walls. Water rushed past. The mountains had flushed purple, the sky a flat palette of blue streaked with veins of scarlet and red. Instead of heading back into town, I turned left and took us along another road which ran next to the river.

After a few minutes of walking down the road, I noticed everyone but Charles had fallen behind. Soon the two of us were walking in a brisk stride. We chatted; Charles had relaxed again, his voice playful, as if he'd gotten over the whole ordeal. "You hear from your big man?"

I didn't answer at first. "He's pretty busy, I think. But the Jagans have a lot of support."

"You really interested in all that stuff?"

"Some. When I was growing up, we always had these very serious talks at home." Laughter, small and light, flew from my throat. "Maybe too serious. My father didn't think much of a man unless he went half blind from reading."

Charles joined in my laughter. "So what about you? Talking so smart, like a college girl."

I groaned. "Oh, Charles, that's a boring story. I gave up after two years."

"You going back?"

"Back?"

In Charles' voice was the shape and tone of admiration,

though for what I wasn't sure—especially coming from a
man. But in Charles' innocent question, my own future,
its uncertainty, came rushing to my feet, the thought of
Roland boiling up from below like some reckless debris.
As we continued to walk, I could hear river scud over
stone, its sound growing louder and louder until a wild,
accusatory clatter took up in my head. Over and over
there swept around us the sound of water against rock,
crashing, disappearing into a gulf of silence. After a while
we were walking on a quieter street and I was able to calm
down. I'd become aware again of my surroundings, the
houses spaced far apart with big looming fields in
between. At least I hadn't fallen apart in front of him.

"Go ahead. You tell me if I'm sticking my nose where I
don't belong." His voice went soft. "You know Sarita and
I have grown fond of you."

"That's all right."

"And your man there, he's a good sort. But I tell you
one thing, Sarah." He touched his temple for an instant.

"Yes?"

"If Roland ain't all he seem, don't blame the poor bastard. Where we come from, things is different between a
man and a woman."

"Goddammit," I blurted out. "Why won't any of you
talk straight with me?"

The words had shot out of me, raw with anger. It was
the exact question I wasn't supposed to fire at him. But
now I had, and we had no choice but to stare at one
another, Charles rubbing his knuckles in his palm, me
with my arms across my chest.

"Sarah, Roland is crazy about you. I never saw that boy
so happy the day he come over and tell me about you."

I smiled.

"But no marriage is perfect, none don't have its secrets.

All that lovey dovey stuff is for the movies. Sarita and me—"

"I know all that," I interrupted. "What I want to know about is Roland."

He toed a small rock in the road, back and forth. The rock made a dusty, scraping noise, which irritated me until he lifted his face and showed me his eyes, tiny black irises, shrinking to pinpoints of black. Whatever old secret Roland had kept from me I didn't want Charles to be the one to tell me—nor did he. The only shred of dignity I did own came through a prideful, knowing and womanly silence, when in fact I was ignorant as sin. And he knew this too.

"Forget it," I muttered. "You don't have to tell me."

Now the others came wading out of the darkness, like bathers emerging after a long swim, shadows streaming off their arms. We stood in front of an old mailbox crooked on its post. The house behind us was an uneven sprawl, its windows blank of lights. A hump of bushes obscured the view, but we could see the place was substantial, with a wrap-around porch and three stories capped by a wide, sloping roof.

"Now there you go," Charles remarked. "That's the kind of place we need."

Sarita stifled a yawn behind him. "Come on, Charles. It's a long ride home."

"Wait a minute, woman."

Pushing through the gate, he took a few uncertain steps and squatted before something stuck in the ground, about the height of a newly planted sapling. The rest of us came from behind to see that it wasn't a tree, but a wooden FOR RENT sign. Stencilled underneath, in bright red letters, were the words ED ROWE EXCLUSIVE.

"Shit," Vijay hissed.

Charles was already striding up the path, elbows flopping at his sides. Sarita barked out behind him, "And where you think you're going?"

"Inside," he yelled back.

"You out of your mind? That's somebody's home!"

But he kept walking up the path and soon all we could see was his white shirt floating up the stairs.

"He going to get us in a lot of trouble," Sarita whined.

He was gone a long while. Sarita began to pace, nervously buttoning her jacket, while Claire decided to squat next to a tree. We all waited. Not a single person passed on the road. We stared at the shivering evergreens, the sky, furrowed with silver clouds that moved back and forth across the moon like hands behind a lit lampshade. After a while our feelings of uneasy trespassing gave way to boredom, then irritation. It had been so long, we'd almost forgotten why we were here in the first place.

"I'll go in," I said, and started up the path.

It was odd, following after Charles, but it was as if, during our conversation, Charles and I had made a cautious circle of ourselves, fingers touching. There were secrets, Chinese boxes fastened one into another, which seemed to keep opening meaningfully between us.

I scraped up the stairs, looking around me. No one around. When I pulled the screen door, it rattled off a hinge, as if this place was barely tethered to the land it sat on. And then I was inside a foyer where the air hung stale with dust.

There was no telling where Charles might be. The rooms were pitch quiet and when I called out his name, the sound I uttered might have been buried underground. I started forward, first to the left, then right and stopped, confused. I began again, using the cold, smooth walls to guide me. As I walked, the house seemed to me more like some troubled rumination of a home. Each hall led to another hall, or a room with a door on the other side. There was no figuring its layout, no end to the corridors.

In the kitchen, silvery moonlight broke across the sink taps and stove burners. The cupboard doors were flung open, as if someone had just hungrily rummaged through its shelves. I could make out an old fashioned pantry and an antlered lamp hanging from the ceiling, perhaps of burnished brass. It was here I finally began to hear sound—the *shush* of water once again, sucking and burbling into pebbles. A breeze pushed against my ankles and I turned to find the door open. Outside I found Charles in the middle of the yard.

"I knew it would be you." His voice was a high, tight wire.

"Charles, we better go."

"It's empty. No one lives here."

"I know."

"What you think?"

"I think we better leave." I picked my way across the wet grass and stood next to him. Now that I was up close, I could see his eyes were two excited flickers, one hand mashing a handkerchief against his neck. Strips of moonlight fell about the curly hairs which edged his throat and excited face. "Sarah, it's got eleven bedrooms. Eleven," he whispered again.

"More than we need."

"I don't ask for much. Every month I pay the bills and turn the rest over to Sarita. She'll tell you different, but it's true. I like nice things, I want them like the rest. But I got plans. I looking to the future, one that's right here under our noses. You understand me?"

He did not even wait for an answer, but pressed on. I could not quite believe what I was hearing; Charles was the most earthbound, practical man I knew. But it was as if this house had blown open a musical charm inside him. "One of these days, I tell you, I'm going to own two of these houses! I'm going to have myself over twenty bedrooms!"

"Charles," I giggled, "what are you and Sarita going to do with that many bedrooms?"

He stopped and the air between us slid into silence. Then he grabbed my arm and squeezed my wrist, shaking it before he let go again. "You know how old Sarita was when I first saw her?" he asked.

"No."

"Seventeen! Her father brought her to me in Canada. It was done before she'd even finished her schooling."

"It seems to have worked out."

"Worked out, yeah. But that was before, when we didn't even know about things we now can't live without. Sarita can't do her hair without a curling iron. She got to have one. Or now it's a fan. 'How we going to live in the city this summer without a fan?' she asked me the other day. This coming from a woman from Trinidad!"

This last exclamation was uttered with both annoyance and pride. As always, a bone of desperation showed behind Charles' face. Sarita might wear skirts from Saks, but she also made no secret of her repulsion for her husband, poking his rotund stomach, letting us know she didn't often deign to sleep with him. And so Charles was forced to live in a strange, nervous equilibrium, always having to renew his claim on his wife, taking her abuse as his reluctant debt for her father's betrayal. And it was in knowing ourselves this way—as people who took no love for granted—that Charles and I had touched minutes before under the dark, revealing trees. Once more, in this same quality of friendship, he put his hand on my arm and whispered: "Don't mind what I say, Sarah. Sarita's a good woman. She was raised modern by her family. She wanted to go to school in Paris and be a fashion designer. All that was dashed for her."

"It's all right, Charles."

We both turned to walk up the kitchen stairs. The house spread before us, wide as cypress trees, its roof lingering over our heads. We both knew that the day's fumbled search had brought us to this dark, vagrant mass that now drifted before us. We were greedy to touch it. That was the kind of people we were, not so much homeless as longing to shape with our hands, build ourselves up from the outside in. When he turned to me and asked, "If I say to the others we going to rent this house, you back me up?" the answer was already there.

I let myself pause an instant, listening to the stream outside, hearing a faint rhythm start to beat inside me, one which would carry me through these long days of waiting for Roland and even more, into that lost, blasted wreck of myself. "Yes," I said out loud and took us through the door.

6

That Monday Charles tricked Rowe's secretary into releasing the phone number of the owner—Landowne, a rich lawyer in Philadelphia—then I hunted down Landowne through the Philadelphia Bar Association, negotiated one hundred off the price, since the pipes needed fixing, still two hundred more than the Club had agreed upon, so I secretly emptied out the remainder of my old Ridgewood Bank Savings account and made up the difference. To the rest of the Indo-American Club, the clean triplicate lease delivered by messenger two days later represented a sheer cunning that brought this house to us, mysterious as a gift.

Everyone was used to their own underground of apartments and off-the-books jobs, navigations that rarely broke the surface of the real America. For the West Indians especially, too many polite and not so polite refusals made them forget there was any other way. Not that it was all illegal—half of them had come over like Roland as students, and those like the Srinivans were nicely set up with a two-bedroom apartment, TV and Consulate car rights. Yet for the poorer and less-connected Trinidadians and Guianese, even if they came with the bluish stamp of a student visa on their passports, a year or two later, when they didn't want to go back, they found themselves stepping into air, into the ceaseless flow of an anonymous, white world. For someone like Vijay, worried that the Immigration Department might catch onto his other marriage, he got by through word-of-mouth jobs, business deals he'd worked on the side. He'd gotten so used to the act of concealment that my brazen pursuit of this house could only strike him as audacious and frightening.

On Memorial Day Weekend, the five of us squeezed into Vijay's car and sailed up Route Seventeen, brimming, full as an ark. A few hours later we could see that even in two weeks the Catskills had lost their bony, wintry shape, trees swollen with green, while everywhere sprang up untidy bunches of hyacinths and wild lavender. But as the car rolled to a stop, we all fell silent. Charles turned off the ignition, the engine heaving to a quiet. We stared again, as if to clear our vision.

"You must be mad!" Sarita cried. Unrolling the window, she thrust her head out. "How could you let some Yankee fellow talk you into this?"

None of us could wrestle up a reply. Sunlight filtered through the emptied paper bags of hard boiled egg and nan we'd consumed, warming our necks. This was not what we imagined when we signed the lease. But now we sat on the sun-scorched upholstery, eggs cold in our stomachs, our crate of scrub brushes and sponges, Charles' new toolbox forgotten in Vijay's trunk. We stared at this horrible house, our fumbled gift, and felt ashamed. Torn tar paper hung like burnt paper from the porch rafters, the roof a slouching muddle of shingle. At least half the windows were jagged with broken panes, the lawn powdered with glass bits that glinted into our eyes.

It was Charles who struck out first—door swung open,

kicking at the ragged loop of a bicycle tire, bending to tear off the FOR RENT sign from its post. The rest of us shook out our trouser legs and damp skirts and followed behind in numb silence. Inside it smelled like an emptying drain, mouse pellets squashed underfoot, floorboards damp and scarred from a flood the year before. We filed up the sagging main stair, each bedroom filled with old mattresses and piled up linens. We wanted to push our fists through the softened sheetrock, but didn't. There was a stiffening in each of our necks, a quick signal, then we picked our way back down again and began the ferry of items out of the car.

Only Sarita refused to cooperate. Slipping off her shoes, she stared in dismay at the screen door, which had tilted off its frame, while Charles came heaving up the stairs, arms loaded with a crate. "Move that sweet behind of yours, Sarita. We all of us got a lot to do."

She flicked open a silver case and lit a cigarette. The rest of us were forced to circle around her, dropping our belongings on the flattened newspaper Claire had spread in the hall. I listened, crouching in the hall.

"You crazy, thinking this place worth lifting a finger for!" Sarita cried.

"What kind of nonsense is this? Here Sarah and I bust ass to get this place and make our dream come true!"

"Hah! You a dreamer, all right. You a child wasting our good money. My Daddy would weep if he knew the hare brained schemes I got to drag along with!"

"If you want to know what's a waste of money, it's that camel's hair coat you bought this spring!"

Her voice went into a cry that shred through the shutters. "You just like the rest of those rotten Indian men, hiding they booze and they pay check from they wives!"

"Foolish, spoiled girl!"

Through a narrow slat, I watched Sarita's face go into an injured pout while Charles' back ebbed to the side. The cigarette was flung to the floor, ground out. Then she grabbed up her matching suitcase and hat box and went flashing across the lawn, halting at the fir tree. She sat planted on the suitcase rim, another cigarette lit.

"You come back here!"

"No! I want to go dancing and go to the theater and eat in a restaurant. I didn't come all the way from Trinidad to clean a bloody floor."

There was not much for us to do but ignore her. Soon we fell into the ordinary rhythms of work. Charles and Vijay dragged out the mattresses and flung them over the porch rail. It was my job to beat them with a broom. From inside I could hear the swoosh of water, then a bracing scent of disinfectant—Claire was on her hands and knees in the living room, the tail of Vijay's workshirt dammed at her navel. Every now and then, I would let down the broom to rest my arms, and gaze across the lawn to Sarita. Still she sat under the fir tree, still she smoked.

I wanted to be mad with her, but somehow I couldn't. Sarita looked foolish, trapped in this elaborate cage of anger; in her tiny waist and its smart piping, the swift jerks of her chin, I could see the tragedy of her marriage. Not just the arranged part—that went without saying for a girl from Trinidad—but her little dramas, so embroidered, ornate with desire, lost on the coarseness of Charles. He was a man who understood things, dollars, plans. I heard him inside now, smashing out useless windows—gleeful, thrashing at the sheer ugly flesh of this place.

And then came his heavy tread from behind. He had changed into an old pair of overalls, bib loose over his stomach. He waited a moment, surveyed the yard like a planter disturbed by one impudent head in the fields. He made his way down the path, one foot dragging slower than the other. Sarita did not move, her magazine forgotten, back straight.

The arguing started up again—Sarita's voice a bright, golden thread, fraying itself around Charles who stood quiet as a pillar, arms across his chest. Her voice thinned; her neck drooped. "It's not fair!" I heard her utter. But as she rose, I saw there was something bared and awful and beautiful between them—the weight of his shadow, her crumbling cigarette ash.

Later we could hear Charles in the upstairs bedroom, flinging open its windows, now scrabbling across the roof. Sarita and I listened, waiting for the ominous crash of a body flying through wood. But there was only a stuttering clunk as he kicked off some rotted beams. When he came back downstairs, a crumbled flower pot was balanced on each palm. "Now not one of you say a word, ladies. But I tell you. I got the real idea." He dropped himself down on an old wicker chair we'd dragged out of the cellar, sinking like a tropical prince into his unravelling throne.

"So?" Sarita had settled into another wicker chair, feet tucked under. She picked at the crust of a sandwich, her face smooth.

"So this." He picked up a chicken thigh, sucked for a moment before going on, using the bone to point upstairs. "See that porch roof?"

"Got more holes than your head, man." Vijay stood slanted in the doorway, waiting for Claire to hand him a sandwich.

"We can fix it." Dropping a chicken bone on the newspaper spread at his feet, he leaned forward, eyes bright. "I'm going to build a terrace. A nice, Caribbean-style terrace."

The rest of us stared at him. "That thing going to fall apart the minute you take a step!" Vijay laughed.

"You got no imagination, man! Of course I can build a terrace there."

As Charles set down the bottle, his eyes flew to me. His pupils had shrunk, same as when we stood under the trees fifty yards away not more than a week ago.

"It's not such a bad idea. But maybe you should ask a carpenter."

"Why bother?" Vijay's tone was smug.

"Because I aim to fix this house up so nice, Landowne feel he got to sell to me."

"Oh, that's a very smart idea. Saddle us with a mortgage for a heap nobody else want."

"The place is old, Charles," Claire pointed out. "A terrace—it's probably not safe."

"The way I see it, a house that's too old, too set in its ways got to be changed. We got to make something new."

"But a *terrace*!" Sarita's voice quivered. "Who needs a terrace in this here place?"

"A terrace something beautiful. It stick out, way high up. It like having a whole lot of days in front of you, all the days sailing past like ships on a sea. You a captain of the air, of everything, when you got yourself a terrace."

Silence fell; his own words had embarrassed him. He swung his knees around, facing me. "You all a bunch of pessimists. The only one here who going to back me up is Sarah." He wagged a finger. "Sarah here an optimist. That's the one thing I know about her."

The others turned to stare at me, as if Charles and I were hoarding a secret we'd mistakenly let out. We both didn't know how to react. Embarrassed, I pretended to clear up our things, but Sarita, sensing danger in the air, jumped up from the step and using her foot, pushed me aside. "Go on, you two dreamers stay and take a rest. You talk about your damn terrace."

Claire and Vijay rose and went inside too, leaving Charles and me on the porch, the both of us shifting to the steps. We didn't say much. Dusk braided through the trees, a glistening fringe of purple brushing against the grass. The muscles in my arms and legs, though sore, felt rested. I was safe, I thought. Not alone. Around me lay the sounds of others clattering behind walls.

"How come you and Roland don't spend much time together anymore?" I asked.

Charles laughed, kneading his arm. "Well, I think that bum was kind of ashamed of me."

"Ashamed?"

"You got to understand the kind of family Roland come from, Sarah. The Singhs always worrying about they reputation. And that Uncle Lionel of his, he a big man. Roland feel bad for the kind of boy he been, all his mistakes. He want to prove himself ten times over."

"But what did he do that was so wrong?"

At this, he halted and there pushed between us a dark thing, what could never be said between us. A wedge of sparrows lilted off the roof gutter, breaking apart like bits of blue wood in the air.

"What about me?"

Charles didn't answer at first. He opened and closed his fingers, rubbing them. "It's like this, Sarah. A family down there like an organism. You leave, you still expected to feed it."

"But he's married now."

"I know."

"And I want to go down there. I didn't tell you this before Charles, but I applied for a visa."

Charles did not seem surprised by this revelation, only

weary. In the kitchen someone was letting the drain out, water scooping down the pipes, gurgling with a hiss onto the grass outside the kitchen. "Why don't you wait, child. Let's see what happens in that crazy place. Is not time to be doing anything rash."

I didn't answer. There it was, then—another raw seam exposed, making me wonder if my marriage would always be like this, rent with histories, secrets, Roland had not, like me, wiped out. The old panic came sweeping upon me again as I tried to pick something, *anything,* which seemed familiar and sure, finally settling on Charles' old work boots, slumped next to a step.

"Do you think he would like the house?"

Charles laughed. "Why you asking that?"

"I don't know. Maybe I thought if he saw this place, he would start to think differently. There's possibilities here. You find an old place, fix it up. It's not that hard. Maybe he might even change his mind and want to settle here. God, do I miss him."

The muscles in Charles' shoulders bunched together, dark as grapes under his cotton shirt. Once again, there came between us a blunt edge I wasn't supposed to bring our conversations towards.

"I tell you, Sarah, there a lot of things that make up your man. I once seen him work a whole day in a cane field to help his neighbor. But he despise his own dirt road. He hate that uncle of his, but he admire him too. I think he got to be down there, figuring out who he really is."

"What was Roland like when he was growing up?"

"Roland was a star. His family put all they hope in him. Maybe by being with me and Vijay too much, he afraid he would go backward. Back to being a barefoot boy with his kerosene lamp. I tell you one thing, though. You make him feel lucky, Sarah. More ahead of things."

We both laughed, mostly because it hurt; because I knew the word lucky meant something akin to being white, reminding me of everyone else's view of me. It was as if I was seeing myself through a kaleidoscope, inverted, slivered, everything but the simple whole of me: twenty-three years old, wanting my husband back.

The phone was ringing as I trudged up the stairs with my week-end bag. I fumbled for my key, but by the time the door swung open, the ringing had stopped. Exhausted, I threw down my things, and tore off my dress. In the bathroom I checked my underwear. Already I was three weeks late. But it seemed crazy. Not with Roland gone.

Then I flung open the creaking sofa bed. A few books rolled off and went thudding to the floor, a fan of papers sifting to the floor. Irritated, I scooped them into a pile—newspaper clippings, letters from Roland, the airmail paper pale as water, streaming through my fingers. I tossed them down again, rolled back onto the mattress, blanket wound around my shoulders, satin edge cool against my cheek. Before I knew it I was asleep.

Into a reach so deep, the bells began. They snaked into my dreams, upturning stones which seemed to rub at my feet. With each new peal, I seemed to be rising to hoops of brightness, drawing me up again. Now I was lying belly up. The bells chimed on. It was the phone making such a racket. I reached a hand up to the table, fumbling with the receiver.

"Sarah? You there?"

The voice was distant. Behind was a purring racket of machinery. "Darlin' I been trying to reach you for days. Can you hear me?"

My mind swung awake. "Roland? Is that you?"

"Yes, sweetheart."

"Where are you calling from?"

"I'm in a little village west of the Berbice River."

"I can't believe it."

"I'm here. Everything going to be all right."

There were a few minutes of blurred crying. "God-dammit Roland, what is going on there? That talk about the racial fights—"

"What you talking about? Why you listen to that propaganda! Everything's great down here! I got myself a job!"

"What kind of job?"

"I'm down here helping with the unions. Cheddi trying to break the old union that really a cover for the sugar interests. He got a new labor bill he going to pass next month. It's really happenin', Sarah, we got ourselves a real people's government. Do you know, Sarah, when I travel out to the villages they come and kiss my feet when they learn I workin' for Cheddi?"

I laughed. "I thought a little hard work would knock that boasting right out of you."

Roland also laughed. "Come on girl. You know I'm the same fool as always."

We laughed together—reminding me of the sound of our bedroom talk, the pitted holes we so easily tripped into, lighting up the ugliness and desire in both our hearts. "It's all those mangoes you're getting a bellyache over," I went on. "You can't think straight."

"I'm thinking for the both of us. Don't you be worrying. How things up there?"

"The house is beautiful, Roland. You have to see it." I giggled. "Charles is already talking about buying the place."

"Is that right? You going to forget about seeing my family house one day?"

Suddenly a desire to tell everything to Roland, about our crazy search, the long hours working in the house, came rushing to my lips. "Roland, everyone says it's nuts for you to stay down there. And I do understand but—"

"What?"

"I've been following the news. It isn't all good. The newspapers are so nasty."

There was a pause on the other end. "What kind of talk is this?"

"Charles says Cheddi will never be able to hold together an alliance like that. You've got the Indians against the blacks and your uncle and the big bauxite companies—"

"What that damn fool know? All he sees is a dollar bill and a couple of acres! Is that what you want?"

"The party line again," I grumbled. "Maybe it's what *I* want."

"Now you going to put this down too? You always said it's time I went into action, no more hot air."

"For six weeks?"

But he was interrupting me, the old rage spilling through his words. "I'm doing something real, dammit. Can't you see that? Can't my own wife back her husband up?"

"I'm not a saint, Roland."

Silence fell. The receiver was cold in my palm. A venetian blind rattled against the sill. "I miss you," I said.

A hesitation. "I miss you too."

"When do you think—"

"Sarah, I can't talk too long. I been working twelve, fourteen hour days. And they keep me on the road with this trade union business. But what I want to tell you is this. You the real hero in all of this. Don't think I don't know that."

"Spare me the pedestal." I began to cry again. "Just tell me—how much longer?"

"One month more, I think. Once they push through the labor bill, don't you worry, I be on the next plane home."

"You sure?"

"What you think? I'm not going to let you alone with those island boys much longer. I know how they think. Every one of them probably after you right now."

"Roland, give me a date, something—"

An explosion of curses in the background, a crush of angry voices. The line warbled, went faint. Roland was talking but I couldn't make out what he was saying. I shouted at him to speak up, but it didn't help.

"What's she like?" I shouted.

"Who?"

"Janet Jagan."

For an instant, there came a blank channel of sound, then peals of Roland's laughter, warm-hearted, sunny with delight. *"That's* what you want to know? I can't tell you, sweetheart. I don't see much of the lady."

"But you must have talked to her. At the office. What does she wear? Do people listen to her?"

"What you say?"

Sound was growing thick and raspy. Soon all I could hear were my own questions, booming on the line.

It was an ordinary, glum-looking house. Brown shingle with a chalky, cracked green trim, a slate roof and a funny steep attic that looked like a collapsible hat clapped on top. Too large for one family, too small to be a hotel for the summer season, it languished somewhere in between. A rustic addition sprouted on one side, built shakily of thin, potato-colored walls, tufts of electrical wire bristling out

of the sockets. Only the house never had any showcase
pretensions; it was more used for rich Manhattanites
intending to "rusticate" in the woods. Down in the basement were boxes of children's books, broken cribs, rotted
baseball mitts, reminding us of past lives, of people having moved on to plusher, more fashionable summer inte-
riors.

The house sat on a good ten acres of land, much of it
weed-grown, with a shaggy patch of a lawn, wood stakes
sunk in the back from an old badminton net. About fifty
yards from the rear porch a clump of azalea bushes rose up
in wild bright clamour, then gave way to an incline and a
tumbled flat of rocks. A stream rushed past though this
summer, it ran low, the mud banks on the other side
leeched and dry.

The other neighbors were mostly townsfolk, since this
part of the Catskills was sparse for summer visitors. If we
took the road to the left and traveled back fifty miles, we
descended back down through the summer colonies of my
childhood, garish billboards rising like luminous painted
moons. In Phoenicia, though, they weren't much used to
strangers. There had been a small boom in summer houses
in the twenties—that's when this one was built—but
lacking in the more glamorous attractions like a big lake
with a sand beach or a town with a cinema, the appeal
quickly faded. And they were too far from the racetrack to
have much of a draw for weekenders. The town survived
the Depression, the post-war boom, looking pretty much
the same.

In the next couple of weeks I began to throw myself
into the house, which now seemed so important to all of
us. I could hardly wait for Friday evening when we met
outside Vijay and Claire's apartment building, tumbled
into the convertible and shot up Broadway and out of the

city. We arrived four hours later, the house cooling in the dark. Somehow, the place improved. The first and second floors were whitewashed, unsavory droppings scraped out of even the most obscure of corners. Windows were picked clean of glass shards and stuff from the closets, poked out like wax from ears—broken tennis rackets, moth eaten blankets, an old volleyball net—sat in a greasy heap in the front yard. The kitchen counters, though spidery with cracks, glowed clean. Big problems we ignored, such as the tap water, which kaleidoscoped from rusty-brown to pale yellow; the clogged fireplaces, shedding bits of nest and soot; the blistered spots on the ceiling. At night we lay exhausted under cold, threadbare blankets, sniffing strange, moldy intestinal fumes that seemed to drift like a fever through the pipes.

The terrace became a curiously fragile subject between Vijay and Charles. For two weeks, as the air turned warm, Charles sawed and hammered and stripped. On the huge dining room table he flattened blueprint paper and sketched drawings. A rickety structure cropped up—the old tarpaper lay peeled, showing a rotted cross-hatch of beams; a few new rails poked into the air. Only any time someone offered to help Charles, he turned them down. It was as if, having bared himself for his new pet dream, Charles was an open target for Vijay's simmering resentments. After dinner it was Charles who paced the living room, sketching his plans, and Vijay who shot them down. I watched Vijay turn secretive, even spiteful. Once I handed him a can of tile grout and a palette knife for caulking the bathroom tile, he disappeared into the bathroom, but when I came upstairs a while later, I found him stretched in the tub, flipping through *Life* magazine.

But Vijay's deceits seemed small, dark with mistrust. Though I could hardly blame him—Charles could be impossible. Ever since he'd found the house for us, he made the presumption to define us as a family, with himself at its head. The instant we arrived in Phoenicia, he reigned like a noisy mother, rapping on doors early Saturday morning, waiting in the kitchen with a pot of coffee on the stove, a list of our house chores.

It was a good time, watching myself toughen and persist. I found myself with more energy than ever before. My arms turned brown and muscular; I let my hair grow long enough to tie up in a ponytail that swished on my neck. I had never even held a hammer before. With Charles I learned to crouch down under the greasy innards of sinks, fix faucets, set out mousetraps. It surprised me, this strength, this love of house. The house was like the shock of sex, a cool-limbed rest after when bodies are returning to themselves, restored to their difference. And gradually my old pain was leaving me.

A green truck with ladders hooked to the sides came thundering and creaking to our curb. The house was empty, but for myself and Vijay, who sat on the porch steps, fiddling with a fishing pole on his lap. At breakfast this morning he'd announced he wanted to buy himself some line and tackle. This only gave Charles an opening for his long-awaited attack. "In case you hadn't noticed, old man, we got a house to finish!" Then he'd jumped up from the table and demanded Vijay's car keys so he could go into town to get some supplies.

Now, two men clambered out of the van, both in tobacco-colored pants. The older man showed an impressive line-up of pens clipped to his shirt pocket; a thick tool belt bumped and knocked on the slim hips of the younger one. They came up the walk, squinting at Vijay, who was trying to untangle his wrists of fishing line.

137

"We're looking for Charles Magalee." It was the older one speaking. He had a gruff, flat upstate voice.

"What for?"

"Appraisal." The younger one nodded towards the porch. "On the roof there." He squinted, taking in the scrappy flags of tarpaper that nearly brushed Vijay's head.

"It's a bloody mess, huh? Not worth it, huh?"

"Hard to say," the younger shrugged. "We got to take a look first." His hands rested on his belt and I could see his thumbs, cracked and hard, curving backwards, almost over the knuckle. To me, these men breathed competence, the slow, unwavering intelligence of craft.

We brought them inside, picking past the patched holes in the floor, up the stairs which wobbled a little under our feet and through Charles and Sarita's bedroom. By now Vijay had shrunk back with fright and admiration. I too was a bit amazed. These men were so large, so strong and alert! Before stepping through the window, the son grasped its frame and tapped, as if listening for an inner echo. Their movements terrified us. We could hear plaster crumble, imagine the beams drifting with rot and still these men strode as if this were a bridge linked with air. Crouching down on his knees, the younger one snapped open a ruler and started to measure, shouting out figures to his father who scribbled them down in a notebook. Within a few minutes they came back inside.

"Should I put the questions to you or wait until Mr. Magalee comes back?"

Vijay puffed his chest out a little and said, "Me."

The man licked the end of a pencil stub and jabbed in the direction of the sun-drenched roof. "Your supports aren't bad, they're solid oak. Oak studs. The one on the left could use some reinforcing but that's not your main problem. It's the lateral thrust that's the kicker. You're gonna to have to build maybe a second deck over the paper. Maybe a cross-hatch configuration. And all the rails got to be replaced, of course."

The both of us stared at one another, his words scrambling like gibberish in our heads. "It's a lot of money, huh?" Vijay could hardly conceal the glee from his voice.

The father shrugged. "Not all that bad. It's the materials that'll get you. Our labor isn't so high."

"How much?"

Again the father flashed him a sobering, tolerant look, as if trying to quell an over-excited boy. "Can't give you more than an estimate right now. Maybe somewhere between one hundred and one fifty."

Vijay's eyes widened.

"Don't quote us," the son warned. Vijay took a step back, as if corrected.

In a daze we watched as the men handed us a business card. On it was a picture of a man carrying a ladder and their names in script underneath: Larry and Phil Joseph. Only we had no idea who was who.

"That settles it," Vijay said to me as we were watching them climb back into the truck a few minutes later. "None of us got that kind of money."

"Not really," I said. "There's the fund."

Vijay's eyebrows raised. "What you talking about?"

"Charles got some money together for the repairs." I looked at him. "I thought you knew. I thought everyone knew." I went over to Sarita and Charles' dresser and inched open a drawer. Folded into a neat roll in a pink stocking in a cigar box was two hundred dollars, some of it Charles' own money, some of it extra from members' dues. Vijay looked at the roll of bills, then reached his hand out and lifted it to his lips, rubbing it against his large, white teeth. A grin spread on his lips. "Taste bitter," he laughed.

The house has changed us, I thought the moment my eyes opened the next morning. Blue lozenges of light fell across the sheets, the sink basin glazed white, inviting and bare. Pushing off the damp blankets, I washed myself with cold water. My face shined back at me: browner, tougher than I remembered. The waistband of my skirt fit snug around my stomach.

We'd become an odd, resentful family: the women stayed lumped together, but Charles had made me his uneasy partner, as we sat on the porch steps together, sketching plans. Claire too was becoming mysteriously wedded to the place—last night I heard shouts from her and Vijay's room. Early this morning she slammed out of the house on her way to another one of her sales. It was as if she were building herself up, fork by fork, glass by glass, in some huge and desperate evasion. And Sarita also hoarded her coy secrets—the day before she got dressed as if for the city, in a linen skirt and floppy hat. Later when I went into town to pick up a few things, I spotted her in a drugstore phone booth. She tilted her face away, as if she hadn't seen me. I was beginning to wonder if the house spoke to each of us, but we'd stopped being able to speak to one another.

Downstairs was quiet, the screen doors hooked shut, everyone else still asleep, except for Claire. I found last night's dinner under foil in the refrigerator, the noodles thick, congealed.

Dinner had been awful, almost perfunctory. Claire cooked American, the palate too bland, which always flattened our moods. She carried in her cheese and noodle casserole, while we poked at limp salads in an orangey pool of French dressing. Something was definitely wrong.

It was not so much the food itself as the fact that we were not really eating together, each of us islands in the brightly-lit dining room, nothing exchanged between us. Charles loomed at one end. Sarita bristled every time he forgot to wipe his mouth. Vijay couldn't seem to keep his eyes on the table.

Later, as I pushed through the swinging door, Charles was throwing down his napkin, grunting at Vijay, "I don't know what happened. The contractor was supposed to come round the other day about the roof."

I'd frozen. My hands were full up with cups and saucers for coffee, Claire nudging behind with the coffee pot. I don't know why—something told me I shouldn't say a word about the visit. Already, there was the business about the hidden money and I'd stuck up for Charles too many times. Sure enough Vijay shrugged and said, "Nobody come today." He twirled a toothpick between his teeth. "Besides, I thought we said that terrace going to be too dangerous to build."

"That's what I aim to find out, man. I going to tap his brain and do all the work myself."

"What makes you think you can do that?"

"And what makes you think I can't?"

I could see Vijay hesitate, as if trying to drum up another objection; this one was slipping too quickly. He shot me a stormy, warning look before continuing on. "There's the money. You can't be spending our money just like that!"

Charles had put down his spoon and looked quizzically at his friend. "I know that, Vijay. What gives you the idea I would go ahead without asking you all?" When I ran into Vijay later that night in the hall, I asked, "When are you going to tell him they did come?" "Don't rush me, woman," he growled. "Everybody always rushing around here."

I decided to head into town, rather than eat breakfast with the group. This way I could buy some sewing supplies at the store and get started on new curtains. Already it was hot outside. As I swung down the road, flies droned and ticked in the nubby-headed weeds, and the air smelled of slightly scorched grass. The doors of the Five and Dime were locked shut, so I went across to Roberto's for coffee, settling down with my cup in a window booth, watching the turpentine-yellow light thin to clearness. Pinned over the door was a sagging banner which read CELEBRATE OUR BOYS COMING HOME AUGUST 18 FIREWORKS AT DUFFY FIELD.

How different the Catskills seemed here: local men dressed in plaid flannel shirts clomped inside for their morning coffees, swapping talk, their voices blowing with spaciousness and familiarity. My own parents rarely strayed outside their circle of bungalows. When they did, their foreignness rubbed against the slow, broad grain of these outdoor people. Back at our bungalows were husky women with thighs soft as water, sharing gossip, boasting of each triumph in the face of America's indifference— which son was a dentist, which opened a new business in California. Inside those light summer evenings the older generation's expectations rumbled as a fearsome storm: the young folk must do better, right the past which had nearly destroyed them. And then there was my own father, strange misfit that he was, walking along the shore, talking to no one.

Remembering Samuel, my chest lurched with a hot, certain pain. I could forget for weeks at a time, but then it would be upon me—a small explosion. It was hard to ignore that my parents would be sharing these same hills. Was my choice really that horrible? I blew on my coffee. I was so lost in thought that I didn't catch the voice talking to me. Not the friendly syllables cascading around me, but a tight and wary sound.

"Hello."

I looked up: first a bow tie then suspenders bending like two strips of licorice. I was staring right into the face of Ed Rowe.

"Oh, hello."

"Settled in?"

"Pretty much."

He laughed, but not nicely. "I guess you got what you wanted, then. I'll say one thing. That Magalee fellow is pretty determined."

My fingers tightened around my cup. "We all wanted to rent the house, Mr. Rowe."

"Obviously." One thumb stroking a suspender, he peered closer. "So how'd you end up with these folks? What's your connection?"

The word *connection* tumbled through me like a coin through a long, empty chute. I took a last sip of my coffee. "My husband," I heard myself mumble.

"He one of those fellows?"

"He's down in his country right now."

"Where's that?"

I hesitated. I didn't know how much I wanted to tell. "Guiana." Then I added, "He works in politics." The words were meant to give Roland the hue of legitimacy, but an instant later I regretted them.

"So he's foreign, too."

"Yes."

There was a pause, as if he were gauging me. "We got so many of our boys far off in Korea. Jimmy down the road came back with a game leg. Eighteen years old, poor kid, couldn't even dance with his girl at the prom. Funny world, these days." Then his interest seemed to dip away.

It wasn't only me he meant to focus on. I noticed his newspaper was still spread open in a booth across the aisle, a curl of steam rising up from his coffee cup. "I see a lot of work going on there. You building?"

"Not building. Fixing."

"I saw some beams up on the porch."

"Repairs," I insisted again.

A smile broke across Rowe's face. "No need to get defensive, ma'am. I was just wondering, that's all. The house has been the way it is for so long, it would be funny, seeing it different. And I know Frank Landowne is real attached to the place—"

"Mr. Rowe," I interrupted. "We have an agreement. We're not doing anything wrong."

Rowe's hands shot up near his face and he spread his fingers wide—the same gesture of helplessness he'd made weeks ago when we stood in the gravel lot of the old camp and he lied to me about the houses. The wrists were puffy, sunburned red, creased white. He found me peculiar, a white woman living among dark-skinned foreigners. "Hey now, " he was saying. "Don't make me out to be the bad guy. We're a friendly place here. Everybody gets along and we just like to keep an eye out for each other."

"Forgive me if I didn't notice the welcome committee." Seeing Rowe's face darken, I added quickly, "Like I said. We're just making repairs."

"Looks like your man is doing a hell of a lot more than that." He swiped at his hair. There was a hesitation, thick hand poised in the air, as if about to make a motion of nonchalance, the conversation released into patter, and I might breathe easy. But the fingers twitched; he tugged once on an earlobe, showing me irritation. "I imagine you might even need a permit for what Magalee's got cookin'."

"Permit?"

Now it was his turn to laugh—hands dropped to his sides, his mouth went slack. "That's right. You want my opinion, you may want to check with Rusty Bauer. He's in charge of inspections and he's a stickler, all right."

"Mr. Rowe, if I didn't know any better I'd say you were giving us a hard time."

"Now, Mrs.—"

"Singh."

"Mrs. Singh. I'm just trying to tell you about the way things are around here."

"I can see that," I said, swallowing. "I'll be sure to tell Mr. Magalee." I paid and left the restaurant and hurried down the road. I'd forgotten all about the sewing supplies.

In the kitchen I found the morning's dirty dishes stacked on the counter and began to wash them. The sting of water on my wrists, hair damp against my forehead was somehow soothing. After a while I heard voices clump together—Charles and Vijay had fixed themselves drinks and now strolled across the grass, shoulders hunched, deep in conversation. I knew they were talking about the terrace: Vijay now stood with his chin thrust out, eyes small; Charles making gestures towards the roof, his hands sketching, making bigger and bigger things in the air.

This wasn't fair. I was tired of these mean struggles over a few boards and beams. The men stripped and exposed themselves in this effort to build, while I couldn't know what lay ahead for myself. Propping the iron pan in the rack, I tugged out the stopper, watching the suds spiral down the drain.

As I was wiping my hands on a towel, I became aware of someone in the room. It was Claire, standing by the back door.

"What's going on out there?"

"Something about the roof."

"It's about the Club money again, isn't it?" She opened the door further, letting sunlight in, showing the ripe curve of her breasts through her dress.

"Why don't you ask Vijay?"

"I know what you think, Sarah. But you have to be patient with Vijay." Her gaze flickered away. "He'll get around explaining everything to me. He always does." She came forward and stood very close to me. For the first time, I noticed a reddish mole, over her right ear lobe. The imperfection seemed to make her all the more beautiful.

"I guess it isn't easy for either of us."

"What is that supposed to mean?"

"Sarah, I don't know much about politics. And I've never met Roland." She took a breath. "But I overhead Charles talking to Vijay before about Roland, about somebody in his village." She hesitated. "I heard something about a woman named Ma Das."

The back of my neck prickled. "Why are you telling me this?"

Her eyes widened. "Because if you knew something about Vijay, I'd want you to tell me."

It was obvious, the tremendous effort her statement had taken. I could see she was gathering herself up, trying to get her point across, but this simply wasn't Claire—she hated things out in the open. The men's voices drifted through the walls. Then I noticed a box sitting at her feet. "What's that?" I asked.

"Some stuff I got at a sale today. Look."

We bent over the box. Crammed inside were odd glasses and bottles, all made of blue glass. I picked up one and held it against the sunny window. Claire was already pulling the rest out of the box, humming a song under

her breath. I had never seen Claire so confident or animated. She rinsed a few and lined them up on the sill, a
blue light spilling onto her hands. "Neat," she murmured.

"Who cares about those dopey guys," I agreed. Then
the two of us lifted up glass after glass and squinted
through the glass bottoms, each view of the yard, the
kitchen, our own laughing faces, hued strange and wonderful.

Pregnant. Pocketbook on my knees, I sat listening to the
doctor tell me the results of my rabbit test. Positive—
over two months now—about the same amount of time
Roland had been gone. Of course. So it was true. I wasn't
crazy. In a daze I walked out of his office, down Madison
Avenue, staring at myself in the shop windows. Did I look
like someone who was a mother? I passed the shop where
Roland had bought me the red dress last year. Thinking
about the moist spots between my thighs that night, my
hands rubbed my stomach. It began there, with our skin
and secrets, and now this fetus, mingling in our juices.
Walking over to Fifth Avenue, I took the downtown bus,
aware of everything about myself—the summer wind in
my hair, the slightest gurgle in my belly.

"What are you going to do?" Nettie asked when I told
her my news at the library.

"I'll send him a telegram." I shook my head. I wanted
to tell her about Claire, about the business of Ma Das, but
I was too embarrassed. "It's so complicated. You haven't
told my parents about Roland leaving, have you?"

"Of course not. They keep to themselves, like they
always have. But don't worry, Sarah. They'll come around.
I bet when there see the grandchild—"

"Let's not talk about that," I interrupted.

"You know, this may sound kind of corny, but I've always admired you, Sarah."

"You make me sound like an English teacher who did a good job teaching Melville."

"You have such a particular air about you. You don't seem to care about what other people think. You don't care even care about what I think. And you've braved this business with your parents so well. But—"

"Uh-oh. I think I hear a lecture coming on."

She didn't answer at first. "It's just that sometimes, I don't know if it's so great to burn all your bridges. I wonder, in all this rush to be right, to go on, if you know where it is you're going."

Her words hurt, more than she probably knew. "It's not so bad anymore, Nettie. I have Roland's friends now."

Thrillingly, Roland figured out a way to send me a bouquet of yellow roses. They arrived at the library a few days later with a small note, *I am so happy for us. Wait for me.* How like him, I thought, fingering the thin, bright petals at my desk. I understood the gesture: I must learn the art of waiting; I must make it as exquisite, as charming as he would. Charles was right; Roland did need to find out who he might become, what was possible in that fragile country of his. He had found a role for himself, doing union work. I didn't understand the details of his job, but I knew it was the urgency of the task that compelled him. I had always known with Roland that a certain loneliness was inevitable, that he would always belong to a force bigger, beyond the both of us, and I must live with the spaces in our marriage. The pregnancy changed everything. It was as if something was continuing between us, branching into our thoughts, even without our bodies touching every night. We would have to move on, beyond ourselves. I began to dream of our child:

I was sure she would be a girl, with long lashes and black, lustrous hair, like Roland's. She was a link between the troubled islands we had made of ourselves. Though I still wondered about Roland and his secrets, about his family waiting in their run-down house in his village. And couldn't help myself: I made a phone call to the British Embassy to check on my visa.

7

In June, the city poured heat. Temperatures climbed into the nineties. Cars moved down the avenues, all glare and exhaust, time broken into fragments of sensation: the sudden shade of an awning, a moist blast from an open steam pipe. When I flipped to a new page on my calendar hanging in the kitchen, I realized Roland had been gone almost three months. The P.P.P. was in power a month. Weekly, his bulletins arrived, thin blue air mail letters with a grainy photo of Kaieteur Fall, purple stamps showing an Amerindian shooting fish. He wrote of the long hours on the road, the color and smell of the mango trees. He scolded me about working on the house in my condition. And he told me about the details of what was going on: the Jagans were pushing forth new bills in the legislature. Cheddi was concentrating his efforts on the upcoming Labour Relations Bill that Roland was doing the grassroots work for. There were other efforts as well: a repeal of the Undesirable Publications Law that Lionel had helped draft. And more daring yet, Janet and Cheddi publicly asked for clemency for Ethel and Julius Rosenberg. A few days after the Rosenbergs were executed, I received a postcard from

Roland: *Those bastards. But keep the faith. Will write soon, my love.*

By noon of our house's opening day a faded green Buick arrived, dragging a tailpipe. Inside were a Guianese couple—the Pilloos and their six-year old daughter Sharon, who came hurtling up the path, sandals slapping, skirt flying out like a crisp parasol. "Slow down!" her mother cried, but the little girl had already streaked past Sarita and me, wrenched open the screen door and disappeared inside, her high voice booming through the rooms. "Uncle Charles!" she shouted. "Uncle, I'm here!"

"You must be Roland's wife." Rita set down a straw basket on the porch. "You a lovely girl."

I could feel her admiring gaze on my arms, my face. I knew what the look meant: my dress was simple, not too flashy. I didn't show yet, but word had gotten around the club. My pale skin was a plus—we'd have a fair child. Her husband Thomas stole up behind her. He was a thin man, dressed in a cotton shirt, gray hair combed to the side, giving him a slightly weary, unhealthy look. He pressed in with a smile. "So you the one gone and married the Singh boy? I remember him with his crooked teeth and glasses. What a temper that boy had!"

"We sometimes have him over for a little meal, you know," Rita put in. "I was always worried about the country boy away from his mother, not getting fed enough. But how that boy could talk! He had grand plans. He still studying?"

"Not exactly. He took some time off to work for the P.P.P. "

Thomas' eyebrows raised. "He over there with Cheddi?" Thomas, I could see, was not too keen on Cheddi. Rita was more openly disapproving, remarking,

"And here it is, he related to one of the biggest men in Georgetown!"

"I don't think Lionel is exactly Roland's cup of tea," I laughed.

The door slapped open and Charles came back on to the porch with Sharon in his arms, letting out a yell. "Now it's that monkey man, Thomas!" He set Sharon down and the two men laughed and embraced. "Sarita, you remember me tellin' you about Thomas! They run him out of the country for his wicked writing."

"It wasn't wicked," Thomas said. "Just telling the truth."

Charles poked his friend in the ribs. "This man got a tongue like a snake and a pen full of venom."

"Are you writing now?"

His wife let out a groan. "Thank God, no. Now he a writer in royal exile."

A wan smile leaked across Thomas' face. "I've moved into another profession, dear. Much less dangerous. I manage a restaurant in New York called the Royal Palms."

"So you haven't heard anything?" I asked.

"Nothing I'd want to be quote on!" he said and winked.

We all laughed, though I was a little disappointed. For a moment Thomas seemed to hold out the promise of linking me to Roland and fresher news. But that prospect dimmed as he leaned against the porch rail, kicked off his sandals and let himself drift with Charles and Sarita into talk of old friends, who had settled where in the States and Canada.

"Your sweetheart getting jealous," Thomas observed of Sharon, who kept very close to Charles. She was a small, brassy-skinned girl with round black eyes who took more after her father's wiry tense look than the voluptuous, overripe beauty of Rita.

"Sharon, leave Charles alone. Don't act so nasty like," her mother complained.

Sharon drew her mouth into a pout. "I am not."

"What you want your new friends to think of you?"

Thomas winked at me. "Charles here promise to marry Sharon when she reach his shoulder, but she can't wait."

"I want to sit on top," the little girl declared, pointing at Charles' head.

With a laugh, Charles reached down and swept her onto his shoulders while Rita protested, "Charles, you really musn't!" But Sharon was already letting out shrieks of delight, her skirt flying up around her dimpled knees as he tickled and poked her. She knew she was a prized possession, for this weekend none of the families with children were coming up.

In fact, only a paltry showing of members showed today. Shortly after the Pilloos arrived, the lone figure of Ranjit could be seen strolling up the road from the bus station, a leather briefcase in one hand, a paper sack of clothes in the other. He danced up our steps with a kind of princely grace, wagged his head at the screen door which still wasn't fastened properly and laughed, "So *this* is our summer haven?" He smiled again, his eyes distant. "Or should I say hovel?" I felt sorry for him, since he looked so ill at ease.

Nor did it help that a few minutes later, a black and white car with Rudy's Taxi painted on the side panel pulled up to the curb with Srini and Tara sitting inside. Flushing, Ranjit stubbed out his cigarette on the porch steps as Tara emerged from the taxi, shaking out the folds of her crisp, starched sari. Srini, meanwhile, was pacing while the driver went around the back and opened the rear hood. Out of the trunk came an astonishing stream of items: wooden folding chairs, blankets, pillows, pots, pans and baskets smelling of spices. Coming onto the porch, Tara instantly launched into a shrill attack at Ranjit; apparently there had been some mix-up—Ranjit was supposed to come to Phoenicia with them, but instead stayed in Connecticut last night and took the strangely independent move of leaving on the early bus. "Is this any way to behave?" she scolded him. "What would your mother think if I told her of your goings about?"

Out of the taxi trunk, like a trove from a caravan of camel bags, came baskets of vegetables, tiffins of nan and salted potatoes, tea cups and spoons—a gesture not so much helpful, as commanding, we realized, the moment Tara shouldered her way into the kitchen and sniffed at the pots hanging on pegs, greasy, corrupted with beef.

Everything distressed them—the news that each family was responsible for cleaning their own room; the rum and whiskey bottles standing in a brazen line on the sideboard, things I don't think Srini at all cared about, but with which they might beat us back, force us to honor them. Even Ranjit, who had taken a whiskey and cigarette after being shown his room—suffered a long harangue. "What would your mother think if I told her of your goings about?" Tara had demanded. "I'm very, very sorry to offend you, Auntie," he mumbled back. The house was in an uproar, Tara now yelling at Sarita about the small bedroom she and Srini had been granted—they were the eldest, after all—and Sharon in a tantrum because her mother would not let her play with the old pistol and holster she'd found in her bedroom closet.

Finally calm descended on the house—the very quality we'd been working towards all spring. Our day settled into a warm, glassed-in peace. Sun drenched the grass like mist; cicadas started up in the branches. The gifts everyone brought—jars of chutney sealed with cheese cloth, chunks of mango glistening inside, and tablecloth fabric for me—meant our summer had finally begun. A change, a relish of long, leisurely time, was filling up our house, splashing into its freshly-scrubbed rooms. The hours now took on a cool, delicious sense of wait, of a breath drawn in and slowly let out as the sky seemed to darken and go light again like a stone experiencing shades of sunlight.

"You must find us peculiar," Tara laughed as she shuffled in and collapsed into a rattan chair, seat bottom creaking. "All our rules and Srini can be a bit fussy, I know. And now our quarrels." She sighed. "Sometimes just the sound of my own voice is tiresome."

"It's all right."

"No, it's not. I can see it on your face."

I did not answer, but began pinning a new hem. The fabric was plum colored, rimmed with gold, falling in a lush sweep across my knees. I stuck the last pin in and pulled it up before my face, the fabric a ruddy scrim with the trees wavering behind. *Shades*—I thought to myself, this was what was now possible. Inside the house, a radio was turned on somewhere—"This is Charles Laughton..."— then it warbled off.

But Tara's voice broke in, splintering the mood. "Forgive my frankness, Sarah. This club is hardly a place for a girl like you. I'm afraid we're a bit, my goodness, what's the word? Old-fashioned?"

"Oh, Tara. If you only knew what I came from." It was time for another test, I knew, one longer and more arduous than Rita's.

"You want to do something. I sense that. This house. Charles showed me your work—all the curtains—you didn't waste a moment, did you? All that energy!" She turned to give me her profile, her chin wobbling in the air, as if to focus on a spot just beyond the edge of the yard, where Srini and Ranjit, changed into more comfortable kurtas and loose white pyjama pants, sat talking in the shade on a rolled out bamboo mat. This was the way it was with Tara—the distracted smiles, her mind working at some distant, leisurely ideal. "I frankly wouldn't want all that energy you've got. And you don't seem to mind being left alone."

"It's not easy. But I've managed."

Leaning forward, the wedge of her stomach made a thick, double fold. Her thighs parted, sari edge clinging to the cane of her chair. "What about your family? They know about the baby?"

I shook my head.

She sighed. "How terrible. To be cut off from your people like that."

Her words stung, but I was determined not to let it show. I kept jabbing my needle into the fabric. "We all make our choices," I said.

"You know, so many of our boys want to marry American women. Ranjit and his friends, chasing after those pretty receptionists. But these marriages don't do very well. Our boys weren't raised for such independence."

My hands hesitated over the pin box. A few went scattering to the floor. "I told you, Tara. I've been perfectly happy here."

Tara remained cool. The comment was meant to ruffle. "And Roland?"

"So far no trouble. It's a popular government."

"What about his studies? It came as quite a blow to Srini when Roland left."

I put my needle down, knowing this was the other knot of discord between us, Roland's sudden departure, the stir he'd created at the Consulate.

157

"It wasn't an easy decision. But you know the story. He wasn't going anywhere at the Consulate."

Her chin gave a wobble again. A quick readjustment of bunched up damp sari, easing it out from under her thighs that now solidly closed. "Well, I must say, yours is a *very* unusual marriage."

Then she sank back again in her chair, as if the effort of our conversation had exhausted her, training a wisp of hair back into its bun. We stayed silent, watching the men shake out their trousers and pick their way across the grass. In the kitchen there was a rough clatter of dishes— Sarita was seeing to our tea. Already the house atmosphere had changed, filled with the polite, segregated chatter of men and women. Even Vijay, tripping up the steps with his fishing pole, stopped in surprise when he saw Claire and Sarita laboring through the screen door with their tray of tea. How chaste, how careful the moment seemed! With a sigh, Tara rose to take charge of the tea things; I had the sense she wanted to forget our conversation as much as I did.

"Did I catch wind of some talk about our bloody Consulate?" Ranjit sauntered up the stairs, popped a sweet into his mouth, then draped himself on the chair Tara had just occupied. The other men were climbing up the stairs as Claire came out with the tea tray. "Can't we have some peace from that awful place?"

"Ranjit, it's not so dreadful!" Srini laughed from behind.

"What do you know, my fellow? You have that splendid office and send lackeys like me scampering around."

"Hardly." Srini settled into a chair; his tone was avuncular, narrow face broken into bland, smiling lines. "None of us know the true meaning of working hard; we are all splendid bureaucrats. And you—you've got the best set-up of all the young ones with that special arrangement of yours."

"What special arrangement?" I asked.

"I'm on a kind of advanced track. The work I'm doing at the Consulate is to be the basis for my dissertation." So Roland was right: Ranjit was a spoiled prince. Even the way he rolled a cigarette spoke of a kind of elaborate ceremony, the habits of exclusivity.

"How lucky for you," I murmured. "Roland never even had time to study."

Charles' eyes glittered across the porch. He sniffed and rubbed his nose with a handkerchief. "Advanced track!" he laughed. "That's the opposite of me, old man! When it come to school, you on the advanced track, I on the 'fall behind' track!"

"Hear, hear!" Thomas put in, head nodding. "In Georgetown you got to butter the right side of the Queen's ass to come study at her libraries!"

At this, both Charles and Thomas tilted back in their chairs and snorted with laughter, relishing their joke, a few more comments passing between them, meant to coarsen the mood. With Srini and Tara, it was as if a gloom had set upon them. Tara had gotten up to pour tea, turning her back to us.

"Now forgive an old woman who knows nothing of world affairs, but I did want to put some other questions to our Ranjit," she said. "So what is this business, gala-vanting around in the city last night? I hear you're always in the company of some American diplomat's daughter."

He was flustered. "*Please.*" His utterance carried a silent plea—*not here*—but Tara knew this. She drew up her chin, staring severely as she set down his tea before his pulled-up knees. I could see he was wondering how he might cut short the public humiliation. Brow wrinkled, he pushed the teacup aside, and jumped up from his seat. "You know what I think!" he gasped. "I think you're worried that I might have a good time with these girls!"

A few small coughs of laughter, then silence. The statement was silly. We could all see it—the childish shine in his eyes; the awkward, hips out challenge. Ranjit's remarks were aimed at myself and Claire, American wives of Indians, inevitably exposed.

"Ranjit!"

"And who can blame me?" To my shock and pleasure, he winked in my direction.

A disdainful look on her face, Tara jerked up and began clearing the dishes, as if to cover over his rudeness. His stab at philosophizing had clearly offended her. The others turned their faces away.

"All right then," Ranjit said. "Let's get ourselves a little cricket game."

"Now there's a splendid idea," Srini laughed, rising from his chair.

"I want to play, I want to play!" Sharon began hopping on one foot.

Amused, Srini let his hand rest on her head. "Girls can't play cricket, dear."

"But I want to!"

"It's a good idea," I put in. "Let her join you."

"It's her father's fault," Rita complained. "He's bought this American nonsense, saying she can do this or that. Then I have to listen when her grandmother complains about the bad-mouth girl I'm raising."

But Ranjit seemed to have warmed to my suggestion. "Sarah is right. Come little girl, it's time we taught you something really useful."

"Oh Ranjit, there she's in a skirt—it's not lady-like!" Rita complained.

"Lady-like! And what century do you belong to, madam?" He scooped Sharon into his arms and announced, "If there's any good I can do in this world, it's to teach a girl how to play cricket." Thrilled at Ranjit rubbing his furry beard against her cheek, Sharon squirmed with pleasure. He let her down again. Hair straggling out of its ribbon, she dashed back and forth on the porch, shouting, "I'm going to learn cricket! I'm going to swing a bat!"

A few minutes later, though, when Ranjit came up the stairs, cricket bat and ball clutched to his chest, Sharon appeared to have an ungrateful change of mind. Now she sidled next to my chair, pretending to watch me sew. She was withdrawn, but theatrically so. Her fingers fiddled with her hair ribbon; she tugged at her bobby sock.

"Let's go, little one."

"I don't want to."

Ranjit tried a beautiful, wide-toothed smile. "You wanted to before. Are you going to break my heart now?"

I noticed the back of her calves tense. "No."

"Sharon, Ranjit gone and set it up for you. Don't be impolite." With two fingers, her mother pushed at her daughter's shoulder blade.

"I want to sew." Her voice was hard, stubborn. She drew nearer to my arm.

Flushing, I let out a nervous laugh. I was sure Sharon hadn't really noticed me, though I took in everything about her; her tiny nails chipped with red polish, the imperious wag of her head each time an adult flattered her. She wrested from me tufts of longing for my own baby, if only to touch her skin, to smell its milkiness. "Sharon, go play with Ranjit. You don't want to sit on the porch like an old lady."

Ranjit still waited, one foot on the steps, his face a bit

resentful. I could see he regarded this small game as a test. If he had failed earlier with Tara, he might prove himself in another tiny, domestic gesture. Girls could play cricket; thus, aunties like Tara were obsolete. The world was an of equation of absolutes with Ranjit, though his gaze was distant, calculating.

Taking Sharon by the hand, I led her to him. The sun lit up his black hair in a glossy halo. A smile passed between us, like the exchange of a password. "There you go. You come sit on the porch with me later."

"I'll give you a ride first," he said. As he reached his long arms out, lifting her high up in the air, I couldn't help myself, I felt a lurch of disappointment. Sharon was suspended for a moment over our heads, feet kicking, squealing with laughter—then she nestled on his shoulders. He smiled at me and I was flooded with a strange, acute happiness.

"Say farewell to Auntie Sarah," he said.

"Farewell!"

"Tell all those fuddy duddies you're going to learn cricket like a boy."

"Don't tell her that!" Rita cried from behind.

"I'm going to learn cricket—" Again she dissolved into giggles.

"Another big-talking one," Rita sighed as watched them walk away, Sharon bobbing on Ranjit's shoulders, ribbon sliding down her back. I was so excited, I wasn't sure I could concentrate on my sewing. "Just like Thomas, putting these ideas in her head."

"I think she's a wonderful kid," I said. "So much spirit."

"Nonsense." Rita's bangles jingled as she smoothed her skirt, picking crumbs from her lap. "He's simply spoiling her."

Reluctantly, I returned to my sewing. It was hard to tell if Rita was annoyed or putting on a face of convention for the sake of our group. She smoothed her dress, adjusted the pins in her hair, eyes on Ranjit as he deposited Sharon on the grass and began to organize a game around the little girl.

On the lawn Ranjit kneeled behind Sharon, hands doubled over hers. From a few feet away, Thomas tossed the ball and the cricket bat flashed comically, like an extra limb. "Down!" Ranjit kept saying, but the ball thudded and rolled behind them. Again Thomas pitched the ball; again she swung too high, nearly smashing Ranjit in the face. Laughing, he ducked away. "She's too little," Vijay grumbled.

For an hour we watched as Ranjit taught Sharon. A disgusted Vijay and Srini slumped in the shade. Thomas bore it out, mopping his head with a handkerchief. My gaze strayed to Ranjit, holding himself in a long, delicate arch as he explained how to grip the handle. The assuredness of his body, his quiet manner excited me. It was hard to ignore, this mild attraction between us. Smoothing the fabric across my knees, I wondered: Are you supposed to stop having such feelings when you're pregnant? Shouldn't I be experiencing nesting instincts, cleaning the closets?

But I was thinking about Ranjit again. At the least we would have the most to say to one another, simply because we were oddly paired this weekend. I was glad. Ranjit could be a bore, but I looked forward to the long warm hours, to supper and talk with a man I knew only slightly, taking my mind off everything else.

A loud, solid crack sounded in the air. It was the ball, finally connecting with wood. Thomas, roused out of his daydreaming, scrambled across the grass and scooped the ball up. Triumphant, Ranjit turned to us on the porch. "See dear mother?" he declared. "Who says your daughter can't play?"

Before I could help myself, I had run to the edge of the porch and was shouting wildly, "Once more!" My skirt clung to my legs; my wrists shook. "Go on, Sharon! Show those fellows! Get a real game going!"

An embarrassed Ranjit dropped the bat down on the grass and went to lie with the other men under the trees. Tara's sharp voice rapped behind me. "Sarah," she scolded. "Don't just stand there. Come help clear these tea things away."

Our days wore on. Not a single rainstorm and the country turned dry. Pale mounds of hay bleached in the sun, fields gleamed like ponds of ice. The deep green of the Catskills showed signs of having lightened; the rivers ran low, knots of silver leaping over shallow rocks, barely cresting the boulders. There were signs posted everywhere: DO NOT THROW LIGHTED MATTER ON GRASS and NO CAMPFIRES, VIOLATORS PROSECUTED.

For weeks our house managed to stay full: the Magalees and Balakrishnans; some Trinidadian families, the Dindyalls and Laljings; a couple from Calcutta, drifting up for a day or two with warm packages of chappatis and teeth-spoiling shandesh, homemade saffron curd—even a few coconuts, which we hacked off and drank the milk from in silver cups. With the arrival of more children, the walls seemed to puff out like cheerful sails. The house brimmed with noise. Caribbean voices lilted over the lawn, scraps of Hindi, the effortless shouts of children as they stampeded across the grass in pursuit of some urgent game. Often, they squatted on hot rocks, dipping nets into the stream in hopes of nabbing minnows flicking like transparent leaves in shallow pools. Sharon especially grew strong and brown. She lay on her stomach on the porch flipping through Marvel comic books, mimicking all her heroes, laughing uproariously when she squatted by the radio. She and the Laljing boy, Johnny, became inseparable. Johnny spun a silver pistol, Sharon a skinned stick and they tore through the rooms as the Lone Ranger and Tonto. Soon Sharon insisted on having her hair cut short like Johnny, and the two took to wearing the same clothes: navy shorts and saddle shoes. Despite the little bell-shaped earrings which dangled from her ears, she now looked hopelessly like a boy. Her mother simply gave up.

The house pipes brought up more rust so we set out pots of boiled water in the pantry to cool. No one called a repairman or plumber, nor was there any mention of the terrace. With Charles' persistence, raw posts continued to appear on the porch roof. Otherwise, a torpor of inactivity set in on the house; holes lay unpatched, taps leaked. A few trips were made to town, but most of the time we kept to the quiet honeycomb of rooms, holding fast to our habits—long meals of curry and rice, half-serious cricket games and endless veranda talks. After a late supper, the men strolled down the road to the bridge, faces invisible in the darkening night while the women gathered around the big kitchen table.

Usually we swapped advice, such as where to buy chutneys and and good ginger and how to use supermarket coupons. Sarita often brought some new prized item to show off—a box of Clairol hair dye, a hoola hoop for Sharon, a Bulova watch Charles bought her on credit at Bloomingdale's. She filled the kitchen with alien finds: freezer-wrapped chicken breasts, boxes of Bisquick, maraschino cherries and Tom Collins mixes. The rest of us nervously tested Sarita's strange concoctions and swiftly grew drunk.

But tensions were starting to show in the house. When the men came back from their walk, still hungry for excitement, they gathered on the porch, where they could be heard drinking rum well past midnight, their voices rising in a raucous cacophony. Eventually, there was an outraged banging of doors upstairs and like a tug sent out to fetch her stray boats, Tara came sailing down the stairs to scold them—but to no avail. The men flicked their fingers, continuing on. They didn't know Tara's language; didn't care, as she did, about the same standards of decency anymore. Port of Spain streets and Madras shut rooms were a long way distant. "Let a man have his poison!" Charles yelled at her one time and so she withdrew, but not without complaining to Srini of the "rough types" they'd thrown their money in with.

And the arguments—especially among the men, about life, about politics, about America, which they all detested and loved. I would often join in, but I knew my remarks weren't welcome. It was so strange: where was my old world, the arguments around the dinner table with those quarrelsome, melancholy people? And poor Ranjit, breaking from the group, pacing around the property, bluish cigarette smoke twining over his head. Tara fretted; from the porch, she would shout to him, "Come, Baba, come!" offering up a fresh-pressed shirt or directing him to a stool where she trimmed his beard, right out in the open. I could imagine him as a husband—impossibly self-centered, a halo of seriousness gathered around his striking face.

It was interesting that Ranjit kept surfacing as significant to me. Perhaps it was because there was a kind of kinship between us, denied by him, longed for by me, which

my act of waiting had brought out. Each night the house
drew us into its deep well of sounds, bringing me closer to
memories, the moment when I had left my parents and
seemed unsure of who I was—who I might become. I
could see he no longer wanted things in the old way, as
they were given to him—but then he was someone, like
me, who had dashed to an edge and now stared in fright
and anger at the broken vista which lay before him. I
sewed a new blue skirt that spilled over my new belly,
dabbed my ears with scent. We would strike up our private conversations, but there was always the same twitch
of his shoulders, a tight, wary glance thrown in my direction, which I sometimes took to be a subterfuge, even a
kind of tease. Or at least, when I was honest enough with
myself, that was what I wanted.

Roland's note sat propped against a water glass, thumbed
and greasy. *Please wait.* The bubble that had since formed
around the word "wait"—after so many weeks, now hued
with secrecy, contingency, turned to shame. I was not
imagining it—the men were starting to avoid me. The
walls spoke of it; the faces in the other rooms turned away.
I could feel my flesh turn thick with effrontery. There was
a danger, as a woman, pregnant, without a husband. I was
becoming a freak, an embarrassment to the group. Talk of
the goings on in Georgetown, old friends, lapses into
Hindi, trailed off when I pushed through the screen door.
I'd seen the same looks around Claire—she bore it
placidly, her round face serene, blank. *Ma Das.* A child,
another marriage, an age-old betrayal—it was also possible with me, I knew, though I never uttered this out
loud—not even to Charles, who would have understood.
Claire tried to blend; she was *good*. But around me there
twitched a suspicious air—the same air which followed

Janet Jagan, I imagined—a woman who makes things difficult. Sometimes I argued. Sometimes my fingers jabbed the air; I tried to interfere, challenge Tara and her silly mother-in-law rules. Today the argument was over swimming. Tired of all the eating, the endless chats, I had gotten up from the lunch table and suggested we drive to a lake twenty miles up the road, where we might swim. "Don't you guys ever want to *do* something?" I complained. Everyone instead waddled out to the porch, argued and yawned and soon fell asleep.

Now an irritable, damp night had fallen—the hum of mosquitoes, moths thudding against lampshades. I was bored, my body heavy and tense, exhausted from so much inactivity. And the long supper had worn me out, left me beached in speculation on my weeks-old note—when did *wait* become *now*? I thought, pushing up from the bed, sweat sliding down my puffy ankles. Would any of those faces dare to tell me what they knew?

In the hallway, I noticed the door to Charles and Sarita's door yawning open. Beyond their bed a shape moved, in front of the half-finished terrace. An ember glowed— then I saw Ranjit in the window, a glass and bottle of whiskey propped on the sill beside him. He called to me.

"Come on, join me here. Auntie has finished her scolding for the evening, so you are perfectly safe to come in." Seeing my hesitation, he added, "Come, come, there's nothing dangerous in sitting with me, is there?"

"I thought it was the other way around."

He watched my legs flashing under my skirt as I managed the sill and sat opposite him. I had just started to show and it seemed natural to sit with my hands latched under my belly, near this handsome man. It was cooler here. The curtains blew at my back. I could just make out the dim outlines of the new railing.

"Comfortable?"

"Much better. These long dinners. I can't believe it's almost the end of the summer and we haven't gone swimming once. You'd think I was trying to start a revolution rather than get us to cool off."

"I can see why you make Tara so nervous," he smiled. "You really are the most charming creature here this summer."

I knew what I should do—the exact tone of sarcasm, a loose flip of hand to keep my distance. But the moment went longer and the darkness made it seem as if we were conspiring together. I watched him breathing; I watched him watch me.

"You still think my husband is a fool to be down there, Ranjit?"

"Perhaps I'm a bit envious. You know what I did for the past week? The Consulate paid me ten dollars to follow the Prime Minister around and agree with whatever he said. Or I spend my days puzzling out equations that seem far removed from what your husband is doing. Though I do have my doubts about what's going on there."

"Why?"

"I'm not that familiar with this movement. Though I wonder about Jagan. For a man from the country, he may have too much fire, not enough common sense. Such as, you don't immediately start in on the trade unions and think the Colonial Governor is going to give you a nice approving pat on the head."

"But he stands for something."

"That's right, and if he doesn't watch where he's standing, the bloody Queen of England is going to make sure he don't have an office to hang his hat in!"

I also laughed. This must be why I liked Ranjit so

much. He was like Charles. He did not seem to care, like so many of Roland's friends, whether I was either a woman to be condescended to, or an American to be condescended to for a different reason. His voice, while almost a whisper, held a quiet vigor. He was someone used to neatly sweeping up big ideas, spreading them out on his thin fingertips. He leaned back against the window jamb and began gesturing in the air.

"Think of it this way, Sarah. This motley crew of ours is fixing up a house. In places like India or Guiana, it's like living in an old house with not much light, a bit of sack cloth thrown across the windows. Then one day a man comes selling looking glasses. They're very expensive and they come from all over the world. So the man of the house, he buys the looking glass.

"All of a sudden he notices how ugly he is. He sees himself in his worn clothes and his leaking ceiling. Then he notices how old his wife is and when his neighbors come visit he can't help but cringe at their bad manners and how they too are very unpleasant. His eyes are not turned in on himself, but on how he's being seen."

"Ranjit, that's ridiculous. You make it seem as if before a man didn't know he was poor."

"Which before? There's all kind of looking glasses that have their times. Your husband's Lionel Lal, he found one kind of glass, the kind the British held up so he grew to hate the color of his skin. Jagan and your husband—they come overseas and they find another looking glass to themselves. This one they dub socialism. Mind you, this looking glass is still one you buy from outside."

Quiet flew between us. "What about Jagan?"

"Jagan forgets a country doesn't see things in the abstract. That's the problem with us over-educated types running back shouting solidarity. The fight down there between Negro and Indian is no small thing. What does a poor fellow know? He sees the Indian shopkeeper cheating him day in, day out. And that's exactly the sort of flaw the British will exploit."

I hugged my arms tight. "Sometimes I wish I could be like Janet Jagan. New York socialist girl in her utilitarian gray, slogging around with the workers?"

Ranjit laughed. "You are quite delightful the way you are, Sarah. But tell me, how do you and Roland manage? There must be confusions."

Laughing, I pushed some hair off my neck. "What do you really know about these things?"

"I know that not one of my friends will stay with the woman he is with here. They'll be letters, telegrams and one, two, three, and snap, a marriage is in the works back in Delhi. My problem is I'm far too honest. If I'm in love with a woman, I want to throw the whole bloody thing off. Marriage disgusts me."

"Marriage disgusts most people," I observed. Everything pressed—the trees and the dark and the oddly reassuring odor of Ranjit, liquor mingled with cologne. We stared out at the hills, hunched like wooly bears on the horizon. Ranjit had drawn closer and I could not bear that my back arched, that I wanted him to touch me.

"Maybe Tara is right," I sighed. "Maybe our marriages are flimsy." I squeezed my eyes shut for an instant. "Roland isn't like Charles. He can't give up one place for another." Despite myself, a few tears leaked out of my eyes. "I don't know where that leaves us. Or me."

We were silent a while. This was the first time I had spoken so rawly of my own emotions—how much my life still hung in an uncertain balance, strung between two continents, the solid and tempting mass of America and a beleaguered, torn scrap of a colony.

"Ranjit, what do you think I should do?"

He smiled. "I would like to say you should kiss me and we can forget all these awful politics for the while."

My heart sped up—I hated to think that this was what I wanted as well.

"Will you hold me?"

It was a strange request. But I needed to have a man's hands on my skin again, to know that I was real. He put his arms around me and kissed me once on my forehead. It was awkward, balancing on the sill, as if we were about to pitch ourselves onto the terrace, the sea of trees beyond. Hearing footsteps on the stairs, I started to pull away, but Ranjit squeezed his fingernails into my arms. "Just know this. I have connections at the British Embassy," he whispered. "If anything should go wrong—" He stopped. The footsteps had neared, Tara's voice sailing across the dark bedroom, calling, "Who's out there? Who's out on that dirty roof?"

"Thanks," I whispered. We sprang apart just as the hall light crowned Tara's head.

"Isn't anyone going to swim?" I asked the next day, as I slid off my sandals. The lake that spread before us was small and irregular, with a narrow sand beach. A scattering of redwood tables were set on a grassy slope. Bramble bushes and fir trees sprang in thick clumps around the rest of the shore. A few families who had already set up their blankets stared at Tara as she trundled across the sand, sari flapping in the breeze.

But I was met with silence. No one made a move to undress, even though it was warm out and people were already splashing in the water. Sarita stayed in her prim buttercup dress, straw hat dipped low over her eyes. Even Claire remained in her blouse and slacks. There was something odd in the air. Annoyed, I settled down on the blanket. I tried to think instead of pleasant things, like Ranjit, though he'd been avoiding me all morning and now sat several feet away, trouser cuffs turned up, showing delicate, slim ankles.

"Go on," he chided Sharon, who sat nested in her mother's lap, having her hair combed. "You go swimming."

"I want to build a sandcastle."

"All right then. Build us the best sandcastle on this beach."

"With towers and a moat?"

"We musn't forget the moat. And a drawbridge too."

"I can make a castle with two bridges," she declared. Twisting around, she cried in annoyance to her mother, "Leave me alone!" and pitching herself out of Rita's lap, she labored across the beach with her bucket and spade. With great seriousness, she began to dig a few feet from the water. I could see Rita was hurt by this small moment of defiance.

"My goodness," Tara remarked. "That child has quite a temper, doesn't she?"

"Sometimes I hardly recognize her," Rita sighed. "Ever since we move here, she gets so many ideas in her head."

"That's the way they raise children here—"

"It's terrible. You can't have these poor creatures in both worlds," Tara remarked. "They'll be positively looney by the time they grow up."

"And what are these two worlds?" Thomas Pilloo laughed.

"Such as, when Sharon grows up, is she off dating with bobby socks and pearls? Or do you send her back to Georgetown?" I was aware of her glance flashing once to me, then away.

Thomas smiled at Sharon, who was absorbed in her digging. "My daughter appears more interested in the Lone Ranger than pearls."

"There, you see! Choice, that most American of euphemisms!" She nodded toward Sharon. "Is that what you would want to foist on a poor little girl?"

"Tara—" Srini warned.

The conversation ground to a stop. My hands fiddled with my skirt. "What's going on here?" I whispered, turning to Sarita.

"Tara saw you and Ranjit." Neatly, she undid the strap of her sandals and tucked her feet under her. Her hat brim wobbled. For the first time Sarita looked scared, her eyes glassy and large. "You got to be more careful, Sarah. You no married to some Yankee."

"But it wasn't like that," I protested.

"That may be. But I got a motto. No funny business in front of these folks. I'm not crazy."

Furious, I heaved myself up from the blanket and began to undress. I could feel everyone's eyes on my spine, taking in the scoops of flesh that sprang loose as I undid my skirt. The backs of my thighs widened, my stomach seemed monstrously large. I fumbled with my blouse buttons. In exasperation, I yanked it over my head and flung the blouse at my feet. My body had never felt so heavy, so obvious.

"Sarah, what are you doing?" Sarita asked.

"I'm going swimming."

"In your condition?"

"It's all right. I'll stay in the shallow water. "

The whispers grew more agitated as I picked my way down the slope. "What is she off doing now?" I heard Tara whisper as I began to walk away. "She can't go galavanting, behaving as she pleases."

"Shh—"

"Leave Sarah alone," Sarita said.

As I was stepping into the water, a rhythm of voices, one high, the other deep, came to me. I turned. Thomas Pilloo, trousers rolled to the knee, was leading Sharon away from her crumbling sandcastle into the lake. Gently he lifted Sharon over some rocks and brought her down in a shallow pool. Sharon squealed in mock terror but one of Thomas' hands cupped the small of her back, the other spread across her belly to steady her.

Watching this most ordinary of efforts between father and daughter, my heart began to speed up. I remembered Samuel sitting on the pebbled shore of our summertime lake, barely able to muster up a wave of encouragement as I used to practice my own stroke.

Where was my safety, now that the obvious had been torn from me?

When I dove, the lake cut open, cold as glass against the wide bow of my hips. I ignored its shock, the fear that I had grown so heavy, I might sink the instant I tried to swim. My arms hit the surface, trying to force down the scene from before. I kept swimming until my stroke grew less clumsy, the water softening across my back. I swam until I was so tired I forced myself to head toward a nearby shaded cove, clambered out of the water and stretched out on a rock. The baby fluttered, then stilled. Here I would at least be alone. I turned my face from the sun. I tried not to cry.

Time passed. I saw things: memories, a photo. Frieda with a dozen other immigrants at wooden desks. Evening school, 1937. Just turned twenty-eight, two months in America, childless, with good legs and firm breasts. Around her neck she wore a strand of nickel pearls. Her mother lived with her in a one-room cold water flat on Pitkin Avenue, waiting by the window for her daughter to return from evening school, terrified less that Frieda would be hurt than that her loudmouth daughter would befriend the wrong kind of people. She did. Jennie Friedman, three faces down, black hair swinging like a pennant at her waist, a copy of What Must Be Done? slid inside her notebook.

Next to the maps and Presidential pictures and high plaster ceilings, as Frieda struggled to make the loops and sounds of English, she all of a sudden made a choice. One night she went home by trolley, dragged out all her low-cut dresses, her fishnet stockings and tossed them into the dustbin. Her mother understood. She began going to shule regularly, sitting shyly with the other women up in the balcony. They didn't bicker any more. An order, a home had been made again.

Why, I often asked, this tunneling backward, a world that would one day swallow me up? It was the room, she told me, Litvaks and Hungarians and a dirty Sephardi all together. Even a Pole, a Gentile—one schwartze but she kept to herself, a nice girl. I thought: it should have been an awakening; instead it made her skin crawl. But there was more. Something happened, another story folded inside: once she was honest enough to tell me of a Hungarian man with whom one night she went out for tea. After, when she cried because his hand had reached the edge of her garter, he told her coldly she should go back to Russia if she wasn't ready for this. And that, my mother told me, was the end of *that*.

But I hated this story, its punishing moral. I begged her to go back to school, to learn better English. "No, I've done my duty. Your father does his. We are simple people, Sarah. Why such airs? We keep to ourselves, we know who we are." The more I dug my heels in, screamed for change, America, its vast blueness, jazz on the radio, the more they turned their backs. I watched other people flaunt dabs of newness: Jennie secretly smoked, Ernie Cohen donned a Yankees cap and learned how to dance, the girl next door went to Barnard and studied poetry. Why was nothing all right for me? The sun beat down in hard, angry strokes; my body twitched.

Frieda, as I'd never seen her before, loomed close. A pretty woman, with a trace of worry around her mouth. Her womb had failed her, as Samuel's strength and resolve had failed him once he arrived here. They loved Saturday evenings, Yiddish radio shows, the sight of me, their new little girl in her starched black dress. I was hope, like new blown glass. My sharp lips resembled Frieda's; my serious green eyes, Samuel's. It was a fair enough match. Improvisation was not their talent, but they made do. Relieved, Frieda poured all her habits, her stories and superstitions into my alert, waiting mind. *Don't open an umbrella in a house. Cross the other way when you see a priest. Watch, you don't look at a boy the wrong way.* I squirmed and pulled away. Frieda grew desperate, angry. She sought from me a signal of approval, as if from a mother. We grew confused, tangled as sisters. There were so many fights at night: "What's the matter, you can't remember a civil hello?" Or from me: "Why must you hang around when my friends are here?"

There was also a coldness cracking the surface of our new family. We did not touch often. I used to hear Frieda remark to her friends, with a chill in her voice: "Like a bookkeeper, Sarah watches and counts what I do." And I would rebuff her: "She measures me, like a bolt of cloth."

But there was one day I remembered, strolling home from my new elementary school, a new handmade flannel skirt flaring around my calves. Swinging from orange yarn was a picture I had painted in chalk gray and red— Mother and Father, Our House. The first time ever. The air smelled of autumn. I was turning the corner with the other children, elbowing ahead, trying to be the first to show off my gift. I prayed Frieda would be on the stoop with the other mothers.

But I went so fast, I fell. My knee was skinned, the drawing crushed in my fist. I began to cry. The other children trooped past, snickering at the klutzy orphan girl, sprawled on dirty pavement. Mama, I cried to myself, unable to wrest the word from my mouth. *Mama.* There was a shout. And then Frieda rose up from the steps, soft white in a pale wool dress, arms outstretched, a miracle, an angel without wings.

When my eyes blinked open, a shadow fell across my face. The sun had gone behind the trees, darkening the face, skinny arms that dangled at her hips.

"Fish," a small voice uttered. "I want the fish." She squatted down and peered into my face. "What's wrong with you?" she asked. "Are you crying?"

My mouth contorted, but I couldn't quite bring up an answer.

"Did you fall down?" She picked at a scab on her arm.

As I heaved myself up, pinpricks of light swam into my eyes. I shook my head. "No, I was dreaming or something."

"About the fish?"

"What fish?"

"In the water. Didn't you see?" She cocked her head, obviously disappointed I couldn't follow along. But I was staring at Sharon's bony arms. They were paler than I remembered, as if milk stirred in the grainy brown of Roland's skin. Her smell drifted toward me—lake dampness mingled with soap. Slowly, I gathered her to me. She did not protest, letting out an amused giggle. She was so small, I thought, the knobs of her shoulders fitting into my palms. She could be mine. I could sense the whole of her weight sink into mine. Relief splashed through me as we nuzzled, hair brushing. "You're wet," she laughed. Her eyes were black lustrous stones. I wanted to breathe her in, taste her skin.

As I pulled our cheeks closer, an uncertain smile trembled across Sharon's lips. "Stick—y!" she complained and began to jiggle with impatience. Feeling her retreat from me, I couldn't help myself; my fingers gripped tighter. "Lemme go!" Sharon tried to twist away, but my hands seemed to have a life of their own; they grew large and grasping, tugging at the milk brown skin and black hair which was fast slipping into air. We began to struggle, Sharon letting out shrieks of protest, while I tried to press her closer. No, I thought wildly. *No.*

A shout rang out. I let go my hold as the bushes split apart and Ranjit came crashing towards us. Sharon stumbled backward, hair swinging in her face, eyes staring in wild fright. The both of us were breathing hard.

"What happened?"

With a sob, Sharon ran to him, burying her face in his knees. I shook my head.

"Did she do something wrong?"

"She came up and surprised me, that's all."

He put a hand on her head and stroked it. "There, there. *Acha.* It's okay. No harm done. It was nothing." Sharon dug her face deeper into Ranjit's trousers, weeping extravagantly.

"It's just a silly mistake," I said, though I could hear the guilt tinging my voice. "I thought I was all alone. I was half asleep—"

"And we were worried. Sarita sent me to make sure you were all right and Sharon decided to come along." He regarded me a moment with shielded eyes. Sharon still clutched at his trouser legs. "I'm truly sorry she bothered you. But she's just a little girl. Very curious."

"I told you, Ranjit. She didn't bother me." In a small voice, I added, "*Please*. About what happened last night—"

He flicked at an insect which buzzed about his lashes. "She did. I can see that. It's obvious we've upset your private mood." He flashed me a brief, distant smile. "At home, we're so used to living one on top of one another, we forget that others like privacy."

"That's not what I meant," I asserted, my temper mounting. "And you don't have to talk to me that way."

"And what way is that?"

"As if I were—" I wanted to say "white" or even "a stranger" but that would seem too crude, too obvious. My face grew warm and I could feel angry thoughts, explanations, pushing against the inside of my skull. For a second, I considered flinging my arms around him, begging him to take me in again. Or slapping him across the face. Anything rude or shocking to make me stop feeling so naked and wrong.

A second later, the impulse had passed. The both of us stared at the ground. "Let's get out of here," he muttered. With a stiff jerk of his head, he grabbed Sharon's hand and started for the trees.

Back at the house, a huge green truck with TOWN OF PHOENICIA scrolled on the cab door sat parked by the curb. Climbing down from the cab was a man, red hair springing in thick clumps, as if unable to settle down on his skull. He looked distinctly unhappy to be here. "Charles Magalee here?"

From inside the living room arced Sarita's shriek, "Charles, is some man come to see you! Hurry now!" Overhead, Charles could be heard muttering; a loud thunk as he dropped his tools and clomped across the porch roof, his face and stomach a meshed triangle as he pressed against the screen door. Then he was before us, wiping his hands on his overalls. The man remained at the bottom of our stairs, balancing one foot on a step. "Good day." He held out his hand.

Charles did not take it. "What can I do for you?"

"You the Magalee fellow?"

"Yes."

"I'm afraid I've got some bad news. You're going to have to stop that building of yours, Mr. Magalee. We can't have it."

Charles' elbow flew back, fingers resting on his harness belt. "What you mean?"

"It's against the law." He flipped open his small notebook. "You can't do construction without a permit."

"Permit!"

"That's right." He used his pencil to point to the porch roof, where a flap of tarpaper blew in the wind. "Even from here I can see you stripped that thing dry of support. It's dangerous."

"But it's a terrace I'm building. And I got some experts going to give me some help."

"Can't do that without a permit. I'm surprised Landowne didn't say something. He knows better. You got to have an inspection first." He nodded toward the porch again. "The main thing is you have to stay off there."

"Blasted, I'm trying to get this thing ready for tonight so the group of us can watch the fireworks."

"Look, I don't want to be the bad guy here. But you

people do things your own way and this is what happens."

The two men shaded their eyes, sun glinting off the truck fenders. I took a few hesitant steps forward and asked, "Can't we just sit to watch the fireworks?"

As he stuffed his notebook into his shirt pocket, he lifted his face to me, a smile curving across his jaw. "Ma'am, I don't even bother with site visits on a weekend. But word got out. Folks around here noticed."

Feeling guilty, my fingers cramped in their pockets. "And you can't make an exception?"

He laughed, sliding his pencil inside his pocket. His eyes were green, I noticed, flecked with bits of yellow. "Exception?" he repeated, and laughed once more before getting climbing into the cab.

After the truck rumbled away, we stood in awkward silence. Sarita didn't even flash her husband an I-told-you-so look as Charles turned around and went upstairs. We could hear the clomp of his footsteps on the porch roof. "He going to get us all kicked out," Sarita muttered under her breath.

Charles came back downstairs, lugging his new tool belt, handsaw and cans of nails. His face looked gray and tired. Then he headed for the dining room, where he poured himself a glass of whiskey and sat down in sullen silence on the porch. All through the evening, Charles' mood turned even blacker. He declined to join us for an early holiday dinner, polishing off glass after glass by himself. By the time we ambled onto the porch, he was gone. He wasn't back up on the roof or in his bed, sleeping off his drunk. We tried the basement, the yard, by the stream. Sarita was by now tugging at the ends of her hair. "That man!" she kept crying. "Why he have to cause so much trouble!"

We all stood in the living room, listening to the stutter

and pop of firecrackers in the distance. Upstairs doors banged open and shut. Tara was shifting their belongings to a different room. Claire was stomping back and forth across the floorboards, though no one knew why. "That's where he went, the bastard," Vijay declared after a few minutes. "The fireworks."

Four of us—Sarita, Vijay, Ranjit and myself—clambered inside the Pilloos' car. I sat behind Ranjit, sensing his reluctance over my presence. As we wound up the steep mountain road curves, drinking in the evening air, I replayed the incident at the lake, hating myself for not calming down Sharon, at least proving I was normal, able to shield in my own childless arms. We tumbled out of the car and I banged into Ranjit's arm and felt his retreat, like a spot of warmth leaving a room when a door is flung open. We were all like doors, banging wide, scattering through the lot.

Spread out in the field was a small crowd—weary parents calling to children, boys kissing girls who kept their hands safely at their sides. Then schools of teenagers, flitting in the variegated pond of blankets and folding chairs, never stopping. Heads turned as we made our way across toward where a band was playing on a small stage. Occasionally a tiny crack like rice against glass could be heard, and the crowd whistled.

I followed the others down the slope, Vijay's elbows jutting behind him like dark arrows. "Excuse me"—"Yes, the front"—"Yes, I'm sorry." Our excuses fell like scraps, dissolving. Families sat knee to knee, six to a blanket as we steered around coolers and hidden stumps of thermoses. I grew nervous. If Charles were here, what was he doing? The band had finished its song.

Vijay stopped, glancing around. The stage was easier to see—a huge banner reading GOD BLESS OUR BOYS pinned across the back. Here about a dozen people sat on wooden chairs in two rows, cordoned off by a twisted crepe paper rope; a few older men in their uniforms. A woman sitting in the last seat with a white pocketbook at her feet flashed us a nervous smile. We came to a stop, listening to the clatter of stands and instruments as the musicians got up. The stage, bathed in a tangerine light, slowly emptied. Several people stared at us. Vijay was sweating and the woman with the white pocketbook had looked away. A man walked toward us, one hand raised, as if quieting a class. "Excuse me," he said, "there's room in the back."

"We looking for someone."

"And who's that?"

"A friend of ours. Charles Magalee."

The man made the gesture again. "The fireworks should begin very soon. You'd better go to the back."

We backed up the slope through the crowd that sprawled on the grass, still scanning, but the dark made it hard to see. Every now and then a sparkler fizzled; children cried. The air pressed at our backs.

Suddenly we caught sight of Charles bearing down from behind the stage. There was a chaotic rhythm to his walk, arms dangling at his sides. And it took a second, but the neat row of faces on the chairs lifted like pinball ducks, then understood it was them he was aiming for. At the same time, I spotted the bow tie, the suspenders, and realized who sat there as well. "Charles, no!" I called out, stumbling forward as Rowe rose from his seat. I pushed through the last clump of picnickers and came to the clearing just as Charles did.

"So, you don't like my plans!" Charles had pushed himself next to Rowe.

"Mr. Magalee, I don't know what you're talking about."

"You can't stop me with the house, you going to get me another way, huh?"

I did not know whether to laugh or cry. Out of the corner of my eye, I noticed the other startled faces sitting on the chairs, unable to make sense of what was happening.

"In Trinidad we got a name for a man like you," Charles went on. "Yankee cheap. You a man of cheap sentiment, Mr. Rowe. What you not see is I'm building something beautiful, something your Yankee hands don't know how to make."

Rowe turned to me. "You had better get him out of here," he said.

"You can talk to me!"

"I don't talk to a drunk," the other man replied.

"It's brown-skinned drunks you want no part of," Charles laughed. "What you think, I going to rub off on you?"

I could see Vijay a few feet away; he was unsure of whether to step forward. And Sarita, gesturing as if to say *Get him out, now matter what*. But I didn't know what to do. Charles edged closer to Rowe, swaying on his heels; Rowe's hands had clenched into fists. From the seats another man drifted up; I noticed a soft pouch of stomach easing over his belt; thick, capable hands. They're just people wanting to have a good time, I told myself.

"What's the problem here?" the new man asked.

"No problem," I whispered.

"Harassment," Rowe said, jabbing a finger at Charles.

"What about my permit?"

"I have nothing to do with that," Rowe said.

"The hell not!"

"Sir, I'm going to have to ask you to leave. We're a peaceable town and we don't take too kindly to this sort of behavior."

The man reached a hand out and placed it on Charles' shoulder, but he jerked away, bringing himself close to Rowe, so their chins nearly touched. The rude and improbable contrast of these two men, so urgently close, made me queasy, and I shut my eyes. "See this face. These eyes, this mouth?" I heard him mutter. "What you not like?" Murmurs behind us; I wanted to shut my eyes.

Before Rowe could answer, there was a cracking noise, a burst of striated light. Chins lifted; the fireworks were starting. An instant later, red shafts shot up into the sky, exploding into a crumbling pattern of palm trees. The two men had frozen, not sure what to do. The next rockets went off, blue comets that shook out their tails in a swirl of silver dots. Flecks sprinkled the sky. Then I saw Charles tip forward, one hand raised, and a cry flew from my lips. But Charles wasn't hitting Rowe. His movements were slow and deliberate, punctuated by flashes of burning white. He threw his arms around the other man's neck, drawing him up like a bucket of cool water, taking in all of him—the flushed pink cheeks, his baffled fists—and with great relish, kissed him full and hard on the lips.

Back at the house, we found Vijay and Claire in the middle of a fight. From upstairs came thumps and crashing noises. A shellacked oval went spiralling in the air, landing with a soft thud on the grass—a hairbrush. Dead silence. No one in the house said anything. Tara rose up from the rattan chair, her plump body folded into disapproval. An hour later, as Claire and I set out forks and knives for dinner, I noticed her red-rimmed and puffy eyes. "What's going on with you?"

"Nothing."

"Are you sure?"

Claire put the pitcher down. "What is this? I'm fine.

I'm just a little tired, that's all." Then she ran out of the room, wiping her hands in her apron.

But Sarita was a bit more blunt about the matter. "Something bad gone happened between she and Vijay," she told me a few minutes later.

It nagged at me all through supper preparations as I stole glances at Claire setting the table. Maybe Ranjit and Tara were right; maybe there were too many confusions in our marriages. I remembered all those afternoons Claire and I spent in the kitchen, wiping the grime off the items she'd bought. Vijay would dance up the steps, hands drumming at his thighs. He'd grown bored; he didn't like all this messing around in the dust. He could not help himself—Vijay had no patience for work on a house. Nails scattered through his fingers; window blinds broke.

But there was also the Saturday Claire had come back from a yard sale, carrying a cardboard box of those glasses, face brimming. As she rinsed them and set them on the windowsill to dry, she had sung "Sweet Adelaide," and we both seemed to forget the rumors around our marriages.

I pressed my wrist to my eyes. Too much was happening at once. First my confusion at the lake, then the fireworks, and now this. Hurrying out of the kitchen, I dropped down on the back steps where I sat by myself, grateful for the darkness which hid my crying. Would nothing stay still?

After a while someone came and sat down next to me. It was Charles, holding a wet compress to his brow; his lip was split and swollen. "What a fool I am," he groaned, taking the compress away. A walnut-sized lump was just starting bulge over his right eye.

"I guess we've both made fools of ourselves today."

"How's that?"

I shrugged. "Nothing."

"Go on, tell me. Take my mind off my own stupid antics."

"Before, by the lake. I think I acted a little strangely. I had fallen asleep, and must have had a bad dream because when I woke, there was Sharon. I was very confused. I mean, for a second I thought she was—" My voice wavered for an instant. "I thought she was mine."

We were both silent. The trees rustled and a blue scent of stream rose to our faces. "I made a fool of myself in front of Tara. I'm not sure why. Something about her—" I wasn't sure how much to let on. "She makes me feel ashamed."

Charles snorted. "Why? She's nothing but a nasty Queen Victoria!"

"I don't know. She seems so definite about some things. Where she and Srini belong."

"I know folks like that. Too pure to mix with the rest of us." He threw the compress down on the porch in disgust. "I tell you, Sarah. I wouldn't say this before. But I'm not so crazy about these Srinivans and the like coming here, bossing us around—"

"Charles, hush."

"What you hushing me for? They can hear all they like. You know that Srini fellow, he tell me tonight he won't come back unless we clean his room?" Charles shook his head. "No, sir. I no come to America to scrub some Brahmin's bathtub."

I began to giggle.

"Sarah, I'm in this country five years now. I didn't come to live among the same old people, live the same way, like Tara and Srini. They rigid. They want to keep everything the same."

"I know. That's the big joke about this. I thought I was running away. And here I am—right where I started. Tara sounds just like my own mother. If there is a God, he's definitely having one big laugh at me now. Hah hah."

Charles smiled. "Look it your Bump. He also want to go backwards." He swept a hand out. "He wants from Guiana something it don't have. It's a little place the British come and trample on us. The men, they can't get out of they own villages. In Georgetown you got black man against Indian—you got everyone fighting."

"You know Roland doesn't agree. He's proud of that little place."

Charles made a clucking sound in his throat. "Don't get sentimental on me." He looked at me severely, then stood with a groan. One of the men had punched him several times in the kidneys.

We remained in silence a moment, Charles standing in front of me, one hand cradling the small of his back, stomach forward. Every now and then a car would pass on a nearby road, lighting up the trees from behind, showing their skeletal branches. I thought about this strange day, dreaming on the rock, about Sharon, and my need to press her to me; the hard ache that had never gone away since my parents hung up on me over a year ago.

"You know what, crazy lady?" His voice was soft, chiding.

"What?"

"You are an optimist like me, that's your problem."

I laughed too, spreading my skirt around my damp, swollen thighs. "Charles, if you weren't another goddamn Guianese man with their goddamn ways, I'd want to marry you."

Before walking away, he touched his finger to my lips.

Then we both went inside. Dinner was ready. I felt better, for a while, at least. Until I saw Claire pull her chair back and slip away upstairs. Sarita flashed me a troubled look. It was no use; something had been stolen from us. Everything was coming apart. We could not help noticing Claire's absence. Vijay sat on a bar stool, taking long gulps of rum from a blue tumbler. There was a lot of rum flowing tonight and even though he didn't join the others in drinking, Srini vociferously joined in the conversation this time, which turned to the fight about terrace. Though the men had roughed him up a bit and Charles' bruise had hardened to a small plum-colored lump over his eyebrow, he asserted, "None of that matter. This still the greatest country on earth. You wait, I going to get my way."

Ranjit sneered, "You are believing that statue of liberty nonsense, my dear Charles! This country has a thin veneer of hospitality. Underneath is a hard heart, turned against outsiders."

"What you know about that?" Charles objected. "I thought you here on special arrangement!"

"I've been treated rather well," he replied. "But it hasn't all been pleasant. No matter what, this is a terribly impatient country."

"Here, here!" Vijay thumped his palm on the table.

Ranjit regarded Vijay with a faint look of annoyance. "You misunderstand me, Vijay. There's something quite breathtaking about this country as well."

"And you like this?" I asked.

"I suppose." He paused. "But I don't respect it. The U.S. is too in love with the present. "

"Or maybe you in love with that moldy old past we long ago get rid of," Thomas laughed.

This was the first time Thomas had actually spoken so bluntly. His brow was wrinkled, as if debating whether to join in the conversation. As he grew more animated, I understood what was happening, for I'd seen it a hundred times with Roland; how he chose a comic mask—like

Vijay's and Charles'—in order not to be taken too seriously, especially among those who faintly disparaged
him. I had a sudden vision of these West Indian men—
shrunken and distorted by their islands, made inarticu-
late by circumstance. Now it was clear, the overhead lamp
burning on our faces. The table was divided, as sharply as
it ever would be, between those who had a place to return
to and those who made the best of being here. The women
hardly mattered. And it was as if Charles and Vijay and
Thomas had no choice; they had to act the fools, creating a
kind of performance of their buffoonery and ignorance.

Charles' face glowed under the lamplight. His eyes had
the impatient glaze of a child who is not following what is
going on. Another bottle was brought out on the table.
Ranjit pushed aside the glass being offered to him. "You
have to understand!" he kept insisting.

Charles let out a roar. Surprised, we all turned around
to see him climbing on to a ladderback chair as he waved a
bottle by its neck. The bruise over his eye glistened. Tara's
hands went to her mouth. "No, *you* have to understand!"
he shouted.

"Charles!" Sarita cried. "Get down off of there."

"You hush up," he replied.

"You going to hurt yourself, man," Vijay shouted.

"You want to talk about danger? I tell you about a man
walkin' on his hands and knees pullin' out rusted nails—"

"I knew it," Sarita groaned, slapping her forehead with
the heel of her hand, her new wristwatch gleaming.

"Who has been up in the air! You hear that, Ranjit?
The air! I'm going to make a terrace out of air! What you
got to say for yourself?" He stopped for a moment, a foolish grin stuck to his face.

"Don't mind him," Sarita remarked. "He's just off and
drunk again."

"Terrace," Ranjit snorted.

No one saw when it happened, but Charles made a lunge for Sarita and she began to shriek, trying to push him off. Rita and Tara looked on in horror. But he wasn't hitting her. He had snatched her wristwatch and was waving it by the band in front of his face. "Bulova original!" he exclaimed. "Swiss engineering!"

"This man must be out of his mind," Ranjit remarked.

"He is not out of his mind," I said. "He's just angry. And he has every right to be angry." Then I stood and walked over to him and grabbed the watch. Even Sarita was surprised at the authority with which I talked to him. "Do you want to go on the porch roof?" I asked. "Is that what you're saying?"

"But we can't!" someone cried.

"More trouble," Tara moaned.

"Be quiet," I snapped. "Charles?"

"Lifetime guarantee," he said with a grin and plopped down on his chair.

Somehow, we all struggled up from the table littered with overturned cups and dirty dishes, up the creaking stairs, across Sarita and Charles' bedroom, dipping our heads as we climbed through the windows, out onto the half-built structure. "We got ourselves a terrace!" Charles bellowed into the dark.

Its beams gleamed pink in the dark. We stood on the old and new planks, shoes scraping on sawdust, not sure what to do, since thunder rumbled in the distance. A dry wind blew across our arms. Tara began to muttering that this was dangerous, but no one made a move.

Lightning began, far off. First a few pale cracks in the distance. Everyone trembled, knowing it was crazy to be out here, but the air remained dry, the trees rustling overhead. Then more and more, crackling like static over the ridge of mountains. To soothe everyone's tempers, Vijay went downstairs and brought another bottle. Soon we were passing around drinks. White explosions went off over our heads, brightening our faces with eerie streaks. Sharon squealed from on top of her father's shoulders.

Sarita brushed up against me and whispered: "The news is out, I guess. Claire is pregnant. She's known for a while, but couldn't pin Vijay down."

I squeezed my eyes shut a moment. This all seemed so crazy. Another pregnancy? It had never occurred to me that Vijay and Claire might have children—they were too much like children themselves, their marriage more like a whim, an indulgence, especially with his other wife back in Trinidad.

"Vijay is furious, so she's not sure what to do."

"What about—"

"Don't ask. That man gets himself in hot water faster than anyone I know. It going to boil over soon enough."

Soon Rita Pilloo edged near, so we stopped talking. But the first time the lightening flashed nearby, it illuminated in the bedroom window a pale, oval face. A moment later I realized this was Claire, watching us. It was an image I knew I would carry from then on, for at that instant it was clear Claire had been told the truth about Vijay's other wife and his kid. And Claire, staring through the window understood that we, her friends, had always known.

Another jagged burst of lightening seared across the sky—this one the closest yet. The rain was coming soon. Even after the sky had faded it took a second for me to adjust to the darkness again. I could not distinguish who was who. Somebody moved next to me, an elbow bumped against mine. I shifted forward, felt someone's shirt brush the back of my hand. The first drops began to fall.

That was the last of it, as if the many directions we were all moving toward, like some hidden design, had finally taken hold. From that night on, I would call up that moment when we stood bumping in the dark, eyes momentarily blinded. The next Tuesday the Srinivans called and quietly asked for their deposit back—the Phoenicia house became lopsided in favor of those from the Caribbean. And one night Vijay showed up at the Magalees' door and handed them the keys to his car. Charles told me he could not finish his sentences. We found out from the Pilloos a few days later that Vijay was flying back to Trinidad. Claire had already gone back to Milwaukee. And when we went up to the house the next weekend we found the roll of money gone from the cigar box. Everything changed very fast, almost too fast—soon Sarita started staying in the city most weekends; one evening, I passed her in a Village cafe, holding hands with a bearded man. I kept walking. I never said anything.

Charles kept on though—at the house every weekend. Sometimes he got drunk, ranting about his unfinished terrace and Ed Rowe. By morning he couldn't remember what he had done. I went up every weekend as well. It became a little joke, the two of us like fixtures, old people in the place, he in his faded overalls, me with my sewing on my lap. I did not like this role—the unattached auntie, put to the side for the moment. At night, I lay in bed in the Phoenicia house, listening to the voices of men talking on the porch, And I waited, thinking about alliances taking place far from here, trying to gain the strength to do what I needed to. Slowly an idea began building in my mind. It was just a matter of time.

And then came the sign I was waiting for. One afternoon, Charles brought me a letter, passed through the Guianese grapevine in New York. It wasn't even an airmail letter, but sealed in a yellow envelope, the corners smudged. I tore it open. It seemed to have been written hurriedly, the letters spikey, as if written on a moving vehicle.

> *Dear Sarah,*
> *I am writing to tell you I would rather you do not write me*
> *through the Party office. I must be careful because it looks*
> *like my work with the unions may catch fire the wrong way.*
> *Politics are changing fast down here. Lionel is not too*
> *pleased to learn of what I am doing and I don't want him*
> *using his influence against me. I will explain later You*
> *must not worry. There is still time yet.*
>
> *Love, Bump.*

"What's going on?"

I folded the letter into my pocket. "It's not so good," I said.

"Anything I can do?"

"Yes," I said. "I need a favor."

"Whatever you like."

"Would you drive me somewhere?" I said it in such a way that it was not a question.

"Of course. Where do you want to go?"

"I'll show you tomorrow."

After lunch the next day, Charles and I took off. I wasn't exactly sure of the directions, coming from Phoenicia, but I knew enough to go south, away from the range. As we went down in elevation, it grew warm and I took off my sweater. We passed small white houses trimmed in green, motels with flashing neon signs. An occasional cube of turquoise blue, people sunning on towels. Old farm- houses, paint blistering; once a caramel-colored pony cantered up close, nudging between the fence slats. We stopped at a corner store for two bottles of Coca Cola. The sun had started to strike down behind the trees, throwing spindly shadows on the ground. It was around two o'clock. Charles and I hadn't said much but now, he turned to me and asked, "Are you going to tell me where we are going?"

A truck passed, pulling an empty horse trailer. My stomach was in knots. "To my parents," I replied.

8

About a half hour later I began to recognize where
I was. The town was much smaller than Phoenicia, just a
grocery store, a fruit stand selling peaches and corn and a
gas station with two battered pumps. Through the trees I
could see glimpses of the lake and people walking up the
dirt paths from the beaches in flip flops and straw hats.
Small bungalows with red trim sat back from the road
with a circular gravel courtyard in front. Already barbe-
cues were starting up and the woody smell of smoke hung
in the air.

"Where do I go?" Charles asked as we passed another
semi-circle of bungalows.

"Keep going," I said. "It's the one on the end."

The tires spat gravel as Charles swung into the drive.
He turned off the ignition and we sat a moment, engine
ticking. We had parked in a wide stretch of a driveway
which dipped down and ended at a dock. It gave me a
sickening, giddy sensation, as if we could coast downward, plunging into the water. I noticed children jumping off the end of the dock.

"Do you want me to come with you?" he asked as I got
out of the car.

"Do you mind waiting?" I asked him.

"Go on. I'm going to take a nap." He stretched out on the front seat.

As I walked down the hill to the lawns, it was as if I were sinking, inch by inch, into a steamy bath of associations. I heard the voices—Yiddish, a man joking as four friends slapped cards on a fold-up table. I recognized every shape and nuance of this moment—the wide backs of women, their husbands in an irritable slump, while children streaked across the sand.

By my parents' bungalow, a woman approached, carrying a straw beach bag and towel. A moment later, I saw an cigarette flick from the woman's fingers and remembered Jennie having her furtive smoke in my parents' hall. I slowed. When Jennie recognized me, she dropped her things and threw out her freckled arms.

"Look who's dropped in from the sky!" she cried. "My God, stranger, how are you?"

"Hello, Jennie." She grasped me very tightly, so I almost couldn't breathe.

"My God, and look at you! When are you expecting?"

"In November."

"But still so skinny! What's the matter, don't you eat?"

I smiled. "Those are muscles. I've been working."

"What do you mean 'working'? What kind of work is this?"

"Hammering, fixing. We have a house for the summer."

"Whose we?"

"Some friends." I gestured to the car.

Jennie squinted. Her face was flush and healthy, a band of sunburned flesh running across the bridge of her nose. She squeezed my elbow. "Listen, darling. It's so wonderful to see you. Do your parents know?"

"I just decided. All of a sudden." I added, "I need to talk to my mother."

Jennie was quiet for a moment as she struggled with what to say. That was Jennie, always calming us down with her humor. Whenever I would fight with my parents, Jennie would say, "Always know you can come to my place to cool that temper of yours."

"I don't know, Sarah," Jennie was saying now. "Your father—"

"What about him?"

Jennie picked up her bag and towel and squeezed my shoulders. Her mouth set into a firm line. "Go," she said. "Hurry now. Knock on the door. They're there."

I walked across the lawn. On the steps I turned around once. Jennie still stood in the dappled shadows. She waved, urging me on. I turned back around and rapped on the screen door. Nothing. I pressed my face against the screen. In the gloom, I could make out the low tables by the sofa, two chairs. A radio played somewhere.

"Hello?" I called out.

No answer.

"Ma? Papa?"

Pulling open the door, I went inside. "Frieda!" I called. "Samuel!" My voice was flat, without an echo. I followed the low buzz of a radio and found myself at the bedroom door. Before I turned the knob, I looked around. A cut-glass bowl of nuts sat on a table, the newspaper sat on top of a crocheted shawl. It was as if I'd been here yesterday, everything was so much the same.

I pushed through the door where Samuel lay sleeping. The first thing I noticed was his hair had turned completely white. As I crept closer, I began to think I was not looking at Samuel at all, but a shrunken version of the same man, curled under the sheets. The skin of face pink-transparent, tight against the bone of his cheeks. His wrinkled hands tightly clutched the blanket. "Samuel?" I whispered again. He let out a wheeze; a faint flutter of lashes.

The screen door slamming and footsteps announced my mother's arrival. "I went to get some cooking oil from next door," she shouted through the walls. "We ran out." I could hear the snap of the icebox door while Frieda continued to talk through the walls, though Samuel didn't move during all of this. I stared at my father. He appeared to be in a deep sleep, but it was not a peaceful sleep. His crabbed mouth, the tense flank of his neck, made it seem as if he were withdrawing into a bitter core of self. His breaths were slow and even, but raspy. Over the rungs of a chair hung his prayer shawl, fringes dangling. A thick leather book and a glass of water were set on the table. I watched him a few moments more, then shut the door and came to stand in the kitchen doorway. Frieda stood flipping potato pancakes in a pan on the stove.

"Hello Ma," I said.

My mother whirled around, still holding the spatula. Her eyes flew to the bedroom door.

"Don't worry, he didn't wake."

"Nothing can wake him when he's on those pills." She still had on a straw hat, and red rubber flip-flops with big daisies. Her face was made up with two spots of rouge, bright pink lipstick. Her hand lowered. "My God, you scared me, Sarah."

"I didn't mean to."

We stood for a moment staring at one another. Neither of us knew what to say.

"Your pancakes are burning," I finally muttered and walked over to the stove to turn down the flame. I grabbed a sponge and wiped up the spilled batter on the floor. "Why didn't you tell me he was sick?" I returned the sponge to the sink.

"What, after a year I should suddenly tell you everything?"

"He's my father."

Frieda looked away. Her floral pink dress had splashes of pink that showed off her deep sunburn. The skin around her eyes was pale, wrinkled with tiny veins. Tears started to spill down her cheeks. "And you didn't tell me about your news, either."

"No I didn't." We stood in silence. "You look good," I said.

"I have headaches sometimes. And my back went out."

"Aren't you going to say something about me?"

Frieda put down the spatula and squinted at me. At that moment, I remembered my mother's gaze; always scrutinizing, always judging, reminding me that I wasn't her flesh and blood child, after all. More a disappointing visitor.

"I've never seen your hair so long. And so brown you are. You've been in the sun."

I nodded. "We have a house."

"You and your husband?"

Without replying, I hugged my arms close, pivoting around to gaze through the windows. Outside, people strolled up the path from the lake, arms filled with coolers and wet towels, surrounded by an amber, late afternoon light. A breeze lifted the curtains; they were cream-colored, with a pattern of blue daffodils.

"No, with some friends."

Frieda looked at the frying pan on the stove and then at me. "You want something? This many months pregnant and you look so skinny. Don't you eat?"

"Maybe something to drink."

She went to the refrigerator, pulled out a bottle of seltzer. As she handed me the glass, her mouth twisted into a frown.

"I get the message. If you want me to leave, I will."

"Don't be ridiculous. You did it, you came. Why should you go?" Her hands were trembling.

"Because."

"Stay." A distracted nod. "Your husband all right?"

"He's been away. There was this election—" I took the glass.

My mother didn't say anything, but went back to the stove, a blue flame jumping up as she turned the knob. She stirred some batter into the pan and began to cook. It was an achingly familiar scene: my mother at the stove, ample back to me, one hand on her hip, talking in a rush over her shoulder. I knew she had to cook to keep her mind busy. I cradled my glass in both hands, then nodded toward the door. "So what's wrong with him?"

Frieda's hand paused before flipping a pancake. Outside someone shouted for a ball. "It's his stomach. But it's all right now."

"You sure? He looks so pale."

"Too much sleep, that's all. He doesn't sit out in the sun enough." She bent over, lifting the pancake edge with the spatula, then flipping it over. There was a sputter of oil in the pan. This was Samuel's favorite, with applesauce. How solemnly my mother had always prepared his food, each meal a ritual! I lifted the seltzer glass to my mouth. On the radio in the other room, the music ended and an announcer's voice burst out. Bedsprings groaned.

"He may be getting up."

"I can go now."

Frieda replaced a curl which had fallen from its careful hairdo. "You know, you could have called beforehand. It doesn't make it any easier, barging in like this!"

I didn't reply.

"I don't know what you mean to do here."

"I have questions."

"Such as?"

"About—" I took a deep breath. "About things. What you said to me, a while ago, right here, at the lake. You remember? We sat on the float." I hesitated. "I've been thinking about them."

Shrugging, Frieda went over to a cabinet and pulled out a plate. "How wise you make me sound, Sarah. It's your father who is the thinker. He takes things very seriously." Expertly she flipped two pancakes onto a plate. They were golden brown, still bubbling with grease; my stomach jumped with hunger. I watched my mother's elbows jab the air as she stirred the batter and spooned some more into the frying pan. The smell of potatoes drifted toward me.

"Tell me. What did you mean before, about knowing yourself?"

"You have regrets, nu?"

I stared at my hands, twisting my wedding band on my finger, the edge rimmed with grease. "No regrets. Only questions. Like, do you and papa have secrets? Things you never tell each other?"

She shrugged, then let out a laugh. "Sarah, a man and a woman, after so many years it's hard to keep a secret."

"But big ones. From before—"

Frieda turned around, her eyes alarmed. "Where is he?"

"I told you. He went back to his country. This new government is very important. It means a lot to him."

"You're afraid he won't come back. There you are, how many months gone—"

I jiggled the water in my glass.

"That's what I meant by not knowing. You cannot know how those people really are."

"What are you talking about?" I jumped up, my chair nearly toppling over. "A Jewish man doesn't leave his wife for a few months? You think they're all such mensches? Did I ever tell you about what Stuart Markowitz said to me that time you invited him over for supper?"

"What?"

"He wanted to know what my bra size was! He asked me, when you went into the kitchen."

A smile crept over Frieda's face. "He asked you that?"

"He said it was very important to him, because it appeared I was a little on the flat-chested side. Not that I did not have other lovely attributes—"

"He knew what he wanted," Frieda laughed. "He was looking for a wife. Not an experiment."

"Is that what you think my marriage is?"

"Oh, Sarah—" Frieda made a helpless, loopy motion with her hands. Once again, I was reminded of how beautiful her hands were—like elegant, fussy white birds, the cold flashing eyes of her rings. "I have no idea what it is. I know only what I see."

"And what's that?"

Wiping her hands on her apron, she stood opposite me. Her eyes regarded me for a moment, then she brushed her knuckles against my cheek. They felt like feathers, rubbing.

"Only that you look more confused now than I have ever seen you. You don't look like someone who trusts what she says."

I opened my mouth to say something, only I had no idea what that might be. I was exposed all over again, in that helpless, horrible way that only Frieda could do to me. And then I began to cry—quietly. I never ever did this in front of my mother—I wouldn't let myself. But now it was released in me—stupid, pitiful little sobs.

I felt Frieda watching me, then she reached out a beautiful hand and tried to pat me on the shoulder, but this only made me feel worse. I pulled away. Frieda returned to the stove and flipped the last of the pancakes on to a plate. She placed them in front of me. "Eat," she said.

"But it's Samuel's."

Salt and pepper shakers and a bowl of applesauce were put down in front of me. She slid a fork between my fingers. Her voice was soft, without rebuke. "Come. It's getting cold."

Sitting opposite, she watched as I began to eat. It was hard at first. Frieda's eyes were on me, and all I wanted to do was cry some more. But I forced myself and her face untensed. The pancakes slid down with cold applesauce.

"These are good."

"Of course they are!" Frieda laughed. "What do you think, I suddenly became a bad cook?" Opening the refrigerator, she pulled out a plate with half a roasted chicken. Cutting off a few slices, she added some challa bread. As I finished the last of the pancakes, Frieda gave me the chicken and bread. "I can't," I giggled.

"Yes you can." There was real pleasure lighting my mother's face as she watched me eat. For an instant, I remembered the moment when Roland had brought me his meat pattie and I had accepted its strange flavor, tasting him. Now I swallowed, pushing the memory down.

"So what other atrocious things did Stuart Markowitz say to you?"

"He wanted to know what my grade point average was and if I thought Ernest Hemingway was really a Communist." I smiled. "He was simply awful, ma." As I laughed, it began to hurt, realizing I had called Frieda "ma." I began to cry all over again, wetting my shirt front.

"Stop it," Frieda murmured. "You're dripping on the chicken. And don't worry about Stuart. He married a girl with very big breasts. She weighs two hundred pounds."

"No!"

"Yes. Her father owns a drugstore chain and she's not even observant."

"And what about that other one, what's his name—"

"Leonard. Leonard Stein. He was much nicer, I think."

"He had body odor."

"His mother was very sick. Maybe that was it."

I shook my head. "No, I'm sure he never bathed."

"You're so judgmental."

"Hah! And you?"

Frieda smiled. "You hardly gave them a chance. You hardly gave anything a chance, Sarah. From the day you arrived, you were always fighting me about something. You always had a better idea. Do you remember what you did with that closet?"

I shook my head as Frieda reached an arm across the table, hesitated, then brushed a loose strand that had fallen across my cheek. "Watch, don't eat that long hair of yours."

"What happened with the closet?"

"There you were, all of seven years old. You were so little for your age, I was shocked. I thought maybe they had made a mistake, you were really five and they had lied to me. But when you opened your mouth and began to talk, I thought you were eighty years old!" We both smiled.

"Remember I took you to buy some dresses that day?"

I nodded.

"After we came home, I showed you how to sew the little loops for your skirts and hang everything nice in the closet in your room. I could see you didn't like me telling you what to do, but you were used to being obedient in your own way. The next morning when I woke up, I found you inside my cabinets, rearranging everything."

"You yelled at me because it was Saturday and I wasn't supposed to be working."

"That's true. You weren't. You were disobedient on two counts. To say nothing of the fleishe and milche dishes you mixed up."

I began to laugh, very hard. A wedge of chicken got stuck in my throat, so I took a swig of selzer, running in a cold sizzle down to my stomach. Still laughing, tears began streaming down my cheeks. "Don't you see? It wasn't meant to be. I wasn't meant to follow everybody's rules. I was always getting it wrong."

"It was your father who would really get mad."

In a second, my laughter evaporated. I watched the curtains blow full and wide in the windows; the daffodils seemed to scatter in the air. "It was him who told you to hang up on me, wasn't it?"

Frieda pressed her knuckles against her teeth, mouth twisted to one side. "Always such extremes from you, Sarah. It didn't have to be so bad."

"How he can go on and on about morals? Mr. Big Shot with God, he's so pure he's got a special appointment. What a hypocrite." I crossed my arms. "Fine. I don't care that he doesn't want to see me. I don't want to see him either."

Frieda jumped up from the table and cleared my plate. A silence fell between us. I saw my mother standing for a moment with her back to me, leaning on a counter, napkin wadded in her fist. When she turned around again, she was using the napkin to blot her eyes. "You can say such things!" she blurted out. "Why not test everything you think or say? You have your whole life ahead of you to find out if you mean it."

"What's that supposed to mean?"

She tossed the napkin into the wastebasket. "Six months." She spat the words out. "Six months to reckon a whole life."

"What about six months?"

"Your father has six months to live."

It was as if a wall had suddenly swung into my chest, knocking the breath out of me. It couldn't be. Life didn't come in such stingy portions. "That's impossible," I said. "It must be a mistake."

"No mistake. He waited too long. By the time the doctors found out, it was too far along. It's in his liver, his pancreas." Frieda looked out the window, pulled a tissue from the sleeve of her dress and blew her nose. "Jennie has been wonderful. She was the one who said we had to rent the bungalow for the whole summer. I wasn't going to do it. I wasn't going to move him."

"Why didn't you call me?"

She began to shred her tissue. "It's been a year, you have no idea. He's been sick, hardly talking. So much on my hands—" She shook her head, adding, "I was going to. It just all happened so fast." Again a shake of her head. "Too sudden."

I stared at my own hands, which looked large and ugly in my lap. I thought of the feel of Ranjit's hands on me the other night. None of it seemed real—Roland, my friends, the brown-shingle Phoenicia house, Charles waiting for me just up the road. They flickered, fading into dream-like cells. All I knew was my father, shrunken under those sheets, waiting for me.

"I want to come home," I declared.

"What for?"

"Just because."

"Always such pronunciations from you. Such a big scene. What you do or don't want. Sarah, he's dying. This isn't some kind of reckoning for you."

"But what am I supposed to do?" Putting my fist against my cheek, I began crying all over again.

"You should stay with your husband."

"That wasn't what I meant!" I stopped. My mother had shifted to the other end of the kitchen, wiping the bread knife on a towel.

"Look," she said, after a while. "The only thing you can give your father is some respect. Maybe that didn't matter to you before. Now that's all he he's got. Every morning he gets up and pees into a little cup. Then he eats a hard boiled egg and dry toast. I read to him from the newspaper, he takes a pill and says some prayers. Then he goes to sleep. For lunch I give him whatever he likes, no matter what the doctor told us. In the afternoon he sits out by the lake with us. He can hardly walk the few yards there. And his eyes are going. It isn't much, Sarah. There's no big scene here. Nothing. If you're looking to be forgiven—" She broke off. "That's not for me to say."

"What about you?"

"I will do whatever he asks. It's only right."

I took a breath and waited. "Will you tell him about my visit?"

Her voice was soft, gliding on the words. "Of course."

Shutting my eyes, I felt my mother come up behind me. I could smell Frieda, her face powder and sweat, a mother with capable arms and a way of talking just for me. It was a good feeling, making me think that we might be the three of us together again. I would sit reading by Samuel's bed, while Frieda sewed. The hushed room we could make for ourselves, which only we three could occupy. As I stepped back, my fingers grasped something rough and soft at the same time. I opened my eyes to discover Frieda's towel in my hands. Frieda had gone over to the bedroom, ear pressed to the door.

"He wakes now," she whispered. "Time for his pill. You must go."

For an instant, I was confused. I took a step forward, calling out my mother's name. The corridor blinded me, it was so dark. But Frieda led me to the back door and brushed her cheek against mine. "Go," she repeated. "I will talk to you soon."

A moment later I was standing on the steps outside the bungalow, dazed by the bright, blinding sunlight. Children swam in the lake, moving like hidden fish in and out of the shadows. The beach was nearly deserted. Despite all the food I had just eaten my stomach was hollow. I took a step down. Then another, each step deliberate, taking me further out of the circle of shade thrown by my parents' bungalow. Ahead lay the gravel drive, rising gently toward the trees where the car sat waiting.

The first time I saw my father again he was wrapped in a plaid blanket on a chair on the bungalow lawn. It was a Sunday; Charles had driven me here, and again remained by the car, napping on the front seat. Now, I touched my father's hand, which was cold and papery. Dread whirred through me—already he seemed dead. His lashes whirred open and he craned his neck back, squinting angrily. "Who is that? Frieda? Sarah? It's you, Sarah, isn't it?"

"Yes, papa. I've come to be with you."

"What do you mean be? What is this, a philosophy talk? You're standing next to me, that's all."

I smiled. "Do you want me to sit?"

"That might be better, yes." The seat creaked as I sat down and pulled my pocketbook on to my lap.

"What, you can't put that thing down? You going to leave already?" He was shaking his head. "So impatient, so impatient."

"I am not leaving."

We bickered some more, until Frieda came out with a tray of gefilte fish and crackers. I ate them, though I was hardly hungry, and I left with heavy heart, since Charles needed to get back. Yet the next Sunday, I forced myself to put on a new dress, carefully make up my face and do the trip again. As Charles pulled up before the bungalows, he said to me, "You all right?"

"Not really," I admitted.

"You want to turn back?"

"No."

I stayed all afternoon and this time I managed to keep from fighting with Samuel by reading the newspaper aloud. His eyes were very bad. Soon I began to take off a few days off from the library, taking the Greyhound bus up to Phoenicia during the week and splitting my time between my parents and the Phoenicia house. I never actually slept at the bungalows.

Samuel never asked me anything—not about Roland or the pregnancy. There were a thousand things I was dying to explain about myself, but then again, now there seemed nothing to say. The days slipped by. Samuel's eyes began to get worse.

Mostly we sat out on the lawn in folding chairs while Frieda and Jennie paddled in the shallow end of the lake. Samuel would remain bundled in a blanket and his prayer shawl which he clutched like a small child with a favorite toy, the lake breeze bowing his thin hair up on one end so I could see flakes of peeling scalp underneath. I read to him from his books, running my work-roughened fingers over the page, slowly pronouncing the Yiddish words I had tried to forget. It was strange how in only a year's time, being with Samuel was like meeting an old enemy on a road, his sword gone. I had not really come back—it was too late for that. All those crazy months, sticking by Roland, marked some choice in myself; I somehow knew that I was leading myself away from my father's God, who punished; who told me that underneath ran the same stark view: you were either inside or out. After this summer, I knew there had to be a better way.

One afternoon the three of us were sitting quietly together. Suddenly, Frieda began to ask about Roland. I was shocked. Nervous, I glanced over at my father, afraid he would lose his temper. But no, he stared serenely ahead, hands in his lap.

"So what do you think?" my mother asked. "He can get a good job when he comes back?"

"I don't know, ma. Roland has to finish school first."

"There's a bill, Jennie told me about it, for men—"

"That's the GI Bill, ma. Roland isn't even a citizen yet."

"And when is he going to do that?"

I sighed, rubbing my hands along the chair arms. "Ma, I don't think you understand—" I hesitated, not sure how much to tell her. "It's not very safe for Roland right now. He's sided with a bit of trouble."

"What kind of trouble?"

"Ma, please. I didn't know when I was going to tell you this. But I'm going to have to go soon. That's what I've been wanting to tell you."

My mother's voice grew shrill. "What do you mean, go? You going to run off to a foreign country five-months pregnant where it's dangerous?"

"I know how it sounds."

"And when did you get this brilliant thought?"

"I don't know exactly when. It came over me slowly. That's what I learned this summer. It's not so terrible, to wait. At least I've learned a little bit of patience. Not much, but some. If you wait, you find out what it is that you need to do. And I have to go. I have to find out some things. "

At this, my father stirred in his chair, a look of recognition breaking across his face. He grabbed my arm, his bony fingers shaking my wrist.

"What is it, papa?"

"There, there," he kept saying, pointing toward the lake.

"What is it?" I repeated.

But he just kept jabbing a trembling finger. I squinted. All I could see were clouds pushing across an empty sky. A rush of swallows hit the trees overhead. "What papa?" I whispered.

He smiled. "Light," he said. "Now you understand?"

But all I could do was look at my father's eyes. They were sealed in a grayish film, not a speck of black pupil, cloudy with cataracts. He was smiling, mumbling about something, I realized, he could not even see.

In the large, gleaming lobby of the British Consulate no one waited. Not the men who hurried by in double-breasted suits, or the women clicking across the marble floor or the tourists wandering up to the visa window. Or even the delivery boy who hurried up the stairs with coffee on a tray. Everyone knew where they were going. Across from the stairs on the second floor I found a door marked Colonial Administration and entered a large outer office broken into smaller compartments. The secretary's face turned to me. It was oval, with skin like a cracked bar of soap. When I explained my situation, emphasizing that the Guianese I was inquiring about was in fact my husband, her brow went smooth. She stopped rolling her pencil. There flitted across my mind the secretary's view of me: some poor, hapless kid jerked around by a foreign student. *Difficult*.

"The situation is very tense there, you know," the secretary remarked. "They've got the troops on alert. It's considered an emergency." Then she added, "You've heard about the protest the Jagans did? Those folks are crazy."

"I know about that. But I haven't gotten any letters."

"Mail service has been a problem." She tugged out a slim book wrapped in brown paper from a drawer. "Ah, here it is. So what was the number you were looking for?"

"Cheddi Jagan's office. No, I guess he's not there anymore. Then the one for the People's Progressive Party."

A faint crack of perturbation showed on the woman's forehead. "We don't keep that number. What about your husband's family?"

"It's a village. They don't have telephones."

"He didn't leave someone else's number? A relative or something?"

"Well, no."

The woman let out a sigh and shut the book. "I'm really very sorry. You'll just have to wait until things settle down. We're simply not giving out any visas right now."

I moved away from the woman's desk, left the office and stood over the bannister, watching people criss-crossing the lobby. It seemed absurd, that I couldn't write to him or hear his voice or what was worse, this infuriating bureaucracy wouldn't give me the number of the P.P.P. Since the beginning of September, I had written four letters and none of them had been answered; one of his had arrived, but clearly he hadn't read mine. And now the *Times* clipping, folded into my purse, dated October 7:

BRITAIN MAY LIFT GUIANA'S CHARTER. It went on to explain that the queen was considering revoking the constitution. It was clear the Jagans had gone too far in their reform efforts—that much I pieced together from Roland's note in August and the Jagans' demand at the last Assembly session that the British give up their full power. The *Times* article made mention of trouble about the labor bill. But this stretched my sacrifice more than I could ever have fathomed. I went back inside the office.

"I forgot, there is someone," I stammered out. "Roland has an uncle. Lionel Lal."

The woman's eyes widened, as if she could not take in the information that Roland was connected both to the Lals and Jagan.

"I'm sure he could locate him," I went on.

"Why don't you call from home?"

"You said so yourself, things are very confused. If they hear it's from the Embassy—"

The woman shoved back her chair and smoothed her skirt. She nodded to a chair. "I'll check with my boss."

I sat a long time. Through the frosted panes of the inner office, I could see the blurred outline of the secretary as she bent over a desk. On the opposite wall hung a map of the world, each of the colonies colored with the bright red and blue Brittania colors. I shifted in my chair. I didn't like to think about the British, though in fact Roland was still a British colonial, since he didn't want to apply for U.S. citizenship when we married. That would have been the end of it, he'd told me. And up until this point it hardly mattered except at the Indian Consulate. But a faint signal of distress was working away in me, knowing it was through this office—those Roland despised and felt ashamed by— that I must locate him. I squeezed my ankles together.

"Mrs. Singh." A man was standing over me. He wore a

green tweed jacket and brown slacks. His manner was brief, but friendly; he held a hand out. "I'm Gregory Tutkins. I'm sorry to keep you waiting."

I followed him into his office where he shut the door behind me. There were no windows here but we were surrounded by what felt like Chinese boxes made of cloudy glass; in the other boxes hummed the staccato rhythm of typewriters. "Please, sit," he said, gesturing with the stem of his pipe.

"So," he remarked as I settled down. "Lost contact with your husband?"

"That's right."

Tutkins lit his pipe before speaking and the smoke twirled in snowy skeins over his head. "It's a terrible situation. Only the other day I had a man in here hysterical about his family in Georgetown. It took all the devil out of me to explain things are not what they seem."

"What are they then?"

He shook his head, and smiled. "It's merely a natural reaction. That's what happens when things are pushed too fast and too far."

"The P.P.P. won an election. They'd like to accomplish what their platform stated. What's too fast about that?"

Tutkins flashed me another smile. I noticed his front teeth were crooked. "Don't get me wrong. I'm very sympathetic to this push for independence, Mrs. Singh. With moderation, of course."

I did not reply. I had a sense Tutkins had brought me into the office for reasons other than the ones I intended. He puffed a few times on his pipe and the smoke flattened like a wide brim around his head. "So. What do you know about Lionel Lal?"

"I know he's my husband's uncle. Roland lived with him for a spell in Georgetown."

"Lionel has been around a long time. He's quite an experienced legislator."

"I gather that."

"But your husband's working for Cheddi."

"Yes."

There was a pause. Tutkins lit his pipe again. "Do you remember, by any chance, the bill he helped draft?"

"I'm not sure which one you mean," I lied, staring at my hands again. My fingers looked puffy and small in my lap. "I don't follow that closely. Politics is my husband's business."

Tutkins' chair squeaked as he leaned forward, resting his elbows on the desk. On either side were curbed two neat stacks of papers. It occurred to me that Tutkins was a nice-looking man, with ginger-colored hair and an incongruous scattering of freckles, but there was something cold and unpleasant in his manner which made me not want to talk to him. "Lionel helped with a very good piece of legislation. Are you familiar with it?"

I shook my head.

"It was called the Undesirable Publications Law. Certain books must be seized as dangerous articles of consumption. Simply put, it was intended to gain an upper hand on what could grow into an ugly situation."

"What kind of situation?"

He smiled, as if I had asked the prize question.

"Perhaps independence does lie in the colony's future, but that doesn't mean its suddenly on its own." He laughed. "We don't want to be naive, do we?"

"What has this got to do with books?"

"Have you ever looked up the dictionary definition for governance?" He didn't wait before continuing on. "To exercise sovereign authority. To control the speed or magnitude of; to regulate." He put his pipe down. "Control is key, Mrs. Singh."

I understood what Tutkins was doing—seeking my sympathy as someone apart by virtue of being white, never fully invested in this parcel of history, even if I was married to an Indian. He was testing me, wanting to see if my sympathies had stiffened me into a purer, political stance. The analogy to Janet Jagan flashed across my mind. As I shifted forward in my chair, a prickle of unease shimmied up my spine. "Mr. Tutkins. My husband?"

"I realize you're most anxious. It's just that your husband is in an odd position. Tell me, why didn't he go work for his uncle?"

I wasn't sure whether to reveal the truth—that Lionel hardly knew Roland was alive until this election—but that would seem to rank him very low in Tutkins' eyes. "There were some differences in opinion," I finally offered.

"Is your husband a Communist?" -

"Not that I know of."

Tutkins laughed. A sudden, giddy burst of typewriter chatter from another room. The longer we waited, the more I knew he wanted something from me.

"I know, it's a stupid question in a way. But it does make it easier, knowing these things. Because it will be a trifle touchy, with the executive order signed yesterday." He raised an eyebrow. "They're quite serious in London. I probably shouldn't be telling you this, but I've just got word that we're sending a warship from Jamaica."

"Which means?"

Tutkins raised his eyebrows; his irises were a hard, transparent blue. "Perhaps I didn't make myself understood. You've read the news. Jagan and his fellows are making trouble; there's talk of strikes, big problems with the unions. We are approaching a moment of clarity, when the extremists are being shaken out."

"But what has that to do with Roland?"

"Nothing direct. We simply have to know who is on what side."

"And do you really believe the sides so clear over there?"

Tutkins frowned. My question had revealed I understood more than I was letting on, but I hardly felt triumphant for this recognition.

"Look, I could give Lionel's office a ring myself. But I needed to get a sense of how close your husband is to Cheddi Jagan."

I could not tell if Roland was in any serious danger. The talk of the warship frightened me. "My husband was a union representative, Mr. Tutkins. He drove miles in a beat up old truck to tell people what their rights were. He grew up in the bush, that's why they sent him there—he can talk to the local people, think the way they do. He hardly knows Cheddi Jagan at all." Then I added with some vehemence, "It's a *job*, Mr. Tutkins. There's nothing extreme about that."

"Of course," Tutkins replied, embarrassed by my insistent tone. I wondered if I had worn out the small bit of privilege I had come in with, as an American. He was standing now, shoving his pipe in his jacket pocket and holding a hand out. The tone of his voice had changed; now it was a public sound, dismissive. "Mrs. Singh, it's been such a pleasure to meet you. And I do hope this works out. Please don't fret. I've been through this before. Every now and then I had a case like yourself, a marriage such as yours. It's really very awkward. But I can assure you, from experience, the situation will clear up very shortly. We'll do everything we can."

"Then that means I can go down?"

"Excuse me?"

"My visa request. If you recall, last week you told me

you were taking care of the matter personally." I smiled as widely as I could. "That is, if you believe I can be of any help with your"—I paused—"efforts at control." I had said the last words with distaste, but it was exactly the tone needed—as someone willing to risk anything.

Tutkins hesitated; I had caught him unawares, since he didn't think I would take him up. "You realize what you're saying?"

I stared at my hands again. "Yes, I do. But I am useful to you, Mr. Tutkins. There's no one else in my position. A white woman whose first loyalty is probably to her husband, not his uncle, though I have a connection there too. A perfect go-between. Or another Janet Jagan, even. I'm sure that's what the P.P.P will think."

My audacity surprised even me. But I was thinking on my feet and knew I had to do something, quickly—the offer would be gone a moment later. And it worked. Tutkins rose from his desk, went to the door and leaned against it, arms crossed against his chest. He looked suddenly tired. I felt giddy, as if I were clutching a rope that had flung me out over water. I swallowed.

"All right, Mrs. Singh. There is something you can do."

9

In the end, when I cannot sleep for the knot of shame hurting my eyes, I say to myself: I saved a man. And a child. That's all. I brought them here, to our house, and that was my gesture, all I was capable of. As promised, Ranjit helped me. Tutkins explained his very simple plan: he would supply a stack of "Red publications" and I was to drop them off at the P.P.P. offices— easy plants. The next day, the army would sweep in, pick up my evidence for their planned White Paper on the attempted Communist plot to take over the country.

The only thing was, I had to get my own cover. I called Ranjit and he made some mysterious phone calls to other offices in the Consulate and got us the faked papers. Roland's new name was Bharat Singh, from Punjab. A joke—a bad joke, given what I was sent to accomplish. Bharat Singh had led an insurrection the century before in the Caribbean, against plantation owners. But it worked, because I was able, at the same moment the British Navy boats were sailing into Georgetown's harbor, to fly down under Indian diplomatic immunity. How ironic. But it all makes its own ordinary sense. Was this any different from how others found new homes? Migrations, patterns, false papers—how many of us began this way—like Samuel, with his new name from Bucharest, or my own name, made up by a social worker, the original certificate slipped into the pocket of a mother I never knew.

The trip was long. Twenty-five hours strapped in uncomfortable seats, buffeting through tropical storms, the baby inside me in a flutter. I changed flights several times on different islands, stepping into smaller and smaller propeller planes. By the time I arrived at Atkinson Airport, I'd peeled off my cardigan and stockings and felt shrunken, delirious with fatigue and waiting.

But there was Pandu by the gate, crazy hair straggling out of a straw hat, long arms waving at me, brimming with nervous excitement. He was miraculously gracious to me, clutching me by the elbow and using my suitcase to nudge a corridor through the pulsing crowds. All I remember of that moment was his nails digging into my skin and the faces, so many dark faces with beautiful, white smiles. And the soldiers huddled tensely at the corner outside the airport building, their arms pale in a hot sun which drenched my eyes blind.

"You have something for Mr. Lal?"

I put my hand on his arm; to be safe, I had not told him about the meaning of the package or our first stop. "First the P.P.P, Pandu."

We did not drive that far, though the airport lay several miles outside of the city. To me, Georgetown resembled a great heap of freshly cleaned laundry—its corrugated tin roofs glinting white in sunlight, clapboard buildings with their painted trellises and verandas. In between sprouted bougainvillea and the bruised red of flamboyant trees, the Caribbean a calm blue stone beyond. Now I understood why, when Roland first arrived from his village, he believed Georgetown to be the most beautiful place in the world.

For a city under siege, everyone moved peacefully, men steering their rusty bicycles through the broad streets, the slow-hipped saunter of women balancing baskets on their heads as they strolled down back alleyways. As we parked the car in a slumbering, residential street, a man pushing a wheelbarrow shouted out a cheerful, ordinary greeting and teased me about "me movie-star eyes." And I was surprised at how long it took for someone to come to the door of the office. A young woman greeted me. I lifted up a hand in greeting, my bag heavy, thick with printed pamphlets. I had read a few on the plane—they were pretty standard propaganda, terribly written.

"Can I help you?"

"I'm Roland Singh's wife."

Her face broke into a smile. "Imagine that!" she cried. "You such a pretty girl, too! Come, sit, sit, rest yourself!" Shutting the door, she went to a chair piled high with newspapers, and dumped them on the floor. It was a small, cramped office; books and mimeograph sheets spilled off a wall full of crude wooden shelves. I couldn't see how my papers would make much of a difference. The girl looked no older than nineteen. She wore a plain cotton dress with a belt that showed off her small waist; gold bangles shone on her wrists.

"My name's Radhika. I'll make you some tea, darlin'. When you come here anyway?"

"Today."

"You must be tired as an old tree and carrying that baby! How you get here in times like these?"

"I got my ticket months ago."

She disappeared for a few minutes behind a doorway hung with shutters. I sat, wondering if now was the time to set the papers out. But I couldn't—not yet—when Radhika returned with a cup of tea and two biscuits balanced on the saucer. "We don't have much here. And no one's around, with all the trouble. Those big fellows left me to mind things." She cleared another chair and sat.

I was struck with how ordinary Radhika seemed. I could imagine her at our Phoenicia house, lounging in a rattan chair, having a chat with Sarita. She even looked a little vain; dabs of color on her nails, a white flower clipped in her lustrous black hair. I don't know what I had expected, after all these months. It was Roland's fault, in a way. His talk made this whole business seem frightening, remote, not made of ordinary people who slept and fought and pinned flowers to their hair. Now I was very curious about her. I wanted to ask questions, but I was scared I might betray myself.

"So you know Roland?"

"Of course we do! He a bush boy and my family is all town. He and the Mangal boys play cricket and Benny go on the road too. When you go visitin' Roland you go by my brother's place in New Amsterdam, they all can meet the new Singh wife."

I smiled, grateful at this instant inclusion—just like with Sarita and Charles. I sipped my tea. For a moment it seemed possible to stay here forever.

"Now I haven't seen the boy in such a while. Where he at?"

"His family," I lied.

"That's right, I hear something like that." Radhika pushed some hair out of her face; I could tell she had no idea Roland had gone into hiding.

The phone rang. Radhika jumped up to answer it and as she listened, she scribbled something down on a piece of paper, talking in a dialect I couldn't quite make out. When she came to sit with me, she seemed distracted. "It's terrible," she said. "All this nonsense they sayin' about us. Every day it get worse. Now they sayin' we starting a strike with the rice growers."

I set my cup down and swallowed. My fingers tapped my bag. "Roland says he left some belongings in the back room wrapped in a blanket. Do you think you could fetch them for him?"

"He said that?"

"Yes, he sent a wire the other day."

"You sure?"

"I'm sure."

She shrugged. "I'll go look then."

I knew I had only a few minutes. Quickly I opened the envelope and hands trembling, scattered a few pamphlets in a bookcase behind her desk, the rest in her wire mail basket. There were flyers too, about a strike, which I shoved under a stack of books.

Just as I was sitting down again, she came back into the room empty-handed. Her face looked perplexed. "I don't know what he be talking about. Is nothing there."

"That's okay," I told her. "You know Roland. So absent-minded."

Her gaze went to her desk and she frowned. My heart sped up; she was pushing papers around. Dizzy, I shut my eyes. She mustn't find them. When I opened my eyes again she was pushing something between my fingers—a small snapshot. "See here. This is Roland and my brother and me."

The photo showed Roland and a tall, handsome man standing under a palm tree, both dressed in cricket whites, their hair wild and unkempt, their smiles wide. Radhika stood about a foot away, her arm half-raised, as if laughing at the person who took the photo. They looked like brothers and sister, caught in a moment of play.

"That was before things get bad," she murmured.

"Sundays we go have a game. But now it's different. Politics got its own hunger and we got to feed it. Even if we don't want to."

"Thank you."

"What you thankin' me, darlin'? Is not every day a girl come from America way and we see her for ourselves."

As I slipped the photo into my pocketbook, I almost wanted to tell her everything, get it over with, stop what I was doing. If she knew, she would hate me. She would know I was like all the other white people. But it wasn't like that, I wanted to say. Instead I left a few minutes later—Pandu screeched out of the driveway. We never looked back.

It took the maid a long time to answer when I knocked on Lionel Lal's door. As I stood on the porch, bag against my hip, my mind went limp with fatigue and relief; I had almost forgotten what I'd read in the newspaper, the six hundred troops scattered throughout the country, talks of strikes smoldering in the estate fields.

Lionel never came to meet me. I sat in a front drawing room with a wooden fan spinning overhead, its bare floor slatted with shade from the half-drawn shutters. The maid, a slender girl with her hair wound about her head in tight braids, shuffled in and set down a silver tray with a fresh pot of tea and triangles of buttered toast. Then she slipped away. I thought I was in a novel; not in the Caribbean but in England, except for the tree with its glossed oval leaves poking through the shutters, the damp air which pressed at my neck and arms.

After a while a man tiptoed into the room; he was some sort of assistant to Lionel and dressed in a baggy suit, black hair greased to the side. When he said hello, two gold teeth gleamed, and I had the sense he would have liked to be more charming, but under the circumstances, it wasn't possible. Instead he jiggled coins in his pockets, waiting as I slid out the other two manilla envelopes Tutkins had given me. I told him about my visit to the P.P.P; he nodded. Heart pounding, I edged forward on the divan to ask, "And my husband?"

The man started, his hand jerking out of his pocket, palming his hair back. This was not part of our deal—all Tutkins promised was to let me go down, and for Roland to leave the country, even with the state of emergency. Finding him was my problem. Only Pandu, who sat waiting across the street had whispered to me before I left, "Ask him. He acts like he doesn't know, but he does."

"You realize that if you bring him anywhere near here, we'll be forced to detain him?"

"I understand."

"And Lionel in no way wants to be accused of—" He hesitated. "I suppose we might call it nepotism?"

I smiled. "Lionel could hardly be accused of that."

The instant I blurted those words, I regretted them. But I could not help myself. My wrists were sore from carrying so many envelopes in my handbag, and I was irritable and hot from this coy game of secrets. None of it seemed real; all of it seemed a terrible indulgence in story making. The man looked at me and this time his stare was not friendly. "It's true." He tilted his head to the side. "You do resemble Mrs. Jagan."

"So I've been told."

"Do you know her?"

"Not at all. But I wonder about her."

He laughed, his teeth glinting. "I suppose it's Mrs. Jagan going to be doing her wonderin' now!" In that instant, the line between us relaxed; I heard the country lilt forcing itself up, spurting into his colonial-town pronunciation. And I knew underneath he was soft, as soft as my husband, even with these stiff posturings. After scribbling something down on a piece of paper, he handed it to me. "This here the name of the woman he stay with, she go by a name Ma Das. He took sick several weeks ago, that's why no one call him in. But you get there right away and we don't bother him. I can't guarantee much more than that. They going to make a sweep soon."

By six the next morning Pandu and I had left. This time I noticed a battleship cruiser moored in the harbor, a dark and massive shadow behind the two-story houses, which now seemed flimsy as paper. Over the radio we heard the most recent news. The Colonial Governor had taken over the government; as planned, piles of propaganda were found in the party office to suggest a failed "Communist coup" by the Jagans. I had no idea if my "propaganda" mattered; I simply tried to push the whole business from my mind, concentrating on small things: the road humming before us, the slip of paper in my pocketbook.

The land surprised me. It was vast, not at all cramped, as I'd imagined, shimmering green cane field spreading on either side, the rutted road like a long brown and pink-speckled body. We drove and drove. Green floated into brown, back into green again, tipped olive from the shade of palm trees. Sometimes we went for miles without seeing houses. Then a cluster of stilted buildings would drift up around some canals, brown sack thrown over their windows. Every now and then a road block made a clumsy appearance and a couple of soldiers peered inside. Usually they were surprised to see me. "You realize the situation, don't you?" they asked, with irritation. "You shouldn't be out." At one village a man rapped on the rear windshield. "Lady Jagan!" he laughed, showing a wide, toothless smile. Pandu put the car into gear and hurtled off.

We reached the ferry depot several hours later—New Amsterdam a sleepy jumble on the other side; the river flat, brown and sluggish. A man in the office strolled outside and told us the boat was scheduled to leave at two; fifteen minutes later he said it would be four and finally we were loaded on at four ten. I got out of the car and leaned against its hot hood, feeling the throttle of engine in water, the first real breeze against my arms. Everything— the men working the boat, the trees hanging limp and lush over the riverbanks, clusters of buildings up ahead, seemed shocked into an unreal, dreamy state.

By now Pandu thought it would be too late to continue on into the bush, but I insisted. We took a break in the empty restaurant of a hotel where we ate tinned kippers on toast and something resembling an omelette with instant coffee, the taste sooty on my tongue. Here, unlike Georgetown, the tension of events could be felt. This was because we'd reached the Berbice, Pandu explained, where Jagan grew up, and where much of his support had come from. Outside the street lamps were turned on early, and people could be seen dashing back and forth in front of the shops, talking in groups. As he dried his glasses with a rag, the barman was crying. We finished eating and got in the car.

What I remember most is the dark. It fell all of a sudden, a swift curtain of black silk, sweeping open my terror. I had never seen or felt anything like it before. Empty fields, a moonless sky and intermittent, frail glimmers of kerosene light rising up like phosphorescence in water until they too were washed away, wriggling off the rear windshield and we were left in a terrible wash of darkness again. My eyes ached from trying to peer ahead, to see into the oily black that slid off our hood. After a while, I stopped trying, settling back in my seat. I listened to the creak and groan of the car as we jounced along, headlights sweeping along the road's ruts and curves.

We finally came to a larger village, where I could make a cross-hatch of roads and houses, lanterns set out on the upstairs verandas. We slowed. To our right a large house seemed to bristle up from the mud, white and ungainly in the night. The windows were all alight. "That's the Singh family house," Pandu mumbled and then he pressed down on the accelerator, so we surged forward and then it had slipped away.

The house we parked in front of was much smaller, rougher in appearance. It sat on stilts in an alleyway, next to a low concrete building and another modest box of a house. As we emerged out of the car, a few chickens poked their heads out from under the bottom house and waddled toward the trench which lined the yard, making squawking noises; the air was very still, smelling of mud and gutter water. Pressing a handkerchief to my mouth, I followed Pandu up a narrow flight of stairs—a ladder almost—through an unpainted door and inside.

For an instant, I thought I would suffocate. The dark here was even worse, still and without a breeze. Then I heard a rasp of a match and Pandu lit a kerosene lantern. The room flickered to life, throwing trembling shadows onto the wall. He lit another and now I could see very well. It was a small place, but clean and well-kept. A stone floor, with some rice painting on the threshold. A table sat in the center, with a half-finished plate of chicken and rice in a large metal plate; a small arrangement of cane chairs around a rug to the side. An open door led to a kitchen where I could see iron pots on a two-burner wood stove; freshly cleaned glasses set out to dry on newsprint. Pandu, though, pointed to another doorway, hung with printed cloth. He gave me a nudge. "Go," he said. "Go inside."

Even through fevered eyes, Roland was able to joke. He reached a hand out to me, his palm hot and dry in my moist one, and let out a wry laugh. "So, nosy lady. You come find out the stinking mess your man make of things?"

"Did you have any doubts I would?"

"Not really."

I didn't know what else to say, his appearance so shocked me. The skin of his face was drawn against bone, showing the hollows of his cheeks, his lips a swollen, discolored brown. I patted his shoulder. "You should rest," I told him.

"But I want to hear how you get yourself down here when most of this country under wraps!"

"I made a few phone calls."

"And who let you in at a time like this?"

Hesitating, I told him, "Your uncle."

A scowl knit his brow and he sagged back into the bed, as if suddenly exhausted. "Don't talk to me about that man," he grumbled. "He the ruin of me."

I was relieved he cared more about his anger toward Lionel. If he had asked me anything—about Radhika or how I paid for my plane ticket—I would have blurted the whole business out. And I don't know how we could have happened then.

There was a small thud behind us. I turned to see a small child squatting in the corner, grinning at the bucket she had knocked over, tossing a small doll with yellow hair to the floor. The little girl ignored the doll and stared at me, rocking on her haunches, black eyes large and wide. Two clips held back her hair, which hung

231

in thick, wild waves. Around her chubby wrists were two gold bangles. I wanted to utter some noise of protest but instead pushed my voice down into a tone of reasonableness. "What's she doing up so late?"

"You're not surprised," Roland said.

"The packages Pandu sent?"

He looked away.

"I knew, Roland. I knew in my heart even before I could say so. "

Roland released a weak smile; already, his attention seemed to have wandered. "Her grandmother's gone visitin', but she be back soon, put her to bed." He nodded in her direction. "Come Sarla," he whispered. "Come meet me wife. Time you two got to know each other."

I got up and went to the child, who was still watching me, elbows jerked back at her waist, as if ready to sprint from the room. Yet she didn't protest when I put my hand on her head, stroked her hair. We regarded each other in silence a moment, like old friends or rivals, she fiddling with the bangle on her wrist, me with my fists in my pockets. The next thing I knew I squatted down, slid my hands under her armpits and pulled her against me, my heart thudding in my ribs. She dropped her head against the bone of my shoulder, sucking at her index finger. I wanted to hate her, this child with his round cheeks and wavy hair, but her smell was intoxicating, of milk and spices. Her rump sagged downward against my arms. It was as if we had stood this way a thousand times, and when I let go, she wobbled for a second like an upset bottle, then turned her face to me, confused. "You stay?" she asked.

I couldn't answer.

"You stay?" Her voice veered higher.

"Yes," I managed.

I slept that night on a string cot with a pillow made of coconut husks, listening to Roland's raspy, shallow breaths. Sarla lay on a bundle of blankets in the corner, not far from the foot of her bed, a shimmery tent of mosquito netting pinned around her. She slept still as a tree, brown legs pulled tight to her chest. Before leaving, Pandu had explained to me her mother was still nursing when she died; I could see that even though they found her an *ayah* and she lived with her grandmother, she showed the signs of a child who was once abandoned, clutching herself fiercely, her face calm with defiance, even in sleep. I touched her hair, her eyes, then left her alone. I understood.

For five days, I woke as if someone had rapped a board across my eyes, and rose slowly from bed, pushed across the house to see Ma Das toiling across the road, a brass pot balanced on her head. She would not let me help her with anything; it would shame them to make a white woman work this way in the open, she told me. The most I was allowed to do was sit on the front steps, thin cotton dress spread like a tent over my knees, and peel guavas or comb coconut oil into Sarla's hair, making the curls lie flat against her small skull. Ma would join us, and she spoke unsentimentally of Roland and her own daughter's affair over five years ago. "It happen one summer he come back, Yankee boy from school talking big man politics," she told me one afternoon while pounding and flipping roti dough on a board. "But Bimala a girl with too much moon in her eyes. The world, this world can't change so fast. And I tell her no use plucking the tree before it know how to lean in the sun. Let him come back for you, send you a sign he reach back to his past and future the same time. But she no wait. And so we have this little one and

233

she ask after him and the Yankee woman with green eyes we hear about."

I remained silent. I hated Roland for bringing this shame to me, unlike any other I had known.

But I had no choice. I sat, hot sun spilling down my neck, the sounds of the village creaking around me, Roland's previous life cracked open between my fingers, in talk, in memory. I assembled the pieces, what I could learn. In the afternoons, Roland would wake, and having nothing else to do, I sat with a pillow resting against my back while he talked, telling me things he'd silenced before. I tried to imagine it—the boy who came back one summer and sat on the verandas with the old men, eyes flashing with anger. At night we could hear the sounds of music coming from the church dances. The village women would cluck their tongues about the Indian boys who snuck off to dance with the Creole and black girls. That's what Roland did—touch a coarse country girl under the paper lanterns, only all it led to was more deceit.

Now I saw that it mattered I was white. I saw it when I watched the other villagers amble by Ma Das' house gate, hat brims lifting, revealing the shaded browns and soot-black faces of Roland's childhood. He had thought, in marrying me, someone who believed we were more alike than most husbands and wives, he had finally triumphed over the others who drew out his old poison. He had come to believe in my color blindness—up there, in New York. Only there still remained Sarla, crouching in Ma Das' doorway, waiting to catch sight of the white, stiff helmet of the mailman on his motorized bicycle, bringing the packages that Pandu sent every month.

"When did you think you were going to tell me?" I asked him.

He shifted. "I don't know. Sarah, I was so crazy about you. I thought if I said something, I would lose you. I couldn't think that far ahead."

"Well now you have to. We can't stay very long, Roland. And this is getting uncomfortable for me."

No one else knew who I was and it was better, for every now and then a jeep rattled into the village and a soldier would roam about, knocking over milk buckets and lanterns with his gun butt, frightening people. Roland's family had no idea I'd come down, either. One day I snuck down the alleyway and stood in the shade of a coconut tree, hand over my eyes, squinting and watching. After a while I saw one of his brothers come down the stairs. This was Ujai—the jaunty kick to his walk, a newspaper-wrapped liquor bottle stowed under his arm. The shutters flapped once and a woman's face peered out, but that was all.

I said very little. I waited. I woke every morning with a clot of anger on my brow.

On the fifth day, Roland got up from bed and ate puffed bread softened with chicken stew. And the next morning he was pacing in the main room, alert as ever. "It's you, my sweetest," he declared. "You the balm my soul been waiting for."

We dressed him in his good suit and together with Sarla, we walked down the road to his family house. I had to poke an extra hole in his belt; his trousers billowed about his knees like balloons. We'd dressed up Sarla, too, in a yellow dress trimmed in red embroidery done by Ma Das.

Betty Singh wouldn't even come to the door. We were ushered in by the servant to find her sitting in her cane rocker, staring straight in front of her. She was a thin woman, with features more delicate than Roland's, head wrapped in a scarf, profile tilted like an old, worn coin. Even from across the room I could see in her a kind of fury dimmed, her black eyes drenched in regret. "I wish I could greet my new daughter better," she finally uttered. "But my son here done sullied our name, so I can't see my gain for my loss." Roland made a chirupping sound with his teeth and pushed Sarla forward, still holding her wrists with his fingers. "Five years," he said. "And you would think that fool stubborn head of yours see the beautiful gain right here."

He turned to me. "You see, Sarah? What I tell you? This mother of mine living in the dark ages!"

"Baba!" A clatter of noise in the kitchen—coercion through silence, I knew. I too swallowed my words, like his sisters, who flitted around us, setting out tea and biscuits on a table. It was they who made me understand I was family, giving me the best fish at dinner that night, pressing a pair of gold knot earrings into my palm later that night as I sat on the edge of Roland's old bed. "That's for your child. The other girl, she wasn't good," Agnes whispered to me. "Not high class like you. Dark, with common eyes. She thought he take her to America and put her high up!" She released a scornful laugh, covering her mouth with her hand. "A maid's daughter, believing that!" I folded the earrings into my pocket but later, as I closed the netting around Sarla's bed, I tried to brush their cruel words out the window sill, so they might fall like bitter petals under the spreading mango tree outside.

We could not stay very long. By now there was talk of restricting the Jagans' movement in the country and arrests of anyone considered responsible for sedition. And the terrible noises of Roland and his mother arguing began to sound through the house. "How you can say I gone and wasted myself?" I would often hear him cry from another room. "I done more in this year than my damn brothers ever give you! You with your damn airs and your broken china! What that mean, hunh?" It was her silence which most crushed him, I knew; I saw it in his gait as he stumbled out onto the veranda, mashing a handkerchief against his neck.

By noon three days later we had packed our belongings into my suitcase and two jute bags. The minister's son was going to drive us to New Amsterdam; from there we'd work something out through Pandu. Several people gathered by the fence to say good-bye; Ma Das came when the others could not see her, wiping her eyes with a cotton cloth. "Don't mind me," she growled when I stepped forward to hug her. "It's better for the girl. And you wait, I come knocking at your door soon enough." Up to now, Sarla had followed Roland and me everywhere, but when we lifted her onto the car seat, she began to shriek for Ma. Ma took a step back, and shook her head once. Sarla's shrieks rose in desperate, short bursts, but Ma stayed where she was, dirt eddying about her ankles from the car exhaust. As the door swung shut, I took Sarla by the wrists and folded her into me until the trembling stopped and I knew I would never let go again.

Later, at New Amsterdam pier, as the ferry motor began to churn, and the air over the river turned into a flashing band of heat, I turned to Roland and said, "I will try to forgive your lie about the child. But from now on, Roland, you have to do things my way."

He said nothing, but nodded, brushing at his eyes. A few minutes later we had pushed off, and we saw the land shrink and spread, thick, wooly arms of green laced with brown veins, now flanked by sky.

It was on Water Street that we saw them. First a few flutters of white against the bright tin of sky, like something scraped off a surface. Then I realized it was shirts on men, ten, twenty of them, clumped and scattering apart as they streamed off a curb. Behind were more dabs of white and open, excited faces—I had not seen such excitement since I'd come to Guiana. The driver scratched his neck. He was perspiring; we had hired him back in New Amsterdam, and he was not too happy about this complication. "What you want me to do?"

At that moment, two headlights came bearing towards us, weak wands of light in the sun, a smooth tarp of black. A car was moving in the opposite direction.

"It's the Jagans," Roland whispered. "They try to go Trinidad, but they not let out." He craned forward, resting his elbow on his knees, trying to see past the windshield. I looked up; more people were pouring down the street—a basket of bananas toppled off someone's head. A woman stumbled on the corner, falling to one knee. I put my hand on Roland's arm as the sides began to rock. Sarla crushed herself against me. But I kept my eyes open. Up ahead was their car, marooned in a sea of white shirts and straw hats, coasting slowly with two more vehicles following behind, as if for a funeral procession. Despite the chaos around us, there was extraordinary calm to the moment.

I saw Roland's hand reached for the door handle.

"Roland," I said. My voice was firm.

His hand dropped. "Turn here," I ordered the driver.

The car swerved, sending Sarla bouncing against my side. The streets here were paved badly, broken houses leaning into one another. A goat scrabbled in front of our bumper, haunches swaying loose against its hip bones. Sarla began to whimper. I put a hand on her head. "Hush. Roland, you duck down on the floor."

"What the—"

"Do as I say." In the background we could hear the

faint, steady roar of a crowd. They were passing on the other side of this row of buildings, the Jagans' car moving slowly at its head. "*Go*," I told the driver.

"But Mistress, too many people."

"I don't care."

The driver plunged his foot on the accelerator pedal. With a roar we went barrelling into a sea of white. Shouts, arms, startled eyes, a man thrown from his bicycle. The air grew dark a moment and light again. I caught a glimpse of a flag, of a gun, flashing in sunlight. Then we were twisting our heads, looking backward, our last sight of the Jagans' car, a fogged moon against glass. Janet's mouth was pulled to the side, making her look happy, almost giddy. I too, felt a lift in my throat as if a sound had been released from my mouth. Then we were moving again, the road to the airport quiet and still.

As soon I could, when we got back to New York, I took Roland and Sarla to the Phoenicia house. I wanted to lie there one more time, hear it fold around me, forget what had passed. Autumn was strong and full, the yard buried in orange and brown leaves. Delighted, Sarla scooped them into her thin arms, and ran about, shaping neat little piles all over the grass. We'd gone shopping for winter clothes, so she wore a navy cap tilted over her impossible curls, a hand me down zipper jacket from Sharon, which made her look like an old rag man when she crouched down on the ground. I could not stop watching her.

While Sarla made her piles, Charles, Roland, and I took charge of shutting down each room, slowly, as if stitching a wound shut. First the third floor, where we discovered a dead bat behind a bedroom door, wings folded over its gaunt, baby-like face. The house was damp, echoey. I found three mice in their traps. Dust lay trapped like felt under the sofa and a spoon, crusty with marmalade, came clattering out of the mattress Roland and I were to sleep on. It was the opposite of death, lacking in finality. We were closing up for the season, but not without hoping we'd be prying the windows open next year, sun flooding our arms. The Landownes were noncommittal. The lease came back with the deposit and a polite note, "Thank you for the improvements."

And there was so much more blue. Spires of blue smoke twisting over the hills. We burned wood in the fireplaces. Ash and oak and some birch. As a treat, Charles swung Sarla on to his shoulders and helped her pick the hard yellow pears in a tree on the corner of the property. And that night we all fell exhausted into the hapless blue of night. I could imagine each of us in our individual cells of sleep: Sarla in her skinny cot, knees pulled to her chest. The channel of space between Sarita and Charles, deep as a river rift. Roland next to me, hands loose around the dome of my stomach, hair strung like sinuous map lines across the pillow.

We all felt it—a dark blue sleep we entered as the day left us, like heat from a pavement. Slowly, drawing us out, a chilled heart of water beating far off. It was something about the house, its windows drifts of glowing white. Walls lengthened; floor shadows grew thick as grass. The house itself fat with sleep sounds. We were sliding forward in time. In the morning everything would fumble toward an ordinary, present tense clarity: what sandals and socks to wear, how many eggs for breakfast, whether to take the car to town. The men would sigh and grumble and eat. Whole lives were made over rice and peas and linen. Sarla and Sharon would grow mysteriously, shockingly, their eyes sudden mirrors of adulthood. The lapse and exchange of homes, palm trees for fir, mud road for

paved, mango for apple, radio for TV, made for a continu-
ity that could not be found in the details of one place.
Home must be something iridescent, moon-like, liquid
and pure as wind. It was not a place, not seen, not evident
except as movement, change.

I woke when it was still dark, a clot of sheets between my
thighs. Taking a deep breath, I let my anger rise to a pitch
and then sink away. A few more breaths. My head cleared.
Roland's eyes opened and he threw an arm out, tugging at
my shoulder, only I wriggled out of bed, toes cramping
from the cold floor and went to the window. Through the
curtains not even the trees seemed to move. I cracked the
window some more, letting in a chilled scent of evergreen
and morning dew.

"Come back," he mumbled into the pillow.

I heaved myself up from the bed. There was no point in
trying to go back to sleep. Most mornings I woke this
way, furious at him, at us. I spent hours wandering about,
straightening up, fumbling for calm and order in the
dark. Today I went into the darkened hall and listened to
the house. A complaining pipe, an occasional sleepless
groan, bedsprings. The children especially, made the
most interesting, discrete noises. Several times I would
shuffle by Sarla's door and hear an earnest stream of mumbling. It never lasted for more than a few moments, but I
liked to listen, sensing I was entering an impressionable
space, where something unknown was in the making.

In the kitchen I retrieved a pot from the drainboard
and made myself a cup of hot milk. A watery light came
spilling through the window, casting the lawn in frosty
bristles. I could just make out the sound of the stream
rushing past. And there were other sounds—outside—a
squirrel scrabbled across a gutter, the floop of wings as a

bird lit off from a nearby tree. From upstairs, the silence seemed to press at my shoulders. I checked a clock sitting on the windowsill. Only a half hour had passed.

Agitated, I climbed back up the stairs to dress. It was light out now, and I could see the frail remains of Charles' terrace. Through the walls, Sarita groaned in her sleep. Down the hall, someone was waking. Probably Rita Pilloo, getting up to prepare the meals for the day.

Sitting on the edge of the bed, I unpeeled my night gown, letting it fall around my full breasts and lie twisted around my waist. Everyone said I carried the pregnancy well; it was astonishing what I'd done, going to Guiana, but I felt awful, bloated with all these secrets.

Roland's fingers tugged at my nightgown. "Sarah. Just talk to me."

"I don't have anything to say." Standing, I let the cotton gown slink to the floor and pulled on a corduroy smock dress.

"When you going to forgive me?"

I stayed silent.

"You don't love me."

"Really, Roland. That doesn't even deserve an answer." I moved toward the door. What I wanted to say is: I feel too old. You feel too old.

Throwing on a sweater, I tied my hair back in a bandana and went outside. Stepping off the porch, I began wandering around the yard. Here and there I picked up a ball, grimy with dirt, a badminton racket tossed carelessly to the grass. I found a half-filled mug floating with globs of mold and a stale heel of bread and set it down on the porch.

Noises came to me, drumming through the ground. What an echo this place brought. Maybe, soon enough, on the streets people would no longer stare and it would start to seem as if we had always come here. We would buy furniture and pots and pans and stoves and wedge ourselves in, hoping we would fit. Charles would lose some of his coarseness; Sarita would become less angry. And me and Roland and Sarla? I got up and began pacing the property.

After a while I found myself kicking through thickness. I looked down to see orange and brown leaves scattering about my toes. It was Sarla's piles, most of them blown away in the night, now drifting in lacy, burnished patterns across the grass. I pressed my fists against my eyes, blinked. It was not just Roland I was thinking of, but Samuel too. My father had done a terrible thing to me: to have been brought into the humming core of family, only to be banished again. How I sometimes hated the both of them, standing like heros, ideals raised before me, dazzling as a bridge of flaming swords. What did they think? That I would dip my head and surrender in ash and silence? That I would extinguish the life of a little girl?

That was too easy—bitterness borne out of that most womanly of conditions—waiting. The idiom of silence Claire and Sarita and we all learned. For several days upon our return to the States, I agonized, wondering if I should come out with it and confess how I'd gotten Roland out of Guiana. And then days passed and soon it seemed pointless. The old ardor had slipped from our limbs. We had so much to do. Forgiveness? What a high and soaring roof that word promised! All I had was was this man returned to my bed, each day bringing me deeper into grief, as the world I knew gently crumbled. I took care of details like a new apartment for the three of us, medicine for Samuel. And last night, lying in our bed in Phoenicia, listening to the foreign cadences of men's voices down below I could weep openly, for my father; for the end of one life and the shape of things to come.

When I returned to the house, I found Roland sitting on the porch. In these hurried days all we spoke of were arrangements, figuring out how to squeeze Sarla into our life. Now Roland sat bundled into a sweater with a blanket thrown around his shoulders, his hair in disheveled waves. "Couldn't sleep?" I asked.

"You left the bed so early." He added in a hoarse voice, "You always leave early."

I didn't answer. I noticed his hand reach for me, then drop away when I did not return the gesture. We sat in silence, watching the sky grow light through the trees.

After a while, I said to him, "I read somewhere that there's a point in your life where you have to look around the house you're in and get used to living in it."

"That right?"

"That's one of the many profound thoughts I had while sitting here this summer."

"And what else you think about?"

"Us."

"What you think about us, book-lady?"

I smiled. "About how rotten we could be to each other. About the year that's passed." I hesitated. "And how some things are simply over."

He stood and came to me, arms out. I rose too, pressing against the hard leanness of his body. For him too, something had changed. From then on, he rarely talked about the Jagans or Guiana. Roland remained sadder, quieter inside, letting his talk sift into a hole of silence and exile; so did all our friends from down there. We really had no choice. The Jagans flew to England and India to ask for help, but were quickly snubbed. Upon their return both were thrown into prison. And soon enough, more would change in our own lives: Sarita ran off to California with a man from Jamaica. We received a note from Ranjit in

Delhi; he'd gotten engaged to a girl there. We enrolled
Sarla in nursery school on the Upper West Side. Roland
quit the Consulate for good and got a job working for a
local union. It wasn't much, but it was something. Our
son was born at the end of November; we named him
David Ashok. When my father heard, he said, "So! You
have a king for a son. And I hear your floor is so clean you
can eat off it." Two months later Samuel was dead. It
seemed I would never stop mourning my father; I could
never get my arms around the grief. Roland and I hung
on. We fought and made up, discovering that now, more
than ever, we were family.

What I often do, when I need something to remember
who I am, what I believe in, is to think of that summer,
during which the most temporary of alliances had yielded
so much. I think of the house, like a luminous bit of rock
in the dark waters which lie behind. Now that everyone
has scattered, it seems all I can do is hold on to a few
things as keepsakes of that time: the August sun fading
over the Catskills, blue glasses on a windowsill.

This first edition of
House of Waiting
is published by
Global City Press
New York.

It is designed by
Charles Nix.

The typeface is
Garamond No. 3.

Production management is by
Burton Shulman.

The printing is by
Offset Paperback Mfrs., Inc.
Dallas Pennsylvania.

※